Crystal earbobs danced against her pale-as-milk slender neck. She looked extravagant and indulged.

A woman who dressed as if she was due to go to a ball was all wrong for the frontier. Wrong for the hard life in a trapper's cabin. Wrong for him.

Jack focused on the woman as he walked closer.

"I'll give you fifty dollars for her," said the man beside her.

Jack hesitated. Fifty dollars was a lot of money, not as much as it cost to get her here, but enough he could reconsider and send for another bride.

Olivia's eyes widened.

"Unhand her," Jack said softly.

* * *

Bride by Mail
Harlequin® Historical #1187—June 2014

New Harlequin® Historical author

Katy Madison

invites you to her

Wild West Weddings

*Mail-order brides for three hard-working,
hard-living men!*

Three penniless East Coast ladies are prepared to
give up everything they know for the lure of the
West. Will they find new beginnings, new families
and eventual happiness as mail-order brides?

Their advertisements answered, three rugged
frontiersmen await their new brides—
with eagerness, and not a little trepidation!

What have they all let themselves in for?

Read Olivia's story in
Bride by Mail

And look for Anna's and Selina's stories
Coming soon!

KATY MADISON

—

BRIDE BY MAIL

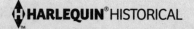

Recycling programs
for this product may
not exist in your area.

ISBN-13: 978-0-373-29787-0

BRIDE BY MAIL

Copyright © 2014 by Karen L. King

www.Harlequin.com

Printed in U.S.A.

KATY MADISON

Award-winning author Katy Madison loves stories. As a child she was always lugging around a book. At the age of eight, after having read over a hundred Nancy Drew mysteries, all the Laura Ingalls Wilder books and a full weekly allotment of library books, Katy went to her mother and begged for a new book to read. Her frustrated mother handed her a romance novel. Katy fell in love with the genre. She quickly discovered where her mother had hidden the rest and began sneaking them out to read.

Now she gets to write romances and live the glamorous life of a writer, which mostly means she stays in her pajamas all day and never uses an alarm clock. Katy thinks nothing is better than curling up with a good book. Visit her on the web at www.katymadison.com.

This is Katy Madison's fabulous debut novel for the Harlequin® Historical line!

Author Note

This is the first of my Wild West Weddings series following three young women working in a cotton mill in Connecticut. When the Civil War halts cotton shipments, the three of them answer advertisements for mail-order brides. After exchanging a few letters that take months to reach their destination, they set out to marry men they've never seen.

In the early years, women were scarce on the frontier. Men often had to send back to the East to find brides. The lure of the West always held promises to Americans of yesteryear. The frontier provided a chance for a new beginning, plentiful land and reward for hard work. But what incredible bravery it must have taken to leave everything behind and go West to marry a virtual stranger.

This first story is about Olivia and Jack. Ever since her parents died in a tragic train accident, Olivia has wanted to find where she belongs. She doesn't realize her inner strength and hopes to find a protector in Jack. He doesn't see her strength either and is certain it won't be long before she flees from the tough life in the Rocky Mountains.

For history buffs, the train accident that Olivia survived really happened in 1853 in Norwalk, Connecticut. The official death toll was fixed at 56, although some bodies were never found and many others were severely injured.

I hope you'll enjoy the adventures of Olivia, Anna and Selina. Please visit me on the web at www.katymadison.com.

Chapter One

Denver City, Colorado Territory
May 1862

> *Twenty-seven-year-old fur trader seeks wife
> and helpmate. Have cabin with cookstove in
> Rocky Mountains. Must be brave woman with
> calm nature.*

Olivia Hansson stepped down to the dusty street. Her shaking hands spoiled her attempt to look calm.

"Here you go, miss." The stagecoach driver set her mother's trunk on the boarded walk behind her.

Tossed from the roof of the stage, her carpetbag thudded next to her feet. The outrider pitched down more bags, raising a cloud. During the harrowing race across the Western prairies, his eyes had held a flinty look, scanning the horizon for danger at every stop.

Raw wood buildings blocked any view of the mountains. The sprawl of buildings with crazy false fronts substituting for second stories was a far cry from Connecticut. The farther West she'd gone, the more often *city* was tacked on to any cluster of buildings, but she was a little relieved the outrider no longer looked as if he feared attack from every direction.

"Gentlemen, grub and beds are available at the saloon," said the driver. He cast a sideways look at Olivia. "Are you being met, ma'am?"

"Yes, thank you." Her husband-to-be would retrieve her. As soon as the stagecoach and crowd cleared out of the way, she would surely see Jack Trudeau.

Her heart skittering, she smoothed a gloved hand over her lavender jacket and tugged the bottom to erase any wrinkles that might have formed. Meeting one's groom didn't happen every day.

In her best anticipation of how the first meeting would go, her beauty would astound him. Not that she really expected that. She pinched her cheeks and bit her lips to force color into her too-pale countenance. She didn't consider herself more than passably pretty, but compared to the careworn women on the frontier, she would do well by contrast. Thanks to her mother's carriage gown, she was better dressed than any woman she'd seen since leaving Kansas City. Surely Jack would be pleased with her appearance.

"We'll head back East tomorrow morning." The driver held her gaze a moment as if warning her to return to a more civilized place.

Her throat went dry. She couldn't afford a return trip. What little money she'd possessed she'd used in a fruitless search for her father's assets.

Her fellow travelers, all men, trudged across the street and into the saloon, but no man waited for her.

The driver and the outrider drove the empty stage through the open double doors of a livery stable. They exited laden with mailbags and toted them down the street. She waited alone.

The wind kicked up gritty dust. Olivia held down her hat and searched for a man wearing buckskins. She resisted the urge to reach into her reticule and retrieve the photograph he'd sent at her request.

When the months without a reply had stretched to December and the pressure to answer another advertisement from the *Matrimonial News* had almost grown too much to bear, she feared her request had put him off. Then Mr. Trudeau's letter had arrived.

Olivia had cautiously unfolded the two sheets to discover his portrait. Anticipation and excitement had thrummed through her just like the Christmas morning when she'd unwrapped a porcelain doll and a miniature china tea set.

The photograph showed a man with dark curls brushing his shoulders, a clean-shaven face with strong planes and a full mouth with the slightest of tilts, as if her request had amused him.

He looked like a man accustomed to danger and the wild. He looked like a man who would think a cabin with a stove was the height of civilization. He looked like a man afraid of nothing, and nothing like a man she had expected to marry.

Her knees had gone weak and her mouth had watered anyway. A tightening sensation like fear had settled low in her gut. After sneaking peeks at the picture again and again, she'd grown sure he was a man who could protect her from the world.

Laughter and shouts emanated from the saloon, but no man from the photograph. Had he been delayed? Her chest tightened.

Her optimism was fast disintegrating. Her friends and roommates had thought her crazy for suggesting they answer advertisements for brides. Perhaps they had been right.

"Howdy, ma'am."

Olivia spun around. Her throat tightened.

"Can I help ya ta find a place?" A man with an untrimmed beard and wearing stained red suspenders approached.

Not Jack. She deflated. "No, thank you. I'm waiting on someone."

A group of bricklayers worked on a building. Men on foot and horseback passed, but not a single woman was in sight. Her spine tightened. Was she alone in a world of men?

Surely her husband-to-be hadn't spent a small fortune on her passage only to abandon her at the last stop. Had an accident or illness befallen him? Was she here in this rough place without a protector?

"Care ta wet your whistle? I can buy you a sarsaparilla across the street." He gestured toward the saloon.

Ladies didn't go into drinking establishments. Even in this wild place, she doubted the rules were different. "Thank you, but I had better wait here."

She turned to dismiss him.

"Who's fetching you?" he persisted.

"I'm sure he will be along directly."

The man crossed his arms and spit a stream of tobacco, narrowly missing the lavender skirts of her carriage dress.

Gentlemen didn't spit in a lady's presence. Pulling her skirts back, she hoped he would take the hint and go away.

He didn't.

Indians moved up the sidewalk. Loincloths and open vests exposed bronzed skin. Their long black hair glistened with blue lights. Olivia drew in a sharp breath at the sight of muscular legs and smooth bare chests covered in strange patterns. Behind the men trailed women wearing buckskin sack dresses. In contrast to the silence of the men, the females chattered in bird-like coos and calls.

They stopped and looked Olivia up and down. Bursting into giggles, they scurried after the men. Heat rose in her cheeks.

"Damned Arapaho." The suspender-clad man spit again.

Realizing her jaw had dropped, she pressed her lips together. She couldn't have said if her shock was because the natives walked down the sidewalk as if they owned it, or if it was because the men wore so few clothes. She felt as if she'd stepped into China or Africa instead of a territory of the country she'd been born and raised in.

Her throat dry, Olivia scanned the street again. The signs around her indicated the ticket office, the livery stable, the BK saloon, and Pike's Mercantile, but no man in buckskins was in sight. Where was her husband-to-be? The bricklayers ceased their work and openly stared at her. Her heart raced and the back of her neck felt as if a cold demon blew on it. She swallowed hard to suppress the outward signs of nervousness.

The scruffy man scratched his armpit. Was the brown stain on his suspenders tobacco, food or just plain dirt?

She shuddered.

One side of his mouth slid up. His gaze dropped to her chest. "You answer one of them ads for a wife?"

Olivia backed up. Her heels clicked against her mother's trunk and she nearly fell on it. She opened her mouth to answer, but nothing came out.

"Might as well come with me. One of us is as good as another."

He had to be kidding. She curled her fingers in so tightly her nails bit into her palms through her gloves. What kind of place was this?

A man in a green-and-white-striped waistcoat and a shiny black jacket pushed the man in suspenders to the side. "Leave the lady be." His pomaded hair was combed straight back and his penetrating eyes appraised her. "Is he bothering you, ma'am?"

Letting out the breath she hadn't realized she was holding, her tension eased. The gentleman would be of assistance. "I'm sure he is just trying to be helpful."

"Allow me to introduce myself. I'm Ben Kincaid." He doffed his hat and made a slight bow.

She nodded but didn't answer in kind.

He extended his arm. "Why don't you come with me, ma'am? I'm sure you don't want to be standing in the street."

"I'd rather wait a bit longer. I am expected." But she'd be grateful if the gentleman would get rid of the man in the dirty suspenders. Ironic that she, who couldn't seem to attract a single man's attention back in Connecticut, had two men vying for her attention. She reached to take the proffered arm.

"You ain't safe waiting here all alone," Mr. Kincaid said, shattering the illusion of being a well-bred man while clamping her hand into the crook of his arm. He insolently looked her up and down.

His bold appraisal made her feel unclean. Her heart thudded in her chest, threatening to break through her ribs. *Where was Jack?*

A frisson of fear sliding down her spine, she tugged, but Mr. Kincaid didn't let her loose. She gave up trying to free her hand rather than create a scene. He was at least preferable to the unkempt man. Or was he?

The scruffier man folded his arms across his suspenders. "Better off comin' with me. Leastwise, I'd marry you."

Mr. Kincaid flashed a big smile. "Now, I have a private room over yonder where you could…freshen up after your journey. I'd be happy to see to your…comfort."

"I'm sure I'll be fine." Olivia wasn't at all sure she would be fine. But at this point she'd opt for tagging after the Indian braves who had ignored her, rather than with Mr. Kincaid, who offered an unsavory sort of assistance, or with the man who needed a bath.

Several men toddled out of the saloon. They took various poses along the opposite sidewalk. What on earth were they doing?

"I'm sure I don't want to keep you." Perhaps she should go down to the mercantile and inquire within, but she couldn't manage her trunk without help. Inside were the last of her links with her parents. She didn't want to abandon it.

She suspected if she asked Mr. Kincaid to assist her, he'd take her trunk into the saloon. Her throat closed and she swallowed.

Her friend Anna would have laughed at the men. Selina would have shooed them off, but Olivia's tongue was tied and it was all she could do to keep from trembling.

Where in heaven's name was Jack, and why was he leaving her alone to contend with these uncouth men?

Horrors that could befall an unprotected woman cast big black blots in her thoughts.

"I'm waiting for Mr. Trudeau. P-perhaps you know him."

Mr. Kincaid's eyes narrowed speculatively. "I ain't seen Jack, nor his mules, lately."

Mules? Olivia again looked around for Jack or mules, but no mules were in sight. A new buckboard wagon and horses waited in front of the mercantile, but no Jack. Her stomach somersaulted.

"Jack's got him a woman already. He don't need you," objected the scruffy man.

Every fiber in her went rigid.

"Now, didn't Jack tell you he had an Indian wife? Shame on him," said the slick man with a sigh, as if he expected no better of Jack.

Her future husband had a wife already? He hadn't said anything about a wife. Her mind blanked as icy dread crept up her spine.

"You'd better come with me." He patted her captured trembling hand as if to soothe her.

She snatched it back and gripped her reticule as if it might shield her.

The men watched her with an intensity that made her neck tighten.

She wanted to crawl under the boards of the sidewalk or run away, but her feet were stuck as if vines had twined around her ankles to hold her in this awful place.

Mr. Kincaid reached out and caught her arm. "You're coming with me. You look like you need to sit down."

The suspender man grabbed her other arm. "I saw her first."

The idea that she could be fought over like a child's plaything made noise rush in her ears. As if she was being swept into a roaring river, she sought the purchase of a rock or a muddy bank. She didn't know what to do. If Jack had a wife, she couldn't go with him, either. Trembles shuddered through her and she fought to breathe.

Jack Trudeau waited for the poky grocer to fill his order. He checked the sack of coffee for nuts and twigs that were often used to bulk up the precious beans. He inhaled deeply of the rich scent.

The mercantile owner painstakingly penciled a list on butcher paper.

A brightly colored array of tins resided on the shelf behind the counter. Olivia might want tea.

"I'll take a tin of tea, too," he said.

"Orange or black?" asked the grocer.

What was the difference? A red tin with a white flower stood out. If his bride didn't like the tea, she might like the metal box to store whatever small things a woman liked to accumulate. "The red one."

Her request for a photograph had struck him as bold, exactly the kind of woman needed on the frontier. Olivia probably wanted the photograph to make certain he wasn't a grizzly, unshaved mountain man. He'd been fortunate to find a man taking photographs of the sprouting Denver City, who'd said he'd take Jack's picture because he reckoned the portrait would help get a pretty wife.

But pretty didn't matter. His first wife hadn't been pretty. She'd been short and dark and built like a tree stump, but he'd loved the way Wetonga's eyes would disappear into upside-down half-moons when she laughed. She had been the wife of his heart.

But Wetonga was gone. He could not raise a plot of

vegetables or keep varmints out of his cabin while he had to go farther and farther north to find the lucrative beaver and red fox.

The worst vermin were the two-legged variety who thought an empty cabin was an invitation to track in mud, sleep on his bed and burn his food into his pots. The pots they left behind anyway. Upon returning from a trapping run and finding his home defiled, Jack had decided he needed a new wife.

He glanced toward the window, where he'd been looking out every now and then to see if the stage had arrived.

Jack shifted impatiently. He'd already waited half an hour to be helped. His bride was due to arrive. He'd promised to meet her, but he hesitated to leave for fear if he returned later he would have to wait another half hour before his shopping was seen to. He wanted to be ready to leave for home as soon as they were hitched.

A group of Arapaho entered the store. As they unwound lengths of cloths, the squaws giggled about a pale-eyed woman with a skirt as big as a tepee.

Jack turned and asked in an Algonquian dialect where they had seen the woman.

A brave stepped forward and said in perfect English, "Pale Eyes arrive on the stage. Many men wish to claim her."

A miner standing near the door leaned out. "It's a right fine-looking lady. Kincaid's got her. She goes to work for him, I'll be first in line."

"Merde!" How had he not heard the stagecoach's arrival?

The Indian switched to a French patois. "Pale Eyes afraid."

Were they playing musical languages? Jack stared

at the brave, who slowly smiled as if they were sharing a great joke.

"Merci." Jack swiveled around to face the grocer as he backed toward the door. "I'll be back before you finish."

Imagining that a scared-horse look was the reason for the nickname Pale Eyes, he trotted out onto the street. A cluster of men blocked his view. He took a few steps closer. A willowy woman dressed in a bell-shaped dress the color of lilacs stood in the center of the throng. Bands of ruffles and bows flared out from her tiny waist.

Her back was to him. Her wide-brimmed straw hat with ribbons and bows covered her hair. One of the ne'er-do-wells who hung about Denver City saloons tugged on her arm. She pulled free and leaned against Kincaid. His bride, or a fancy whore brought in by Kincaid?

He hopped on the boarded sidewalk and headed toward the throng.

Kincaid covered the woman's hand.

The woman who claimed to work hard in a cotton mill couldn't be this waiflike thing clinging to the saloon owner. Kincaid was a worthless excuse for a man. Jack didn't have any use for a man like him, nor would any woman worth her salt.

A reedy female voice said, "Your place is lovely, but is there a hotel or a boardinghouse where I could get a room?"

She wouldn't convince anyone she meant what she said with that waver in her voice.

"Why, ma'am, just come across the street, and I'll be sure that you're taken care of," said Kincaid in a snake-oil-salesman's voice.

"Olivia?" Jack called sharply.

She spun around, and for a second it appeared she had no color in her eyes, except thin black dots at the center. "Mr. Trudeau?"

Crystal earbobs danced against her pale-as-milk slender neck. She looked extravagant and indulged. A woman who dressed as if she was due for a ball was all wrong for the frontier. Wrong for the hard life in a trapper's cabin. Wrong for him.

He nodded.

"Where have you been?" she screeched.

Jack winced. He forced his feet to move forward. "Buying supplies."

Jack focused on the woman as he walked closer. Her irises were of such a pale gray-blue that from a distance she appeared to have the eyes of a ghost. *Eyes more gray than blue,* she'd written.

"I'll give you fifty dollars for her," said Ben Kincaid.

Jack hesitated. Fifty dollars was a lot of money, not as much as it cost to get her here, but enough he could reconsider and send for another bride.

Olivia's eyes widened.

"Unhand her," Jack said softly.

Ben Kincaid loosened his grip on Olivia's arm.

She exhaled and her shoulders dropped. Going limp, she put one hand on the trunk. He thought she might swoon. Could she be any more useless?

"She ain't going to be here long nohow," said a man in greasy suspenders.

His heart sinking, Jack silently agreed. No way would this woman last long in the newly christened Colorado Territory.

Her Cupid's-bow mouth flattened. As if the boards of the sidewalk had burst into flames, she stared down.

Her long lashes fluttered against the carved alabaster curve of her cheek.

Good Lord, his bride was beyond pretty. She was beautiful. Could anything be worse in the Colorado Territory, where women were scarce enough that men wanted to treat them as communal property? Rather than being able to defend his cabin while he was out hunting, her looks would just draw more squatters.

"Seventy-five dollars," said Kincaid.

Jack rolled his eyes.

She stared at Kincaid.

"Do you want to go with him?" asked Jack. His jaw tightened until a twitch developed.

Her head jerked back, and she stared at him as if he'd turned into a rattler. She swallowed hard, but then her chin slid up a notch. "No. I'm not a possession to be sold."

Her voice had moderated from the thin, raspy screech she had greeted him with. She still sounded too breathy and young, but he reckoned he could live with the sweeter sound. Maybe, just maybe, she had a bit of grit. "Then tell him to leave you alone."

She gave him an angry glare, then marched toward the mercantile. The way she floated over the ground in her swaying skirt mesmerized him.

"Sure you won't sell her to me?" said Kincaid, breaking the spell. "Seems to me she took to me a mite better than you."

His blood rising, Jack turned toward Kincaid. "You wouldn't know how to handle a lady if you had one."

"And you would?" Kincaid taunted.

"Yeah, I would." His mother was a lady. And she'd never let anyone forget that her blue-blooded grandparents had fled France during the Reign of Terror.

Jack was off-kilter. Olivia was a huge miscalculation on his part. The last thing he wanted was a woman who reminded him of his mother. God help him if Olivia was as haughty. Watching the stiff set of her shoulders, he didn't harbor high hopes.

She should have been a plain, sturdy woman. Mail-order brides wore calico and sunbonnets, not hoop skirts and beribboned straw hats. Pioneer women were ordinary, not pretty, not pampered. It wouldn't be long before Olivia complained of the dirt, the primitive living conditions and him. It wouldn't be long before she fled—just as his mother had.

Chapter Two

My name is Olivia Hansson. I work in a cotton mill. I live in a boardinghouse with my two dearest friends. They consider me the quiet one. I have light hair and am fair skinned. I am above average height for a woman. My eyes are more gray than blue. Please send me a photograph of you.

Spots danced in front of Olivia's eyes, and she prayed she would reach the wagon. With her tight lacings, she could barely breathe. She needed to stop and catch her breath, but she wanted away from those awful men. Jack included.

Her lungs screamed and her vision closed in. She reached the wagon and gripped the side, trying desperately to breathe. Lying down would be prudent, but she suspected Jack would look at her with even more distaste in his brown eyes. Oh, God, he was even better looking than his picture. Yet his frowning appraisal had implied she was a bitter tonic to swallow.

Her eyes stung. She'd fantasized all kinds of greetings, but for him to look at her with distaste had never even crossed her mind. For a minute she'd feared he would sell her.

Her carpetbag thudded into the wagon bed. Her trunk followed. He'd shouldered it as if it weighed nothing. "I'd hoped to be done stocking up before the stage arrived."

The planks of the wagon side bit into her palms. She couldn't look at him. It wasn't much of an apology, but his tardiness hadn't upset her so much as his not protecting her from the swarming jackals. "I understand. The stage doesn't always arrive on schedule."

She strove to sound rational. He'd asked for a calm woman, and hysteria would not be endearing. Nor did she think fainting would project bravery.

Silence stretched between them. Olivia's heart pounded.

"Men here so seldom see a pretty lady, they don't know how to be civil," he offered.

Had he called her pretty? "I am not used to being accosted in the street." No, she was used to being ignored or studiously avoided by the men in Connecticut. She looked out of the corner of her eye at Jack.

He scowled at the trunk he'd just put in the wagon.

"Or offered up for sale," she muttered.

He glared at her. "I didn't offer to sell you. Besides, you were clinging to Kincaid."

"Yes, well, it seemed better to choose one of them rather than to be torn apart." Olivia chomped down on her tongue. Railing at Jack wouldn't improve things.

"I'm sure they preferred you in one piece." Jack shoved her trunk against the side of the wagon. A rigorous round of cheeps came out of a wooden crate holding a couple dozen half yellow, half brown chicks. They looked like they had a bad case of mange.

Olivia closed her eyes. She knew nothing about raising chickens. She forced herself to open her eyes.

Jack gave her a funny look. "Don't you want eggs?"

Had she given away her apprehension? Determined to put a good face on it, she said, "Of course. I've just never raised chickens."

She should tell him she didn't have a clue how to cook eggs, but the confession froze on her tongue.

"I have to go back in the store. Do you want to stay here or go inside?"

Olivia cast a glance over her shoulder. Men still watched her. "I'll go with you."

Jack strode into the store without a backward look. Pushing at the stitch in her side, Olivia followed.

Her eyes took a second to adjust to the dark interior.

Three scruffy men and the group of Indians turned her way. Everyone looked at her, except Jack. Even the grocer stared over the goods piled on the counter. His mouth fell agape. Was she such an oddity?

Olivia took a step forward. Cracker boxes, pickle barrels and all sorts of dry goods from bolts of material to shovels crammed the space. Negotiating the narrow pathways with her hoops would be impossible.

The Indian women pointed, while this time the impassive native men watched, too. If she tilted her hoops to get through the maze of barrels and crates, they would all laugh.

One rough-dressed man's gaze turned from surprised to speculative. His bold look ran down her front and stopped at her chest. Chills ran down her spine. Olivia backed away. Jack shouldered a flour sack and headed toward the door.

She stepped to the side, out of sight of the rude men inside.

Jack made several trips carrying supplies. He finally paused beside her. "Is there anything you need?"

She shook her head, staring down at the wilting bows of her dress.

Jack folded his arms. "You'll need dresses you can work in."

"I'm not an idiot." She knew the carriage dress was impractical for everyday wear. Her mother had worn it visiting when the most strenuous thing she did was raise a teacup. Olivia lifted her chin. "I have work dresses."

The Indians exited the store. The men left as unencumbered as they arrived, but the women bore bundles on their backs.

"Pale Eyes lazy squaw," said a brave as he passed.

Olivia's jaw dropped. She wanted to escape, but she had nowhere to go.

Jack rubbed his forehead as if pained. He looked off to the side. "The preacher is expecting us."

Her stomach jumped to her throat and Olivia's knees buckled.

Jack caught her elbow. "Are you all right?" The question sounded grudging.

"Of course I'm all right." Her voice sounded breathy and strange to her ears. She locked her knees.

Jack guided her toward the wagon. His hands around her waist, he lifted her into the box, and she felt his touch everywhere. In spite of the warmth of the afternoon sun, she shuddered.

A bright woven blanket covered the wooden bench seat. After arranging her hoops so the front of her skirt would not shoot up in the air, she sat on the woolen blanket and folded her hands in her lap to still their shaking.

She was getting married. Today.

Even though she had come fully expecting to marry

Jack, to meet and marry him in the space of an hour was whirlwind fast. Her pounding heart settled in her throat.

Jack spread thick brown animal skins over the supplies, and then lashed them down.

Olivia twisted in the seat to look at him. The Indian's criticism had been cutting. "Should I help you do that?"

He tied the leather straps down. "Not necessary."

The sun glossed the hides of the two brown horses hitched to the wagon. She bit her lip. He was taking her to the church. The minister would bind them together forever. Or did Jack already have a wife?

Jack untied the horses, not mules, from the hitching post. He swung up and settled onto the bench beside her.

Mr. Kincaid had been wrong about Jack owning mules; he was probably wrong about an Indian wife.

"Mr. Trudeau—"

"Jack," he corrected, just a hint of a French accent coloring his words. "Might as well call me by my given name, because I will call you Olivia."

"Jack or Jacques, the French way?" she queried.

He shrugged. "My mother would call me Jacques, but Jack will do." He clearly made a distinction between the "ah" and "ack" sounds this time.

"Must we be married so soon?" Olivia clamped a hand over her mouth. She hadn't meant to say that. She wanted to ask if he had a wife, but she had no idea how to frame the question.

He drew the wagon to a halt and set the brake. Bracing a boot on the board running across the front of the box, he turned sideways and measured her with his warm brown eyes. "I have a one-room cabin."

"Yes," said Olivia.

"Two days' travel from here."

She nodded.

"One bed. Unless you'd rather live in sin," he said with a slight lilt in his voice.

The point he was attempting to make suddenly became crystal clear. Olivia went hot and cold all over. "Oh."

He turned to face the front. "Figured you'd rather be married."

She ducked her head, hiding her flush.

"I can put you back on the stagecoach, if you'd rather."

From his strong profile she tried to glean a hint as to what he preferred. Her heart sank. Even if he sent her back to Connecticut, her home wasn't there anymore. Not that Connecticut had ever really been home. She'd just been stuck there after the train accident killed her parents.

"We can go to the cabin without benefit of marriage, but I'll be damned if I sleep anywhere but in my own bed."

"I see," said Olivia slowly. She desperately wanted to change the subject. Blurting the first thing that came to mind, she said, "I brought you a shirt and coat." Her voice rose to a squeak. "For the wedding, b-but I need time to finish them."

The shirt she'd made from fresh cotton at the mill, and for the jacket she'd recut one of her father's best broadcloth suits. She'd only basted the seams, wanting to check the fit before finishing.

Jack sighed. "We need to get home."

Home. Her mouth opened and nothing came out. She yearned for a home. But nothing was going as anticipated. She wasn't even sure he liked her. She closed her mouth.

"Look, I have no intention of forcing you to be a

wife in all ways before you're ready. But if you intend to leave, I'd rather you did it now."

Was he as uncertain of her as she was of him? The idea startled her. Nothing had indicated he was anything less than supremely confident.

She wanted to tell him she'd slept with his photograph under her pillow for the past three months, but the words wouldn't form. The detail seemed too intimate to reveal to a man who'd written her three letters. The man would be her husband quite soon. Her head spun.

Silence stretched out.

He scowled. "So what is it to be, Olivia?"

"All right," she said in a low whisper.

Jack stood before the altar in the little brick chapel. The stiff collar of the crisp white shirt cut off his breath. The tight black jacket constricted movement. He hated wearing civilized clothes, but he suspected a refusal to wear the jacket and shirt would upset his tense bride.

The mother-of-pearl buttons had the look of expensive tailoring. Other than being a hair too tight, the shirt fit like a glove. His mother would have been ecstatic to see him so finely clothed. He'd probably never wear the shirt and jacket again. He wouldn't have a need.

Beside him, Olivia trembled like aspen leaves caught in the breeze. He kept his hand near her elbow in case she fainted.

As he said his vows, a sick feeling settled in his stomach. He'd wanted a wife to ease his worries, but she had increased them tenfold. The pale beauty wouldn't stand up to Indians who walked in uninvited. She wouldn't be able to back down men tired of panning for gold and wanting easy pickings from his cabin. She hadn't managed to stand up to the men in town, who had daylight and witnesses to prevent them behaving too uncivilized. He'd never be able to leave on a trapping run.

But he couldn't back out.

Olivia whispered her pledge in a tremulous voice. Her head dipped low. Even though the top of her head was on level with his eyes, he couldn't see her expression. He held his breath, fearing she might yet balk and choose to go back East.

"Do you have the ring?" asked the preacher.

When Jack produced the ring, Olivia jerked her head up. Pink tinged her cheeks.

When he slid the ring on her finger, she would be tied to him and this place.

He caught her hand in his. Her cool fingers were long and delicate like a bird's wings, and fluttering in his grip. What would that fluttering feel like against his skin? Likely she would be gone before he knew.

She'd find the gold band too simple, too plain.

It was too loose. Like everything else about this marriage it didn't fit right.

The preacher intoned the solemn words. "I now pronounce you man and wife."

Olivia swayed.

"You may kiss your bride."

Jack turned to face her, but Olivia stared down at her hand.

He waited for her to look up. The preacher cleared his throat.

Cupping her elbow, Jack eased her sideways, but she didn't turn up her face. He nudged her delicate chin. She pressed her lips together. White rimmed her pale gray irises. Her trembling increased.

He sighed, then leaned forward and brushed a kiss on her smooth cheek. Her hat brim nearly poked out his eye. A tiny squeak left her throat. She blinked rapidly and lowered her gaze.

"Congratulations," the preacher said heartily. "After you sign the certificate, won't you join me in the rectory?"

Olivia swiveled back to face the preacher.

Jack began, "We need to get—"

"Yes!"

"—on our way."

Now she speaks. Jack rolled his eyes. She couldn't make her dread of being alone with him be more obvious. He kept his voice coaxing, rational. "We need to leave while we have daylight."

She gave a short nod, but her lower lip trembled.

"Just one thing, then," said the preacher. "We do things different out here in the territories. I won't file the certificate for a month."

Jack winced.

Olivia froze. Then she turned toward him with her eyes wide.

The preacher lowered his head and cleared his throat. "In case you find you don't suit."

"Wh-what?" asked Olivia on a shallow puff of air.

Jack caught her arm and tugged her toward the door. She looked over her shoulder at the preacher. "Nothing to worry about," Jack mumbled.

But the V between her brows suggested she was plenty worried. She wouldn't make it thirty days. And he wished the preacher hadn't made it so damn obvious she could leave without repercussions.

Hours later, Olivia anxiously scanned the horizon for a dwelling where they might spend the night. Perhaps over the next rise would be a new settlement.

The horses' heads bobbed, jiggling the harnesses. Their backs glistened with sweat as they pulled the creaking wagon over the twin dirt tracks through the long grass. The sun scraped the peaks of the green-and-purple-topped mountains far to their left. With every mile the menacing giants loomed closer.

They hadn't encountered any other travelers. She'd rarely seen such long stretches without a town or a farm.

Jack rolled his shoulders. The basted stitches at his shoulders gaped. He hadn't been willing to wait for her to finish the shirt.

His silence made her tense. His presence made her tense. His despairing gaze on her made her tense.

"Have you known Mr. Kincaid long?" Olivia stared ahead where the trail rose up and up into the robin's-egg-blue sky as she waited for his answer. And waited. She wanted to ask what the preacher had meant, but she dared not.

He scowled.

She wanted to retract her question, yet he would have to acknowledge her sooner or later. What kind of a life would they have if they never talked to each other?

"He seemed to know you." Both men had known Jack, but the other man hadn't given his name.

"Long enough."

Not willing to let the grudging opening go, she asked, "What does he do?"

"He gambles and provides whor—runs a saloon."

"He seemed to want to let me know he was rich."

"Because he dupes the prospectors out of the gold they find."

"He seemed more gentlemanly than the other—"

"He fools women into working on their backs for him, too." Jack glared at her.

"—man." Olivia cringed, her ears heated. "I didn't think he could be trusted."

"No. He can't be." Jack drew the wagon to a halt at the base of the hill and wrapped the reins around the brake handle. "You need to get out and walk."

Her jaw dropped and her fingers curled in. "Because I asked about Mr. Kincaid?"

"No, Olivia." The corner of his mouth curled up.

That look mirrored the look in his photograph. She'd anticipated seeing his bemused half smile for a thousand miles. Her heart skipped a beat. She wanted that look, rather than the look of impatient disgust he'd greeted her with.

"Because the horses have to haul the weight of a loaded wagon up a steep grade." Jack leaped out of the wagon.

Olivia stood. Preparing to climb down, she grasped the footboard. Walking might be a relief. In spite of the blanket folded on the wooden seat, the jolting wagon was not so kind to her posterior.

Jack disappeared around the back.

The width of her skirts made it impossible to see where to step. She would have changed to a more serviceable gown if Jack hadn't been in such a rush to get her out of the church. Reaching back, she searched for a foothold.

His hands closed around her waist.

Her heart skipped.

He swung her down as if she weighed nothing. Awareness of him jangled along every inch of her skin. "Th-thank you."

She couldn't look him in the eye. Her cheeks heated. Her breath hitched. How foolish must she look staring at the wagon? She slowly turned to face him. His hands slid along her waist. A rush of emotions swamped her. He was her husband, but she hardly knew him. They would become intimate, except he'd said he wouldn't rush her.

She stared at a middle button. The stitches around the hole were even and neat, not so small the edges scalloped but not so big as to appear clumsy. Her hopes of a perfect marriage had been in every thrust and pull of her needle.

"Just get over the rise, then you can ride again," he encouraged. Dropping his hold on her, he moved toward the team. Gripping the leather strap between the horses' bridles, he clucked to the horses and started them up the slope.

Olivia followed. The horses pulled the wagon faster than she could walk. Her squished toes protested. Her mother's demi-boots were too small.

The hill stretched out before her like a small mountain. Sucking air between her teeth, she trudged forward.

The wagon pulled away. She pressed at the stitch forming in her side. Before long, spots danced in front of her eyes. To fit in her mother's dress she'd laced her corset tight. While sitting, the extra cinching hadn't mattered.

The wide flare of her hoop skirt hid the best path. Loose rocks twisted her feet while her toes and heels painfully rubbed inside the demi-boots. The steepness increased. Her skirt snagged on a rock. Impatiently she raised her dress high enough to continue.

She plodded forward, one foot after another for as long as she could, only stopping to regain her breath. The wagon disappeared over the ridge. After a few minutes the wagon's rattle and the endless chirping of the chicks no longer drifted back. How far ahead was Jack?

Resuming her trek, she climbed.

The sun disappeared behind the peaks and the light faltered to a shadowlike dusk and then went darker. She took a step, then another. The darkness was not all because of the quality of the light, but the result of her inability to get more than a short puff of air into her lungs. Her foot twisted in a hole she couldn't see and she fell to her hands and knees. Her palms stung.

She stayed like a dog, her head hanging as she waited for the faintness to pass. If she couldn't make it up the hill, would Jack leave her here?

Jack had planned to be another dozen miles up the road before stopping, but Olivia had dropped so far behind, the plateau a half mile past the crest of the hill would have to be far enough today.

He guided the blowing and snorting horses into the meadow. Listening for Olivia, he released them from their traces. The horses needed to be watered, curried and dried before the temperature dipped overnight.

Jack unlashed the wagon bed and retrieved a spade. He picked out the best place for a fire pit. So much needed to be done before the night closed in and Olivia didn't look to be much help.

Wetonga would have already gathered the makings of a fire by now. Hadn't he made it clear in his advertisement that he needed a helpmate, not another helpless animal to care for?

He attacked the sod, turning it over and away from his fire pit. He viciously scraped the dirt. What healthy young woman couldn't walk up a quarter mile of steep hill in less than half an hour? Apparently his wife.

He jabbed the spade in the ground and straightened. As he'd led the horses up the steep grade, he'd seen her slogging forward.

He'd wanted to go back for her, but he couldn't let the horses stand with the weight pulling on them. Nor could he trust them to continue up the hill without guidance. They'd already been huffing and puffing. Stopping and restarting would've put unnecessary strain on his livestock and risked the loaded wagon rolling backward and doing serious damage.

He squinted toward the road. A cool breeze wafted across his brow. The temperature was dropping. He needed to make camp, not fetch Olivia. Why hadn't she made it over the ridge yet?

Her froufrou dress was the height of absurdity in this rugged land. The wide skirt must make walking harder, but her frivolousness irritated him all the same.

He frowned. How the hell was Olivia to know that hoops shouldn't be worn out here? He should have insisted she change. But he'd figured he might as well get the satisfaction of driving a beautiful woman dressed like a princess through town.

So it was his fault that she was struggling to climb a ridge in a dress better suited for a parlor than a mountain pass.

He stomped over to the wagon and shoved aside the animal skins until he found his rifle. Taking a hasty look around, he reckoned there weren't any skulkers about. Too many men in the recent influx of speculators would steal his goods, or worse.

He stalked to the road and back up the slight dip that followed the nasty incline. Many a man would find his pretty bride worth stealing. His heart stepped up a notch.

He jogged to the ridge. His heart pounded as he

scanned the tall grass. The road was empty. More than a hundred yards down a scrap of lilac material lay on the ground. His throat tightened.

"Olivia," he called, and then louder, "Olivia!"

Farther out was a pool of white. His chest tight, he ran down the slope. As he drew near he made out a petticoat and her lilac-colored jacket. What had happened? A disgruntled miner or a rogue brave could have stripped her of her clothes. Jack's heart caught in his throat.

Horrible images flashed in his mind of her knocked out, gagged and bound.

Was she even now being abused in the worst possible way?

His boots thudded against the ground and his hands grew slippery on the rifle. Oh, God, was his wife being raped because he was more worried about his horses and supplies?

Chapter Three

Here is the photograph you requested. I am stand-
ing in front of the offices of The Rocky Mountain
News *by Cherry Creek. The natives say that it is*
unwise to build so close to the water, but their
knowledge is often ignored. Tell me more about
yourself. Would you be willing to travel far into
the mountains?

Now he comes for me, thought Olivia with exasperation. The only way to make it up the hill was to loosen
her corset and remove her hoops, which meant half
undressing. She'd thrown off her jacket, then fought
through the tall grass to a gray-and-green-speckled
boulder for privacy. After struggling for several minutes, she finally got the back of the dress unbuttoned.

The lavender material puffed around her ankles as
she tugged off her petticoats to access her corset strings.

"Olivia!" His voice was much nearer.

Bending down so he wouldn't see her state of undress, she jerked at the strings. The ability to draw in
full breaths was a blessed relief, but she barely got the

strings retied and her dress pulled up before he was upon her.

Her husband would eventually be privy to her undressing, but she wasn't prepared to share everything now.

"Olivia, where are you?"

Drat, the man was practically on top of her.

She rammed her arms into the sleeves and popped up. "I'm here. Go back—" A long black barrel pointed at her. She jerked, bolts of shock zinging through her body, making every fiber tense.

Frozen, she stared. Just beyond the stock his jaw pulsed. After an immeasurable pause his narrowed eyes relaxed. He lowered the gun. His gaze dropped to her petticoats draped over the rock and then rose back to her face.

Her cheeks burned as she held up the unfastened dress. "Could you give me a moment, please," she said in a prim voice.

"Sorry." He turned and walked back toward the path. He stopped with his back to her.

Why in heaven's name had he drawn a gun on her? Shivering with a sudden cold that had nothing to do with the air temperature, Olivia slipped the buttons she could fasten into their holes. She snatched her extra petticoats off the rock, draped them and the excess material of her skirt over her arm and rejoined Jack.

He looped the metal bands of her crinoline around his shoulder. Her jacket was wadded beneath his arm. With the back of her dress half-undone, she needed the jacket to cover the gaping opening.

She hesitated. "Why would you point a gun at me?"

"I thought you might have been attacked," he said. "Next time answer when I call."

His tone was matter-of-fact, but she felt scolded all the same. She nodded. Men didn't carry around guns back in Connecticut. She scanned the tall grass, wondering what vicious animal he'd suspected was lying in wait.

"Do you need me to carry you?" he asked.

"I can walk."

He swiveled toward her. He looked at her as if she'd told him she could fly or some other absurdity.

"I like walking. I walk all the time. I just wasn't dressed for walking." Olivia ducked her chin.

"I didn't realize walking required special attire," said Jack slowly. He pulled at the collar of his shirt. The garment she'd labored over didn't suit him.

"This is a carriage dress. It is for sitting and riding in a carr…" Well, a wagon hardly qualified as high transport. "For riding or visiting, not for scaling mountains." Not for having a gun pointed at her.

His brown gaze slid down her dress.

Her heart did a little jig.

"Do you have dresses for mountain scaling?" he asked.

Good gravy, was her husband an imbecile? Was all that brawny masculinity just a shell around nothing? "No."

"Mmm." The corners of his eyes crinkled as if he were about to smile.

Was that all he could say? Or had he been trying not to laugh at her? She was tired of traveling and being stared at as if she were an oddity. Her palm up, Olivia gestured for him to lead.

Jack gave a tiny shake of his head as if rousing himself from a stupor. "I should have told you to change."

Olivia huffed, a feat she wouldn't have been able to manage before loosening her corset laces.

"But you looked so pretty in your *carriage dress*." He mimicked her gesture as if he expected her to go first, and then looked over his shoulder at the rays that haloed up from the out-of-sight sun.

His compliment was so embedded in criticism, she didn't feel obliged to acknowledge it. Why call her pretty, then look away? If he thought her pretty he would look at her more often. He was probably just trying to soothe her ruffled feathers. Perhaps he didn't want a sulky bride on his wedding night.

A cold wash traveled down her spine. Olivia shivered all over.

"We have a lot to do before night falls," Jack said.

"I'll be right behind you."

His forehead furrowed. "You're not a squaw."

She had no idea what he meant by that. She stared at his broad shoulders as he transferred his gun to his left hand and reached to put his hand at her back.

She twisted away, not wanting him to discover the open back of her dress.

"You don't have to walk behind me," he said.

"I'd rather."

He shook his head. "Stay with me or I will carry you." Then he took off up the incline at a fast clip. She trotted to keep pace. He left the road and Olivia waded through the tall grass. Her thin heels sank into the soft ground.

He tossed her clothing into the wagon, peeled back the hides and then pulled out the peeping box. "Watch the chicks while they forage. Don't let them get away. I'll see if a stream is in those trees." He scooped out the half-feathered chicks and set them on the ground. "The fire pit is over there." He pointed to a patch of bare dirt. "Gather up kindling, too."

She retrieved her matching jacket and put it on. She couldn't button it, but at least her exposed laces were hidden.

Jack walked toward the stand of trees in the distance. "I'll hear you if you shout."

Why would she need to shout for him?

"If you see a bear, or the horses start acting odd, yell." With that he strode off.

The hairs on the back of her neck lifted. Were there bears around? Had Jack had the gun ready because he feared a bear had attacked her?

Bears weren't what concerned Jack. But warning Olivia that she should be wary of all beasts, four legged or two, had seemed unkind. Blood rushed in his ears. He'd been so sure when he saw her jacket near the road and her petticoats on the rock that he'd find her on the ground being violated by one of the low men who'd come West in search of easy money.

Jack had been ready to kill any man who dared touch her. And it angered him that she attracted attention and couldn't fend it off.

The horses needed watering and the camp needed setting up. He slowed his breathing, attuning to what was around him.

The breeze shimmied through aspen leaves and pine trees darkened the woods. He slung his rifle strap over his back and walked into the shade. The tinkle of running water floated through the air. He'd been so focused on Olivia that he'd neglected to bring a bucket.

At least she'd finally showed a bit of spunk. Obviously she hadn't liked him discovering her in the midst of ridding herself of layers of excessive clothing. Perhaps she had been lagging behind for privacy.

A smile tugged at the corners of Jack's mouth. Taking off those ridiculous hoops may have been the first smart thing she'd done. He gathered up deadwood, then started back.

Olivia chased around in a circle shooing the chicks into a tight cluster. With her skirt and petticoats caught in her arm, her slender ankles were visible. She took off her hat and waved it at the chicks.

She looked young and naive as she valiantly kept the chicks from foraging. They peeped and tumbled over each other. Her back to him, she slowly circled.

Great, he'd acquired a sheepdog instead of a wife.

Olivia stepped sideways and fanned her hat at a chick that dared to stray a couple of feet from his brethren. The instant she saw him, she froze.

She pulled her jacket closed and lowered her skirt, hiding her ankles. She pushed a stray strand off her forehead.

The paleness of her hair struck him. The soft-hued blond mass was twisted and woven into dozens of thin braids in an elaborate confection on the back of her head.

Wetonga had braided her hair in two braids or worn it held back by a leather band around her forehead. The first time he'd met her, she'd entered the tepee where he slept, drawn off her doeskin dress and tossed it on the ground before joining him on his bedroll. He suspected it wouldn't be so easy with Olivia.

His throat tightened at the idea of seeing her hair down, curtaining her naked body. Picturing Olivia flushed and naked, his blood heated.

His desire for her hit him like an ax, cleaving him

down to the bone. He'd spent most of the day thinking her too refined to tempt him, but he'd been wrong. Her cool beauty called like forbidden fruit. Her slender fingers, the blush that swept over her cheeks, and the span of her slender waist in his hands all thickened his blood.

But then he'd promised he wouldn't pressure her to be his wife in that way.

He sighed. Perhaps he'd been hasty, but she'd cast a longing look toward the stage office. He'd been willing to say anything to keep her here. Which made no sense at all, since she would be more trouble than help.

"They keep trying to get away," Olivia said.

"They're trying to eat." He resumed walking. "Let them roam."

"Oh." Her forehead furled and she bit her lip.

Jack dropped the wood near the fire pit. She hadn't gathered kindling. "I'm taking the horses to drink at the stream."

"A stream? May I wash?"

"If it is still light enough to see when I get back." Jack brushed bark off his chest. "You need to watch the chicks."

"Will you light the fire?"

"The tinderbox is behind the seat."

Her mouth tightened and her eyes darted nervously from the fire pit to the wagon and back.

"You don't know how to use it," he said flatly. Could she do anything beyond look pretty?

Olivia shook her head. She flapped her hat at a chick straying beyond some larger boundary she'd set in her head.

He sighed. "When I get back, I'll take care of it."

He moved to the wagon, removed his rifle and set

it down. He unbuttoned and stripped off the fancy new shirt.

Olivia gasped.

She studiously looked away, but her cheeks were bright.

He rummaged for his buckskin shirt and drew it over his head. "Might as well change into what you want to sleep in. It'll be dark soon." He remembered to gather the bucket, a sling and a hatchet before tossing buffalo hides to the ground.

If Olivia was shocked at seeing him without his shirt, it didn't bode well for their marital relations. The chances of a lady like her wanting him were slim.

Besides, she didn't know how to light a fire. She didn't know how to dress for the wild and she sure didn't know anything about caring for chickens. "Do you know how to garden?"

She brightened. "We used to have the most lovely roses and irises."

Merde, what kind of a wife was she?

Once he was out of sight, Olivia scurried to the wagon and slid out of her lavender jacket. Hurrying, she changed into a nightgown without removing her shift and corset. While he might not have any qualms about undressing in front of her, she wasn't ready to fling off her garments in his presence.

Chasing the memory of his broad golden-skinned chest from her mind proved impossible. She shivered.

The murky light was dimming by the minute. The shadows of the trees grew black and forbidding. Would Jack be able to find his way back? Were wild animals lurking in the deepening dusk? Or had the stand of trees swallowed him and the horses whole, leaving her all alone in this wilderness?

The chattering trees seemed to warn her this place was not like back East. As if she needed more warning. Hairs on the back of her neck stood on end and her heart beat in irregular jolts. The unseen animals lurking in the shadows, the impending intimacy of her wedding night and the solitude all unnerved her.

What would Jack think if he returned and found her in her nightgown? A shudder racked her body. Sleeping together when they'd barely spoken troubled her. She pulled her heavy brown-twill traveling dress over the top.

The yards of material meant to go over hoops dragged in the grass.

Only a bit warmer, she retrieved the fire-starting implements and carried them over to the pile of wood. He'd wanted her to gather kindling. She glanced toward the copse. She didn't want to go into the darkness. Instead, she snapped off small branches from the wood he'd gathered.

After making a tight little pile of wood, she got out the flint and the metal ring.

Striking sparks couldn't be that hard, could it?

She hit the metal against the sharp edge. A cascade of glowing orange sparks landed on her skirt.

She brushed the hot bits from her skirt, singeing her hand.

"What are you doing?" Booted footfalls thudded toward her. "*Merde!* Are you trying to catch yourself on fire?"

She spun around. She opened her mouth to defend herself but stood mutely. Nothing would have made sense. "I'm fine. I didn't know how it worked."

The horses followed him up the incline with neck-bobbing long strides. "Just wait." Jack set down a bucket near the woodpile. "Let me get the horses staked."

She looked down to see if she'd burned holes in her brown twill, but she couldn't see in the dusky half-light.

How much a nuisance he found her was clear in his voice. Contributing to that impression by insisting he take her down to the water could only make things worse.

"It is too dark for me to go to the creek to wash up now."

"There's water in the bucket. Just don't use it all."

Disappointment curled through her. She'd been looking forward to the chance to thoroughly wash off the dust from the day of travel. Using her cupped palm, she took a drink and used a little of the icy water to wash off her face. Not knowing what else to do, she sank down on the woolly hide.

The chicks peeped happily from their box.

"You put the chicks in their crate?" he asked.

"I didn't want to lose them in the dark." Had that been wrong, too? She held very still as she waited for his response.

"Good."

It was hardly high praise. But at least she'd done one thing right. She breathed out slowly, releasing tension.

Jack groomed the horses and threw blankets across their backs. He walked over and looked down on the wood. "What the hell?"

Olivia winced.

Jack set the broken branches to the side. He threw most of the firewood back on the pile. Obviously her efforts hadn't been worth a darn.

"I don't know how to build a fire, but I can learn."

He grunted, then set about building the fire. Making her efforts look puny, he fired sparks onto a nest of dried grass and the square of black fabric she hadn't known how to use. He blew on it, then shoved the flaring pile under the three sticks steepled in the center.

He made it look simple.

"What is for supper?" asked Olivia. She hadn't eaten since a hurried breakfast at a stage stop.

"Use anything you want out of supplies in the wagon."

Olivia winced.

"There's flour, butter, oats, beans..." He looked up and his eyes narrowed. "You've never cooked over an open fire, either."

She'd never *cooked*. She should tell him, but unable to bear the flat look in his eyes at every revelation she made, she bit her tongue. Shaking her head, she looked down.

"Just sit. I'll get us food in a minute." He coaxed the fire, adding twigs and larger sticks until lively flames popped and crackled. He settled rocks around the edge. "Fires need lots of air."

Olivia folded up her knees and put her chin on them. Jack didn't stop moving until well after the stars were out. He lit a lantern over by the wagon. He gave the chicks water and cracked corn and oats. Then he wrapped the heated rocks and placed them in the crate. When he returned, he held out a couple of things that looked like dried excrement.

Olivia jerked back. "What is that?"

"Jerky." Jack put one to his mouth, sank his strong white teeth in it and ripped off a piece. He waved the remaining strip in her face. "Try it."

She reluctantly took the leathery thing from his hand and sniffed. A faint beefy scent made her mouth water.

With his rifle beside him, Jack sat down cross-legged. "Indians smoke and dry venison strips so it doesn't spoil."

Not beef, but deer, then. Olivia tried to nibble but found it impossible. She had to rip a bite away and then chewed and chewed.

Her civilized eating habits were already gone. What else would be gone by the end of the day? She surreptitiously cast a glance in Jack's direction. He stared off into the darkness as he chewed. Was he thinking of lying with her? Was he looking forward to it?

Olivia knew nothing of what actually occurred in the marriage bed. Her curiosity was likely to be satisfied, but Jack was a stranger. He'd said little. If he was eager to bed her, it wasn't at all clear.

Would Jack be gentle or would he be impatient? Olivia watched him for clues. All she could tell was that he didn't seem terribly interested. He hadn't really kissed her after they were wed. Just a peck on her cheek.

Her mind swirled back to the brief exchange following the ceremony.

"What did the minister mean when he said he won't file the certificate for a month?" she ventured.

"He meant that if the marriage is a mistake, he'll tear up the certificate rather than officially record the marriage."

"What?" She felt punched in the gut. "Like a trial period?"

Jack shot her a narrow-eyed look. "Simpler than a divorce if it isn't going to work."

"I didn't know such things were done." Her hushed voice shook. A coldness crept into her chest and took root. Was she married or not? She sucked in as much air as she could.

"Not everyone is suited for life in the Rockies."

She bit on her lip until she tasted blood. Would this marriage be as temporary as every situation had been since the deaths of her parents? "D-does that mean it would be like the marriage never happened?"

"Officially, yes. There wouldn't be a record."

She'd thought she would finally have a permanent home. The coldness in her chest spread as if she'd been shoved outside naked into a blizzard.

"Did you want him to tell me that?" she squawked.

"No. I didn't think it would be a good idea to alarm you." His voice was tight. Jack leaned forward.

Olivia jumped.

He put another pine branch on the fire. The needles flared and snapped, echoing the turmoil inside her. Her stomach quivered, and even if a decent meal had been offered, she didn't think she could have eaten.

"Don't fret. It is just a precaution in case you cannot handle life out here."

Or he didn't want her. Pulling her knees tighter to her chest, she looked down at the ground. Did he want her to leave?

"Is the jerky that bad?" Jack asked.

Olivia looked at the remaining piece in her hand and forced herself to take another bite. Her stomach protested. Was he waiting for her to finish eating before taking her to bed?

Jack pulled out another strip from a pouch and contentedly ate. The strong line of his stubble-darkened jaw caught her attention. His hair was shorter than when photographed, but the ends curled, defying the neatness of the fresh cut.

She knew so little of him, beyond that he lived in the mountains, trapped and traded with the Indians for furs and wrote of the mountains with reverence. She wanted to learn about him. Perhaps the distance between them could be bridged. "I really want to like it here."

Jack grunted.

Not exactly encouragement to talk.

Abruptly, Jack stood and brushed his hands on his pants. He looked over his shoulder.

His expression turned determined, as if he had an unpleasant task ahead of him, Jack lifted the lantern. "I've made a pallet of sorts in the wagon. We have a long day tomorrow if we're to make it home."

Home. The word felt foreign. She had been heading to a new home in Boston when the train wreck had derailed her life. She wanted to go home, but wasn't sure such a place existed for her. Perhaps sharing the night with him would allow her to feel less like an unwelcome intruder into his world.

Olivia shakily rose to her feet. The stars twinkled in the sky and she couldn't delay any longer. The jerky sat in her stomach like a lead ball. Jack put his hand on the small of her back. She stumbled forward.

The march across the twenty feet felt like miles, yet they reached the wagon too soon. Her heart tripped. She rubbed her damp palms on her skirt. Jack stood so close she could feel his heat. His hand on her lower back seared through the layers of clothing, and her knees turned to jelly.

Setting the lantern on the seat, he slid his hand to her shoulder and turned her to face him. Her body moved woodenly. He cupped both her shoulders. She felt so strange, floaty and yet tense. She wished he would tell her what to expect, that he would take care of her, that she had nothing to fear, but he was silent. Not knowing where to look, she stared at the V at the neck of his shirt.

He slid his hands across her back and brought her against his body. He was solid, warm and, oh, so strong. She didn't know what to do, how to respond. So she did nothing, her arms hanging awkwardly at her sides. Tension screamed through her body as strange tingles spread along her skin.

He expelled a breath before pressing his lips to her forehead.

With a quick movement, he scooped her up.

She gasped.

He hoisted her above the wagon bed's rim and lowered her. A small place behind the seat had been hollowed out, but the space was only enough for one person, unless he intended for them to pile on top of one another as the chicks did. Hot and cold streams ran down her spine.

Setting her down on the pile of skins and blankets, he said, "Good night, Olivia." He returned to the fire, then settled cross-legged by it.

She sat stunned. "You're not sleeping here?"

"I'm not sleeping. I'm keeping watch."

Shadows all around concealed any menace. The strange boulders looked as if they'd been marbles tossed out by the hand of a giant. What lurked in their shadows? Her heart hammered. The wind soughed through the trees. "Watch for what?"

He picked up his gun and laid it across his lap. "Animals."

Bears? Olivia nodded slowly and turned to burrow into the bedding. He was her husband and protector. She could relinquish her worries to him.

Underneath her relief at not facing the mysteries of

the night, disappointment curled in her stomach. She tried to tell herself Jack just had a duty to protect her and the animals. But she suspected she had been such a disappointment he didn't want to make her his wife.

Chapter Four

I haven't traveled since my youth, but I have always dreamed of seeing the Rocky Mountains. I was born in New York. In 1853 my family was moving to Boston when the train had an accident. The engineer missed the signal that the drawbridge was open and the cars fell into the water. My parents did not survive and I never made it to Boston. I would like to know more about your home.

The fire burned low. The temperature dropped. Jack pulled a hide over his legs. In a perfect world, his wife would be nestled beside him keeping him warm, and they'd be farther from the road where Kincaid and his ilk could chance upon them. Predators came in all shapes and sizes. He added a branch to the fire. The pine needles flared.

Olivia's dread of the intimacies couldn't be clearer. Since leaving town, she'd been unnaturally quiet. Several times she'd jerked away from him. When Jack had hugged her, she'd kept her arms rigidly at her sides.

When she'd allowed him to touch her, she always

stared studiously at his chest rather than angle her chin for a kiss.

The last thing he wanted was a wife who submitted but would make it clear she hated every second of intimacy.

But as the hours after midnight ticked by, Jack's concerns diminished. His thoughts shifted to the strange creature nestled in his wagon. Why had Olivia married him? She should have married a banker or lawyer. She had yet to study the mountains she'd been eager to see. She certainly didn't look at him. Instead, she pinned her gaze on her clasped hands in her lap.

The wagon creaked and Jack stared in her direction. He forced himself to look away. The dark copse of trees, the meadow and the road remained empty of threats. The horses bowed their heads, sleeping undoubtedly. If he had made the bed bigger he could have crawled in the wagon with Olivia for a few hours of shut-eye.

As he nestled the chick's warming rocks in the coals, Olivia shifted again. Jack stood and stretched. Fighting sleepiness, he paced.

Was Olivia restless?

After a few minutes, he rolled out the rocks, rewrapped them and placed them in the crate with the chicks. The chicks piled on top of the stones.

Rustling noises emanated from the wagon. Olivia slowly climbed down. For a second she teetered, then found her balance on a wheel spoke. Wrapping the blanket around her shoulders, she approached.

Was she seeking out his company? His spine tightened. He swiveled toward her. "Can't sleep?"

"I should keep watch the rest of the night so you can sleep." Her answer came out in a puff of white mist. She stretched shaking hands toward the orange coals.

She wouldn't know the first thing to look for.

"I could wake you if there is anything amiss." She covered a yawn.

He doubted she'd manage to stay awake. But she was trying. Jack sank down and patted the hide next to him. "Sit."

She stared at the bit of hide left open for her.

Giving her more room, he scooted to the edge, although she didn't need it. His patience, already thin from too long without sleep, cracked. He ordered, "Sit. I won't bite."

She sat down fast. A good six inches remained between them. Six inches and a grand canyon.

Her teeth chattered. While the night air was cool, it wasn't desperately cold. But Olivia was like a hothouse flower that had never had to endure the out-of-doors. This land might destroy her; she was such a pale piece of fluff.

He pulled her onto his lap and wrapped a buffalo skin around them. She tightened like a drawn bowstring. He found her glacial hands and slowly rubbed them. "Don't fight the cold. Breathe deep."

She shuddered violently and leaned away from him. He pulled her back against him. "Relax, I'm just warming you."

"I'm sorry," she whispered.

Jack winced. He ducked his head against her elaborate coif and sighed. Her repulsion made him feel like a coarse, disgusting reptile. Part of him wanted to peel back the layers of material between them and make her his wife, here under the stars with the cold air against his heated skin. Yet he hated to think what her response might be.

He'd planned on waiting until they returned to the

cabin, so she could have the privacy of four walls and the comfort of a bed, but he suspected the wait might be much longer. He'd never felt a strong urge to bed a reluctant woman, not when shared desire was so much better.

Even as cold as Olivia was, she wouldn't appreciate the warmth generated by an exchange of body heat. She held herself rigid. His coarseness might be too much for her. He wasn't a dapper popinjay and never would be. If she'd thought by bringing him a fancy shirt and coat she could refine him, she was wrong.

Her soft hair tickled his nose. She smelled of lavender soap. He traced his fingers over the wedding band. She had a lady's hands, soft, smooth, suited for playing a pianoforte or tatting lace, not hard work. Still he resisted the urge to nuzzle her slender neck. He didn't want to inflict his attentions on her.

She balled her hand and the ring wobbled on her finger. He prodded it back and forth.

"I can get this resized."

"I'll wrap yarn around the inside so it doesn't fall off."

Did she not want the ring to fit? He tensed. "I'm sure the jeweler won't mind."

"Where you bought it?"

"Where I had the ring fashioned from gold I found in my creek." Jack wished he could take back the words. If she thought the gold band too simple, she now knew he was solely responsible. He'd put a piece of his home on her finger and had the ring specially made for her.

"Is there more gold in your creek?"

For the first time since he married her, she sounded eager. Cold seeped inside him, jabbing under his breastbone. Jack stopped rubbing her fingers. "I haven't looked for more."

If she wanted riches, she shouldn't have come to the Colorado Territory. Even if a man had money, he couldn't buy luxuries found in an Eastern city. Or get purchases to his cabin. He'd had a hell of a time hauling in the cookstove purchased from settlers who were giving up.

He hadn't wanted a woman who expected gifts for the privilege of touching her, but he should have given Olivia a wedding gift. She'd brought a shirt and jacket. His puny purchase of a tea tin seemed pathetic. Even though the ring was gold, he hadn't bought it, either.

"Are you warmer?" He heard anger in his voice and regretted that the lack of sleep made his emotions raw.

"Yes, of course." She stood and wrapped the blanket tightly around her. "Thank you." Her voice was stretched taut.

Jack rubbed his scratchy eyes. He hadn't meant she had to get off his lap. He hadn't meant that at all. He stood, too, and he supposed the dark and the tiredness and the disappointment made him say, "Why did you marry me?"

"I had to. The mill closed," she blurted.

Stunned, he stood still. "The mill closed," he repeated slowly. For the first time since they'd been married, she really looked at him. The brassy glow of the fire illuminated her wide soulless eyes.

"When?"

"December. The cotton shipments stopped. Because of the war."

Before she'd written him back after receiving his photograph.

Her pale features twisted in anguish and that perfect Cupid's-bow mouth opened to speak or squeak as she was wont to do. "I had to—"

"Don't make it worse." He warned. The words of caution were for him as much as for her. Her beauty should have been the first clue. She wasn't a regular mail-order bride. But like a sore tooth, he couldn't resist probing it. "The mill closed. And you had no other options?"

"No." She ducked her head again, and perhaps that was better. She hadn't come West because she wanted to be married. No, she had considered marrying him a last resort. Given that she wasn't suited for life out here, she wouldn't last long if her heart wasn't in it.

He leaned over and snatched up the rifle and stalked toward the wagon. Blood roared in his ears, and his stomach churned. She didn't want to be here. The neatly penned words of eagerness were lies.

God, how could he have been such a fool?

Olivia wished she hadn't blurted out about the mill closing. She had picked him from all the other advertisements, but saying so seemed to leave her too exposed. She sank down.

When she received his letter and photograph, she'd been so grateful. She'd thought he wanted her.

But his impatience was tangible. Her shortcomings overshadowed everything else. Not being wanted shouldn't surprise her. She wasn't calm natured or brave, or much of a helpmate in this unfamiliar environment, but she could learn. He just needed to give her a chance.

Rocking back and forth, she fought the chill that was not only from the night air, but deep in her heart. Since her parents' deaths, she hadn't been wanted anywhere.

She would show him marrying her hadn't been a mistake. Just as she had convinced them at the mill she was worth keeping. The shock of hard work had almost made her fail, but she wasn't a pampered young teen anymore.

A decade ago she thought she'd marry a man who wore suits and worked in an office like her papa. Men like that in Norwalk regarded mill girls as social inferiors and steered clear. While no man in Connecticut had ever approached her, the men in Denver City had swarmed her. He had to see that she had value.

Jack returned and nestled an iron skillet down in the coals and set a heavy lid on the top. "We might as well get an early start. Seeing as how we're both awake."

Demonstrating her lack of cooking skills wasn't the best way to show her worthiness. Uneasiness curdled her stomach. She stood. "What should I do?"

He grabbed the lantern and lit it. The light illuminated his stoic expression. He strode back to the wagon and shoved things around. "Just sit. I'll get things done faster if you aren't in my way."

"I know I'm not what you expected," muttered Olivia as she sank down onto the buffalo hide.

She wanted to curl into herself and disappear. "When you sent your photograph, I wanted…wanted to marry you." She could hardly speak to a man for most of her life and now she blurted out the most pathetic details.

The rattling in the wagon stopped. "Because of a photograph—" incredulity rang in his voice "—you decided to marry me?"

Olivia twisted her hands together. "You looked like a man who could face the world and survive." His appearance of solid strength drew her like metal filings to a magnet. Yet his descriptions of the beauty of his home showed he was not a brute. "I thought you could protect me."

"I can't protect you, Olivia." His rustling resumed.

"I spend weeks at a time trapping. Life here is demanding and a woman needs to hold her own. I thought I was clear about that."

He sounded resigned.

"You were clear," she mumbled. She was the deceiver.

"You had choices. There are men in town looking for brides."

"Because not being able to cook would have been an asset in town," she spit out.

"You've never cooked at all, have you?" he asked with a deadly quiet to his voice.

"No. I'm sorry. I didn't think you'd marry me if I told you."

He bent forward and didn't say anything for a bit. Then he picked up the shirt she'd made for him and held it up. "A lot of the miners in California are wearing rags. A shirt like this would fetch a dollar, maybe five. They can get material, but they don't know how to sew."

How would she have known? But that was neither here nor there. She lifted her chin. "I chose you. I only wrote to you."

"Lucky me."

Selina had written to at least three men and Anna never would say how many different advertisements she answered. Olivia swallowed hard. Surely she hadn't been the only one to respond to his request for a wife. He must have chosen her, too.

"I didn't want to live in a tent or a…or a dugout." She had to hold her hands tightly to keep from waving them around to make her point.

"Fine," he said with finality, as if the subject had been exhausted. "It's done now."

But it wasn't done. The preacher had said they had

a month to decide. Jack could still reject her. Tremors rolled down her spine and her stomach knotted. She bit her lip. "Do you intend to take me back to Denver City and pretend this marriage never happened?"

"Is that what you want me to do? Have you decided you've made a mistake?" he asked, his voice rough.

Had *she* made a mistake?

"N-no." She shook her head and stared down at her clasped hands. "I'm not the one who is disappointed."

"Yes, you are, if you expected a full-time protector." He left the wagon and his boots stopped in front of her.

She drew in a deep breath, hoping for an olive branch. Her gaze traveled up his buckskin-clad legs. Her breath left her in an unexpected whoosh. He was the embodiment of the man in the photograph. Strikingly attractive, strong yet domesticated with a pot cradled against his ribs... Just grouchy. His eyebrows knit. He had stayed up all night protecting her and the livestock.

Jack dropped a tin pan beside her. Outstretched in his hand was a chunk of butter. "Here."

She stared at the butter. What was she supposed to do with it?

"Grease the pan with that."

Olivia picked up the tin and carefully took the butter. She smeared the butter in a circle in the bottom of the pan.

Jack dropped to his knees beside her.

He hadn't denied being disappointed in her. She fought back the bitter familiarity of failing to meet expectations. Determined to show she could do a good job, she dragged her fingers in left and right lines. She tried to erase her finger marks only to leave new trails.

He combed a fork through a whitish mass in the pot he held against his stomach. "Get the sides, too."

In the predawn darkness, Jack's gaze weighed heavily on her. Her throat felt thick. Could she just get one thing right? Why hadn't she paid attention to the kitchen servants when she was younger?

Jack reached for the bucket of water and cracked the thin layer of ice on the top. He dipped a towel in the water and held it out. "Clean your hands."

Could he be any more condescending? He treated her as if she was three. Olivia wiped butter residue off her hands.

"How does it happen you've reached the age of two and twenty and never cooked?" Jack scooped a handful of water into the mixture. He ended up with a sticky dough.

"We had servants," she muttered.

"You, Anna and Selina?"

Olivia looked up. Jack watched her as he fashioned the gooey mess into pale lumps and put them in the tin on her lap.

"No, my parents. At the boardinghouse, our landlady, Mrs. Richtor, didn't allow us in the kitchen because she thought we stole food."

The corner of his mouth twitched. "Did you?"

Olivia's cheeks heated and she dropped her gaze. She hoped with the dark he couldn't see her guilty flush.

He reached across and pressed another lump into the tin. His hand so close to her leg made her feel squishy and soft.

She picked the pan up and held it out to him. "The price of boarding included breakfast and supper, but if we bought dinner, no money was left. So we took extra food at meals. I suppose it was stealing."

"What about after your parents died? Where did you live then?"

"An older lady in Norwalk took me in." The elderly Miss Carmichael had failing eyesight and had wanted Olivia to read. Her benefactor had been disappointed when Olivia stuttered. Was she destined to disappoint everyone who took her in?

"She didn't eat?"

Olivia smiled in spite of herself. The movement of her face felt funny, as if it had been a long time since she'd smiled. "She had a cook. After she died I lived in a mill dormitory for a year and a half. They fed us gruel in the mornings and soup for dinner and supper. I hardly ate for the first week. I really missed good cooking."

Jack used the dry edge of the towel to lift the lid off the skillet, put the tin inside and settle the lid back on the pot. With the wet end, he brushed off his hands. "You didn't have any relatives?"

She shook her head. "The only relatives I know of are in Norway, and I've never met them."

He reached out a hand to Olivia. "We have fifteen minutes to wash up before the biscuits are ready."

Biscuits. If she'd seen him assemble the ingredients, she'd have an idea how to make them. "What did you put in them?"

"Look, I'll show you when we get home. Right now we need to get washed up so we can leave at first light." Jack tilted his head back. "It'll be dawn soon."

Olivia looked up to discern what he saw. Were the stars perhaps a little less bright? She'd never spent a night out of doors. She had no idea what signs to look for, or what sounds signaled danger.

"Are you coming?" Jack asked, his hand still extended.

She put her fingers in his. His warm fingers closed

over hers. Her heart jolted. She jerked her hand back as if she'd been scalded.

Jack's expression went flat.

Ashamed she'd responded so strongly, she curled her fingers.

He pivoted and headed toward the trees.

Olivia trotted a couple of steps after him before realizing she didn't have what she needed. "I need my things from my trunk."

She turned toward the wagon. Jack hesitated.

Her trunk was near the back, but unfortunately the latch faced the side. Olivia pushed and shoved to turn it.

"Move," said Jack.

"I have it," she said through gritted teeth. Her shoulder strained. In the months since the mill closed, she'd lost strength, but she was determined to show Jack she wasn't a helpless liability. She could do things for herself.

With his arm around her waist, he lifted her out of the way. Her backside pressed against his hip as he leaned around her. His chest shifted across her back. Olivia fought the hot tremors that raced down her spine.

Jack yanked the trunk around with one hand and set her back down on the wagon gate. "Hurry."

Her breath whooshed out, and she realized she'd been holding it. Though she fought to quell it, a kind of terror settled into the pit of her stomach every time he manhandled her. He was so much bigger than her, stronger. He could snap her in two if he had a mind to, yet that wasn't quite why she was afraid.

She unfastened the buckles and opened the latch. She fished out a paper-wrapped bar of precious lavender soap and a hand towel.

Jack shifted with tangible impatience. "Don't want to burn the biscuits."

She scooted to the edge of the tailgate. Jack's hand at her elbow tugged as well as supported her as she scrambled down. She was eager to wash. She longed for a bath and a chance to wash her hair. Although fifteen minutes was only long enough for the bare minimum.

Jack released her elbow then grabbed his rifle. He lifted the lantern high enough to cast a circle of golden light around them. He led her across the meadow to the thicket of trees. Olivia raised her knees, high-stepping through the underbrush.

As they neared the woods, the smell of pine filled her as well as the crisp scent of fresh spring growth. Norwalk had never smelled like this, nor had the Manhattan brownstone where she'd lived with her parents.

She inhaled deeply. The gurgling of rushing water lured her deeper into the darkness. The air smelled fresh, like after a rainstorm had cleaned the air. Ghostly white spindly trees vied with the thick pines for space. Wisps of fog and their breath hovered in the air. The grove resembled a primeval world not yet inhabited by man.

Except Olivia was all too aware of the man beside her. His every movement set off a fluttering in the pit of her stomach. He set the lantern on a rock and leaned his rifle against a tree. He drew his shirt over his head. Spellbound, Olivia stared at the bare expanse of his chest. His bronzed skin stretched over rippled muscle.

Jack jumped onto a large rock, startling her out of her reverie. She folded her arms over her chest to settle the odd tightening in her nipples.

Cold, she told herself. The damp air around the

stream was cold. Yet *oddly heated* and *loose jointed* would better describe her current state.

Jack leaned out over the edge of the rock and splashed water onto his chest and shoulders. The play of his muscles under his skin was fascinating. He dipped his face in the rushing water and then threw his head back. Droplets arced through the air, catching the light from the lantern and then fading into the darkness beyond the circle of illumination.

He turned toward her, shut one eye and swiped water away from his face with a broad hand. "I thought you wanted to wash."

"Yes, of course." Olivia stepped gingerly toward the edge of the rushing water. The stream frothed around rocks and boulders. The sides lapped at grassy shoals. She stepped close, but her foot sank and tore grass from the soggy bank. With Jack watching her, she didn't want to slip.

Jack lathered up with a brown bar.

Wary of the rushing water and the dark shadows concealing who knew what, Olivia stepped onto a large rock. Her chosen perch was not as flat as his. She wobbled, fighting for her balance.

Kneeling on the surface, she reached down into the icy water and flinched. "That's c-cold."

"Snowmelt off the mountains." Jack stood and brushed water from his arms. He shoved the wet tendrils of his hair back from his face. "Streams around here are always cold."

Scarcely able to look away from him, Olivia cupped water in her rapidly growing-numb fingers and raised it to her face.

"Want this?" he asked. He held out the brown bar.

"I brought my own, thank you." Olivia unwrapped

the perfumed bar of factory-milled soap she'd bought in Connecticut.

"The biscuits are probably done." Jack leaped off his rock and retrieved his shirt.

Although the icy water made her shiver and shake, Olivia lathered her face and neck. Taking care not to get her clothes wet, she rinsed.

Jack lifted the lantern, casting the stream around her into darkness. Undoubtedly he was impatient to get back. Olivia placed the soap back in its paper wrapper and dunked her hands in the frigid flow. Wiping her hands on her towel, she stood. She stepped toward the side of the stream.

Jack leaned and retrieved his rifle. The lantern swung behind him and the illumination disappeared as she stepped onto another stone. The wet surface of the stone provided no purchase. Her demi-boots were barely meant for walking, and the thin heels made her skid worse. Off-balance, Olivia flayed. The precious soap squirted out of her hand and plopped into the stream.

She twisted to retrieve it. Her heel skidded sideways and slipped off the rock. She pitched forward. She caught her soap just before her face hit the surface. The icy blast made her gasp.

Water filled her mouth and nose. The freezing water stabbed with a thousand pricks. Coughing and sputtering, she thrashed. The rushing stream rammed her, knocking her feet sideways. Her lungs refused to fill with air. Rocks shifted under her hands and knees. Each time she tried to find purchase, the bed shifted. The knifing flow relentlessly tossed her like a cork.

God, she didn't want to drown now.

The memories of clawing to be free of the underwater train wreckage flashed in her head, jumbling with the pounding of the creek water. The same sense of imminent death coldly knifed her. Her throat tightened. Silent screams echoed in her head.

She had to survive. Her hands scraped the streambed. If she could reach the bottom, surely she could push up. Her lungs fought to expel the inhaled water. Choking, she convulsed, coughing.

No! She wouldn't die now. Not like this. She scrabbled against the rocky bottom. Her thick, sodden skirts caught the water like sails. Their weight dragged her. The rush of water swept her along. Her head glanced off a rock. Her starved lungs sucked in water as blackness closed in.

Chapter Five

My cabin is on the southern side of a small mountain to the northwest of Denver City. The tallest of snow-covered purple peaks can be seen through the windows. The glass was hard to get out here, but well worth the trouble. A quiet woman might appreciate being able to look out on the majestic Rockies, but it is isolated and far from any loved ones you might leave behind.

Jack couldn't believe Olivia was about to drown in less than three feet of water. She'd surfaced once, but now the current tugged her into the swiftest rapids. Jutting boulders stirred froth. He pitched his rifle and dropped the lantern. To get ahead of her, he hurdled along the uneven bank.

The swollen creek rushed furiously along, tossing and turning her.

His throat squeezed and his heart hammered. He splashed into the water and grabbed a fistful of sodden material. Her weight and the force of the water nearly unbalanced him. His shoulder strained as he braced his feet against the shifting streambed.

He managed to get his arm under her midsection. Her soaking clothes doubled her weight.

Her abdomen heaved against his arm. She thrashed against him. Her heel connected with his shin.

Nearly dropping them both into the drink, Jack reared back. "Stop fighting!"

Setting his feet, he lifted her all the way out of the water.

She coughed and sputtered.

His boots squelching, he lugged her to the bank. He set her down. Hacking and choking, she fell to her knees.

Cold stabbed him. His toes stung. He hadn't noticed the iciness when he'd been trying to pull Olivia out, but he sure as hell noticed it now. Soaked through and through, Olivia had to be worse. Hell, if she didn't drown, she'd probably die of exposure.

He heaved in a couple of deep breaths. "Are you all right?"

He didn't really expect an answer, but she lifted a hand. A flash of white caught his attention. He leaned closer. She held her soap. *Merde,* had she plunged into the water after a bar of soap?

His heart thundered. He should toss her back out in the churning stream. "What were you thinking?"

She coughed and then pushed up slowly to stand. Scowling, she straightened her spine to the rigid erectness of her normal posture. "I was thinking I'd like a b-b-bath."

A bark spewed from his mouth. He couldn't have said if he was amused or angry. Both, perhaps.

Did his wife have a sense of humor under all that frosty hauteur? God help him if she was serious. He stared at her and she stared back.

"C-c-could we go b-back to the f-f-fire?" She turned and took a dragging step toward the lantern. Thank God it hadn't tipped and started a forest fire.

He had to get her dried and warm. The wet cotton would suck the warmth out of her faster than a deerfly could suck blood. She'd end up with pneumonia or worse. Olivia took another slow step. The sodden wet weight of her skirts tripped her.

Olivia squelched a couple of awkward steps away from the frigid stream. Her soaking-wet dress, nightgown and petticoats dragged. She gathered the brown twill hem in numb fingers. Shaking uncontrollably, she wrung out water.

She couldn't feel her feet. Not daring to look at Jack for fear of the disappointment she'd find, she wished herself far away.

Jack put his hand on her shoulder and forced her around to face him. A bone-jarring tremor ran down her spine. Not just cold, but the aftermath of nearly drowning…a second time.

The darkness had lifted to a faint gray predawn. His furrowed brow and flattened lips were all too evident in the low light. Obviously, he didn't think much of her.

Olivia grimaced. Bending down, she continued wringing out her skirts. She should be grateful he'd rescued her from the rushing water, but she resented the implication that she had meant to fall into the stream.

He shoved at the shoulders of her dress. "How is this fastened?"

He answered his own question as he found the buttons running down her spine.

Olivia stood, knocking his hands away. "What are you doing?"

"We have to get you out of these wet clothes before

you freeze to death." Jack cupped the back of her neck and shoved her shoulders back down.

The ribs of her corset jabbed into her lower stomach. Regardless of the lack of sensation in her extremities and the uncontrollable tremors racking her body, she protested, "I won't freeze to death."

She ducked away from his hands and nearly hit her head on a small tree.

"You could, wearing all those wet clothes." Jack resumed his attack on her buttons.

Olivia stepped away, turning so she faced him. "No one freezes to death. That's just a s-s-saying." Only old people who hadn't the money to pay for coal in the middle of winter died of exposure. A violent shudder ripped through her.

He stepped toward her, his jaw hard. He turned her around to get at her back. "Not out here, Olivia. This is harsh country, not a parlor game. In these temperatures, people who get wet while wearing all cotton clothes die."

Olivia twisted away. "I d-didn't know there was a proper way to d-dress for drowning."

"Of course there is." He snapped.

"R-really?" Olivia managed, although surely he'd seen the absurdity of what he said. "I'll purchase p-proper d-drowning clothes next time we're in t-town."

His expression went through gyrations from flattened brows and mouth to an eye roll with a snort. He ended with a tiny curl of his lips. She leaned toward him. But then, as if he'd collected himself, he returned to a scowl. "Wool is better than cotton, but animal skins are best if you risk getting wet."

"Oh." Perhaps that explained his penchant for buckskin. Most of the clothes she owned were cotton.

Jack circled behind her. His fingers gentler, he returned to her buttons. Olivia's pulse raced. He didn't expect her to undress here, did he? Or walk naked back to the wagon? Fear rippled through her. She couldn't do that. She'd rather die.

She swiveled to face him. "My dry clothes are in my trunk."

He caught her and peeled her dress from her shoulders. "I know what I'm doing."

"I need to get b-back to the f-fire." Olivia stepped away, dragging the heavy layers of material. Her teeth chattered so badly she could hardly talk. Holding her dress against her chest with one arm, she bent to pick up the soap she had dropped in the grass. A violent shudder ripped through her. Her fingers refused to close around the bar.

Jack snorted and scooped up her soap.

Olivia turned and tried to walk in a decisive stride, but her sodden skirts dragged.

Yanking her arm, he spun her around. Her midsection connected with his shoulder. He lifted her. Riding on Jack's shoulder like a sack of potatoes was undignified.

"I can walk." She raised her head. Rivulets ran down his back and water dripped from her chin.

"I can walk faster," said Jack.

That may be true, thought Olivia. Between her numb feet and her saturated twill dress, she could barely make any progress. His broad shoulder rubbed against her belly with each long-legged stride. She wished her midsection was numb, too.

Her gaze traveled down his strong back. His body narrowed into straight hips. The bottom of the buckskin shirt brushed his backside. Fascinated by the rhythmic movement of his tread, her stomach fluttered strangely.

Jack clamped down on the back of her thighs. Olivia flinched. Never had any man touched her below her waist.

At their campsite Jack bent, lowering her to the ground. He held her steady for a second, while his brown eyes searched her face. Squinting as if he didn't like what he saw, he said, "Get undressed. I'll see to the fire."

Gray ashes lined the fire pit. Olivia's heart plummeted. She'd expected the fire to remain lit. Hoped.

Jack let her go. Her legs buckled, and she slid down to the ground. She reached for the colorful blanket she'd abandoned earlier.

Jack snatched it away. "Get out of those wet clothes."

With the edge of the blanket, he pulled the skillet to the side and lifted the lid. "Ah, not beyond edible."

She was about to freeze to death, and he was more concerned about his breakfast.

She reached for the animal skin on the ground, but her fingers refused to cooperate. A violent spasm racked her body.

One small branch lay near the pit. Jack bent and snapped off a twig with dead needles. He stirred the ashes. Tiny flecks of orange remained. Blowing and adding dry pine needles, he nursed the cinders back to life and added the lone branch.

Jack removed his boots. She should remove hers, too, but she didn't have the energy. Her eyelids were heavy.

"Olivia!" Jack shook her. "Don't you dare fall asleep."

His voice sounded faraway and tinny, as if traveling through a pipe.

He pulled her up to sit and yanked her dress down her arms. Clarity burst through her foggy mind. Falling asleep was a really bad idea, but so was Jack undressing her. She pushed his hands away. "Stop!"

"You have to get out of these wet things." Jack's voice was urgent. "Come on, Olivia. I won't do anything to you."

"This isn't how I thought it would be," she mumbled.

His hands stilled. She closed her eyes. This wasn't *at all* what she'd thought it would be. She'd thought there would be a fire to warm her, a bed to sleep in and a husband who wanted to undress her for a better reason than to get her out of wet clothes.

With wooden, uncooperative toes, Olivia pushed off her boots. She rolled her wet stockings down and off. The endeavor took much longer and more effort than it should. Metal clinked against metal, but Olivia couldn't make sense of the sound.

"Here, drink some coffee." Jack held a tin cup to her lips.

The hot liquid scalded her tongue. "Hot."

She tried to turn away, but Jack wasn't having it. He planted his palm firmly on her cheek and forced her head back to the cup.

"That's the point. Drink." His serious brown eyes watched her.

She complied, even though the coffee was too strong. Warmth settled into the pit of her stomach like a tiny soldier battling the cold. She blinked a couple of times and took the tin cup and cradled it close to her mouth.

Taking her feet in his hands, he rubbed them. Only the pressure of his hands made it through. Her grayish toes didn't feel as though they belonged to her at all. At least the pain of her blisters and raw spots was gone.

He stared down at her feet in his hands. "*Merde,* Olivia."

"It's nothing," she whispered. "Would you make a bigger fire, please?"

Shaking his head, Jack pulled her to her feet. Her unfastened dress fell to the ground. The air against her wet nightgown made her shudder so badly she feared spilling the coffee.

"You have to get out of these clothes." His tone was cajoling. He tugged at the fallen dress until she stepped out of it. He was like an annoying peddler who wouldn't take no for an answer. "I'll fetch firewood. Can I trust you to get out of the rest?"

She nodded.

"If you don't change, I will do it for you when I get back." Jack picked up the sodden mess. After draping her dress over the wagon box, he swung up into the bed and opened her trunk. He tossed out her scuffs and yanked out clothes haphazardly.

Everything had been neatly folded or rolled. She would never get her clothes situated back inside the trunk.

He opened a pair of drawers and held them up as if to study them.

Olivia winced. "I can get my own clothes."

He draped them over the side of the wagon and added a checked blue dress and black stockings. He rummaged around in the supplies and came up with a hatchet. With a dark look in her direction, he jumped down.

Dutifully she put down the empty tin cup, turned her back to him, then pulled her arms out of the sleeves of her nightgown. She'd take it off when he was out of sight.

Jack took a swing at a branch. A satisfying thud jolted his arms as a chunk of wood flew away. He needed to get Olivia warm, and fast. Her listlessness worried him.

He took another vicious hack. His rifle leaned against a nearby tree. He couldn't believe he'd left the lit lantern and his gun by the creek when he'd carried that stubborn woman back to the campsite. His rifle was never more than ten yards from his side. Mistakes like that could be costly. A delay in getting undressed could be deadly. This land didn't allow foolish blunders.

With a *thwack,* the limb separated from the tree and crashed down.

Olivia was not biddable, for all her meekness. She'd waited until he stepped into the trees before she pulled her soggy nightgown over her head.

Bracing the wood with his foot, he hacked to separate the branch into manageable lengths.

If he wasn't so worried about her condition, he would have lingered longer as she went through the layers of undergarments. He'd forgotten how many different articles of lingerie white women considered necessary.

Interest heated his blood, but he ruthlessly dismissed it. Olivia was working too hard to keep him from being tempted. With one last chop, the log split.

Gathering up the firewood, he headed back toward the ball and chain. How the hell could he have made such a mistake? His marriage to Wetonga had been peaceful and, for the most part, happy.

Marriage was supposed to be better than being alone.

He had the sick feeling that with Olivia he might miss the solitude. And if she planned to throw a fit before removing her clothes, he didn't imagine he'd be getting much pleasure from the arrangement, either.

In his bare feet, he trekked through the underbrush, avoiding sticks and rocks.

When he cleared the trees, he didn't see her.

Heart thumping, he jogged forward. Olivia knelt in the wagon bed. Relief washed through him. He'd feared she might have succumbed to the cold and fallen asleep. That would be dangerous.

Instead, as if she was in no jeopardy, she placed items in her trunk. Stopping to rub her arms under the blanket wrapped around her shoulders, she leaned back on her heels. The blanket swamped her. She might not be out of danger yet, but she was moving.

He closed the last of the distance and released his load. The firewood thumped down on the ground.

Olivia jumped.

He added wood to the lone burning branch.

She scooted out of the wagon and sank down, holding her hands out to the flames. She gasped and jerked back.

"Did a spark get you?" asked Jack.

She shook her head. Scooting back, she looked on one side of her and then the other.

Jack continued building the fire. His stomach growled. He wanted breakfast, meager as it was. He wanted to get on the road home. He wanted a wife who wanted to be married, not just one who'd picked him as the best of desperate choices.

She shivered.

At least she wasn't violently shaking as she had been after he'd pulled her from the water. "Are you warmer?"

Olivia jerked her pale gaze toward him. "A little. The blanket helped."

Apparently she wasn't about to admit that getting out of her wet clothes had made a difference. A smile tugged at the corners of his mouth. "You're worse than my mules."

She blanched. "You have mules?"

"Yes. The horses are new."

Olivia looked over her shoulder. With their tails switching, the horses chomped grass. So far they met his expectations, but he'd kept a close watch on them yesterday for signs of fatigue or poor training.

Jack lifted the lid on the skillet and pulled out the pan with biscuits. They were dark brown on top, black on the bottom and lukewarm. He broke off two and handed one to her. She took her time before reaching out from under the blanket. He popped his in his mouth and reviewed everything he had to do.

"Mr. Kincaid said you had mules," Olivia said tentatively.

Did she find the idea of mules demeaning? She seemed mighty fascinated with that man. "Yeah."

Olivia's gaze darted to the ground.

Jack swallowed hastily. His mama had taught him not to talk around food, but those manners had been dormant for years. He suspected he needed to resurrect them. Wetonga hadn't cared about manners, or at least not the ones his mother had wanted him to learn.

Olivia nibbled on her biscuit.

"Eat." Jack grabbed a second one and tore it into two pieces before he stuffed half of it in his mouth. Telling her not to eat might have served better.

Her chin lifted and she said in a rush, "Mr. Kincaid said you already had a wife. An Indian wife."

Olivia bit her lip as she watched him with her misty gray eyes.

Jack finished chewing. "Yes."

Her expression cracked before she ducked down. Was Olivia fretting about his having had a native wife?

"I did. That a problem?" Would a lady ever understand a man needed companionship? Needed a help-mate just to survive?

"Did?" she piped up.

Cautiously he watched Olivia. "Wetonga fell ill and died two years ago."

"I'm sorry." Olivia swayed toward him.

The condemnatory attitude he'd half expected wasn't evident in her voice. She sounded sincerely apologetic. Certain people, Easterners mostly, thought he ought to thank God for releasing him from the mésalliance.

The blanket slipped off Olivia's shoulder and she set the biscuit in her lap before she struggled to pull the makeshift cloak back up with her right hand.

How like a woman to fret for hours before asking for an explanation. If she was worried he had a woman at home, perhaps that was the reason for her stiffness around him.

He pulled up the blanket and left his hand on her shoulder. "Is there anything else you want to know?"

She pressed her lips together and shook her head. Her stiffness radiated up his arm. He sighed. He had too much to do to worry whether he had offended her, or if his having an Indian wife shocked or repulsed her. Grabbing a last biscuit, he stood.

The sun slanted across the land. Morning was slipping away. He let the chicks out of their crate, then fashioned stakes to spit his and Olivia's boots.

Olivia gathered up the skillet and started toward the woods.

"What are you doing?" he asked sharply.

"I was going to wash these in the creek."

"No!" His panic at her being near the rushing water surprised him. He tried to temper his words. "Just stay here and get warm."

Olivia returned and stared into the flames. He didn't even bother to ask for help as he cleaned out the chicks' crate, filled it with fresh grass and refilled their water bowl.

"Do you want more?" He held out the remaining biscuits.

She shook her head.

One strip of jerky and one biscuit wasn't enough to sustain her. Crumbling the last biscuits for the chicks to eat, he dumped the scraps in the crate. He moved on to the horses. After removing their blankets and stowing them in the wagon, he took the horses and the pots to the stream.

When he returned, Olivia was circling the fire, scanning the ground. She tucked a stray strand of hair into the pulled-back portion. It promptly fell back down, caressing her cheek. Amazingly the confection of loops and twists on the back of her head was intact, although stray bits had worked their way loose around her face and neck. She chewed her bottom lip as her head swept side to side. Her cheeks had regained their color. She had a windblown air more appealing than the high-fashion look she'd arrived with.

The horses nudged him and he realized he'd drawn to a complete halt to watch his wife.

Since she wasn't huddling in front of the fire, Jack reckoned it was time to get on the road. "We'll leave soon as I get the horses hitched."

Olivia drew her hands behind her back, like a guilty child caught stealing sweets.

He led the horses to the front of the wagon. "Gather up the chicks."

"I have to go to..." She gestured toward the woods.

"By all means. Just stay away from the creek."

Olivia ambled toward the stand of trees. She held her skirts back and seemed to examine the ground with every slow step. He was too tired to figure out what she was doing.

Jack hitched the horses. The fire snapped near him. He debated taking her back to Denver City and putting her on the next stage out. He glanced toward the woods.

The next stage wouldn't be for days, and that would leave his cabin empty too long. And she had no place to go. She was his wife for better or for worse. He'd made his vow before a man of God. Jack had thought that was important when he'd married Wetonga. His parents might have gone their separate ways, but he'd never intended to follow that path.

He replaced everything in the wagon and placed the buffalo skins over the top of the load. On top of that, he placed her wet clothes, then he lashed everything down.

The shadows grew shorter. They needed to get a move on. Olivia was taking an awful long time. The horses were hitched, the chicks stowed. He poured the remaining water on the fire.

He needed to refill the bucket and apparently fetch his wayward wife. He headed to the stream. Ducking through the trees, he made his way to the rushing water. Cooler air wafted toward him. Blue flashed through the branches. Too dark of a blue to be the stream.

He shifted a branch as Olivia teetered on a rock in the middle of the flow. Her bare white legs stood out as unnaturally as the blue of the dress. Her gown was folded up between her legs, resembling a pair of short baggy Arabian trousers.

His breath caught. What the hell was she doing?

She seemed fixated on a spot in the stream near where she'd fallen in. The crystal-clear water rushed over the pebbled and rocky bed, foaming and frothing around each boulder. Her expression showed equal parts fear and determination.

Then her searching the ground and the image of her bare white hands circling the coffee cup clicked into place. She'd lost his ring. She didn't have a prayer's chance of finding it.

She stepped into the rushing water. The stream parted, bubbling and surging around her slender ankles. One hand holding tight to the handful of dress pulled between her legs and the other waving wildly in the air, she took a wobbly step.

Dumbstruck, he stood still.

She bent down and dipped her hand in the water. Clutching her fist to her chest, she straightened and waded to a large flat rock and stepped up. Her shapely calves and ankles reddened where they had been below the waterline. Her skirts swung down, shattering his mesmerized stare at her bare legs.

He swallowed hard. She unclenched her fist and slid the wedding ring on her finger. She clasped her hands together and turned her face up the heavens and said, "Thank you, God."

She looked relieved, and his breath whooshed out. Was she glad because she wouldn't have to confess to losing the ring, or did she wanted to stay married? Uncertainty plagued him as she leaped to the bank, sat and pulled on her stockings.

Jack knocked the bucket against a tree branch as he resumed his forward progress. "Olivia," he called, as if he hadn't been spying on her for the past five minutes.

She scrambled to her feet, glancing over her shoulder. "Here."

"Are you 'bout ready? We need to get home."

"Yes, of course." She gathered up the blanket and shook it off before wrapping it back around her shoulders.

He dipped the bucket in the water. Women's work, but Olivia didn't seem inclined to take over.

When she climbed into the wagon, she folded the blanket to put on the seat. The blue-checked pattern of her dress was darker around her ribs. "Dammit, Olivia, you didn't get out of all your wet things."

Why couldn't she obey?

"I'm fine." She stared straight ahead, her shoulders up by her ears, as if she expected him to wrestle her down to remove her underclothes.

He shook his head and climbed on the box and started the horses.

As they drove, his anger simmered. Had she been afraid he'd see her naked? He'd had to skulk around to catch even a glimpse of her skin. White-hot rage flared.

Blast and damnation! She'd made it ridiculously obvious she didn't want him to touch her. She wasn't about to obey him, or even trust his judgment. He didn't care if she thought she was too good for him. He didn't care if she *was* too good for him. It was cruel of her to come. She'd known he needed a helpmate, a frontier woman, a real wife. "Give me back my ring."

Chapter Six

I have no ties to Connecticut, as my dearest friends are seeking husbands out West, too. With the war with the Southern states, we fear cotton shortages will force the mill to close soon. I am eager to start a new life.

"What?" With the rattle of the wagon and the steady thud of the horses' hooves, Olivia wasn't sure she heard Jack correctly.

"Give me the ring." His voice was tight.

After her panic, then knee-weakening relief at finding her wedding band where she'd fallen in the water, Olivia couldn't believe he'd asked for it back.

Was this the end of the marriage?

Surely he wasn't furious because she hadn't taken off her corset. She'd taken off everything else, but she didn't own another corset. The idea of explaining her predicament mortified Olivia. "Why?"

"You'll lose it. Can't always expect to pull gold out of the streams around here."

"I won't lose it," she whispered. *Again.* She certainly never wanted to experience again the terror of wading in the powerful waterway that had almost killed her. He couldn't know how hard facing that deceptively strong stream had been.

"In spite of what they write in the papers back East, this is a harsh land, and people have to work hard to survive here. Gold and silver aren't just lying around for people to pick up." Jack's jaw pulsed.

He must know she'd dropped it in the creek. She slipped the ring from her finger. Her stomach clenched and she wanted to snatch the ring back, but she held out her trembling palm.

Jack's warm fingers scraped the ring from her hand and tremors shot away from his touch. Her palm tingled. She rubbed it against her skirt to ease the sensation.

The weight of his gaze had her curling her fingers into the folds of material.

"Does this mean you refute me as your wife?"

"It needs to be resized," Jack said woodenly.

Sleek brown backs glistening in the sun, the horses plodded onward. The wagon rattled along.

She smoothed her skirts, then drew on the gloves that wouldn't fit over the ring. If she concentrated on little things, she wouldn't come undone. "I know how to work hard."

"But you didn't think you had to."

"I didn't think this life would be easy." She just hadn't expected it to be so hard, either.

Was his distance because he still loved Wetonga? His voice had turned husky as he spoke of her. "Did the ring belong to your first wife?"

"No." His response was abrupt, as if her question was intrusive.

Since her parents' deaths, she'd been careful to not be a nuisance. She minded her manners and did as peo-

ple expected of her. She didn't pry into their business.
But Jack was almost rude. "Why are you so angry
with me?"

He sighed. "When I advertised, I said I wanted a
helpmate, not a—" he waved his hand in a circle as if
an appropriate description escaped him "—fancy show-
piece."

"I see," said Olivia. He'd wanted a woman to show
up in work clothes, not her best dress. The care she'd put
into her appearance had been wasted effort. "You don't
think there is ever an appropriate time to look nice?"

"Not in Colorado." His words lacked conviction.

A dull ache spread under her breastbone. In any case,
he didn't want her. "You have already decided I will not
suit your needs."

He looked at her, his eyebrows flattened. "You cannot light a fire. You cannot cook. You think gardens
are for flowers, not vegetables. You look as if a stiff
wind would blow you over. You've managed to nearly
drown within twenty-four hours of arriving here. You
said you'd like the mountains, but you haven't even
looked at them."

At least he'd left off "what good are you?" but the
sentiment curdled his voice. How many ways could
she disappoint him? Her heart fluttered frantically. She
wanted to curl into a ball to hold all her shattered pieces
together. "They make me feel small."

His gaze weighed on her. Her upbringing: to be an
ornament on a man's arm, hand him his newspaper
in the morning, his slippers in the evening and make
sure the children were seen not heard, left her horribly
unprepared for this kind of life. Being neat and well
dressed were supposed to be assets.

"We're all small compared to the mountains, and

they'll defeat you if you let them. You won't last through a winter. I can't see leaving you to guard the house and tend the livestock while I hunt or trap. If an accident doesn't befall you, you'll get tired of this life and leave."

Where did he think she'd go? She'd hoped—dreamed—of a home she could call her own. Her gaze darted around her. The raw wildness of the Colorado Territory frightened her, but they were married. She'd thought he would protect her.

He'd not only asked for a helpmate, but a brave and calm one. She was neither of those things. She'd never claimed to be, but she hadn't informed him that she was not. "I'm sorry if I misled you."

He blew out between pursed lips.

Olivia looked down at her gloves. "You didn't talk of needing a cook and a person who could tend the animals. I have never done such things."

She looked at the huge horses in front of her. What did they require in the way of care? Could she lead them to water and control them? "So what do we do now?"

"Nothing. Forget I said anything."

But that answer didn't satisfy her. She'd been staying where she was only tolerated for almost a decade now. She wouldn't do it any longer. It was a petty thing to say, but the words were out of her mouth before she could stop them. "Perhaps you should have let me drown."

"Yes. To have two dead wives would have been so much better."

Olivia pressed her lips together. She'd looked forward to having him as a husband, but his disappointed assessment of her lack of skills stabbed her with shards of practicality and truth.

"I didn't know how to do millwork before I began

there. Isn't there a woman nearby who can teach me
how to cook and garden? I can learn."

"Look around, Olivia. There aren't many people
settled out here, and they are mostly men. Our closest
neighbor is over twenty-five miles away. I expected you
to know the basics."

No houses dotted the landscape. Open empty land
lay all around them.

She bit her lip as she considered her options. What
options? She was completely dependent on a man who
didn't want her. But she had her pride. "You should
give me a chance, but I do not wish to stay if you don't
want me."

"It's not that I don't want you—"

"Yes, it is. If you want me to be different or a...a—"
she sought a word that fit "—drudge, then you do not
want *me*. I came out here to make this marriage work.
I've never camped or tried to wash in a fast-moving
stream." She paused, not knowing what else to say. Her
defense sounded pathetic.

The wagon swayed over the ruts, and her shoulder
brushed Jack's. Stiffening, she scooted away from him.

His eyes ran down her side to the space between
them on the bench seat. "You don't want me either,
Olivia. You've made that abundantly clear."

Her mouth dropped open. She wanted to be his wife.
She'd come prepared to be his wife. "Why would you
think that?"

He snorted.

Every time he touched her she felt tickles in her gut
and she felt as if she was coming unglued. Like the
mountains, he scared her with his size and strength.
Raw masculinity oozed from him and unsettled her.

She had shied away from him and the sheer power he had to affect her.

Each time he touched her, shivers ran down her spine and the hairs on the back of her neck stood on end. She was scared, and she couldn't confess it because he'd already condemned her for not being brave.

"I can take you to California to settle near your friends," he said.

She felt as if her face had cracked, and a lump in her throat threatened to choke her. "You won't give me a chance?"

He turned back toward the road. "We'll give it a month, then."

"A month? I can't possibly learn how to be a frontier woman in a month." How could she?

"A month is all the time we have before the preacher makes it official." He dropped his booted foot from the wagon box. The thump rattled through her and jarred her teeth.

The horse on the right nickered and bobbed her head, as if in agreement.

She bit her lip. "Fine. I will do it."

Jack assessed her, his brown eyes slightly narrowed. "Be my wife?"

Resisting the urge to look away and not trusting her voice, she nodded.

His mouth flattened as if he'd hoped to see more enthusiasm. Or had he wanted her to leave?

He tossed the reins in her lap and swung down from the wagon box. "We're leaving the road. Here, take the reins while I pick out a path for the horses. Do you think you can do that?"

She picked up the leather straps. She'd never driven horses. "I'll tr— Yes."

"Hold the reins with enough tension that the horses can't slip their bits."

Jack tramped to the front of the wagon without a backward glance. Had she already let him slip the bit? He was wrong. She wanted to be his wife. She just didn't know how.

Her eyes stinging, she blinked back the sign of weakness. If she gave in to tears, he'd know she was weak and spineless. Straightening her shoulders, she lifted her chin. She would have to show him her mettle.

Jack kicked a rock out of the way. The last thing he needed was for a wagon wheel to break on the rough terrain and delay them even longer. He'd been picking the best path for hours now while the wagon followed. Olivia held the reins so tight that the bits were sawing the horses' mouths. He should take the reins from her, but he preferred walking ahead.

He'd lost his temper earlier and he regretted it. But Olivia had looked at him with ice in her pale eyes. Then, just as he had about gotten his temper under control, she'd swayed into him and pulled away as if he was a leper. She hadn't bothered to deny that she didn't want him, either.

If she had cried, he could have comforted her and said he didn't mean any of it. If she would have let him.

Wetonga hadn't cried often, but she'd cried when he'd threatened to take her back to her tribe. Enormous tears had drifted down her dusky cheeks. He'd known he'd gone too far.

Olivia had not done anything beyond smoothing her skirts as if a wrinkle would kill her. Even if she wasn't dressed as a princess today, she still acted like one.

Probably only pride kept her from admitting their marriage was a mistake.

He didn't know what demon had made him insist on the trial for their marriage. He'd wanted her to fight him about the ring. Instead, it burned in his pocket. He'd wanted her to insist she wanted to be married, but she hadn't. Instead, the look of betrayal in her eyes had made him feel like the worst sort of scoundrel.

"Over yonder rise is a stream. We'll stop for a few minutes and water the horses."

"Good," said Olivia. White marks bracketed her mouth.

She was in pain and hadn't said anything. Not that she said much. Wetonga had chattered like a magpie, never holding back. Olivia hardly spoke at all.

He swung up into the wagon box. "Give me the reins."

She handed them over.

"You don't complain much, do you?" He had to give her that.

She made a small shrug. "Complaining never changes things."

"Depends on if you complain about a thing that can be changed. What hurts?"

She actually looked at him a full second before she dropped her gaze. "Nothing."

"Don't lie."

She gave a tiny shake of her head. "My arms and shoulders. I'll be fine. I'm just not used to driving a wagon."

He needed to smooth the waters. If she could suffer in pain without mentioning it, he could at least make some effort. "You looked beautiful yesterday—"

A short puff left her delicately flared nostrils. She

had a pretty nose, straight and delicate and pink from the sun. The mountains wouldn't take long to strip away her upper-class veneer and leave her skin blistered and red.

He sighed. His compliment felt awkward, but he tried to persist. His mother had expected her looks to be noticed, but she'd left just when he'd started to pay attention to females. "You look more beautiful today."

She stretched her arms out as if to block him. "You don't think that."

"Because you look less civilized today."

She turned away and smoothed back the slipping strands of her hair, trying to tuck them under her hat. When the effort proved futile, she gripped the bench seat with both of her hands. That would keep her from accidentally rocking into him as the wagon bumped over the uneven ground.

God help him, he had no idea how to deal with her. He wanted to give her the ring back, but that would mean admitting he'd been hasty in taking it away or telling her he'd seen her fish it out of the stream.

"Why didn't you send a photograph of you after I sent you mine?"

"I don't photograph well."

It was his turn to snort. "I doubt that." He would have been more prepared for her if he'd seen a photograph first. Or he would have recognized the complete imbalance of their expectations and told her not to come.

"I always look like a ghost." She gestured toward her face. "My eyes don't look right." Olivia smoothed her blue-checked skirt.

"Is that why you don't look me in the eye?"

She gave a tiny shrug as if his questions were of no consequence.

They were in for a long month.

Ahead, a tree break signaled the stream. Jack looked for a place he could pull the wagon through the woods and ford the water.

He drew the wagon to a halt and set the brake. He jumped down and turned around to help Olivia down, but she was already climbing down the opposite side. She moved gingerly and gripped the box tightly. When she reached the ground, she adjusted the drape of her skirts. She turned and caught him watching her. Her eyes widened, and then her gaze darted away.

"The stream is through the trees. Try not to fall in." Jack moved to release the harnesses so the horses could graze and drink while he forged a path.

Rather than moving toward the stream, Olivia lifted the chicks' crate out of the wagon bed. She set it down. Arranging her skirts in a circle around her, she knelt down in the grass. She carefully lifted each chick. Her ginger cradling fascinated him. He loosened the leather straps, all the while watching her.

Her touch was delicate until she said, "Jack," in a tremulous voice.

His name on her tongue evoked an unexpected lurch in his gut. "What?" he asked in a gruff voice.

She held up the limp body of a chick. Her pale eyes filled with moisture. "I think it's dead."

He strode toward her and held out his hand. "I'll get rid of it." He took the carcass by one wing and pitched it as far as he could throw it.

Olivia's horrified expression was priceless.

"I hope you didn't expect me to give it a funeral."

She clapped a hand over her mouth and shook her head. A tear dripped down her face. Was she that innocent?

His response was between exasperation and dismay. He dropped to his knees in front of where she knelt. "You can't be crying over a chick."

"I'm just tired." Twisting away, she wiped her cheek.

He caught her chin in his fingers. Her jaw was delicate, her skin soft. Her gaze down, she stilled like a motherless fawn. He wanted to comfort her, but he half expected her to shove him away. Perhaps the dead chick was just the last straw in a bad day for her. "Hey, I'm sorry."

Her watery gaze turned on him, but she seemed less fragile.

He stared into her gray eyes, the color of a winter sky just before snow. He was caught, mesmerized the way a deer could be hypnotized by a lantern.

"I suspect I was fretting about the loss of eggs." The corners of her lips lifted a tiny bit.

"It was probably a rooster." Rubbing the pad of his thumb across the dampness on her cheek, he wanted to continue touching her smooth, pale skin.

Her slight smile slipped. She watched him without lowering her gaze. For the first time, she wasn't ducking away.

Heat flashed through his blood. He traced her lower lip. The texture was like a flower petal. The moist heat of her breath wafted across his thumb.

He wanted her. She was his wife.

Her eyes widened as he erased the distance between them. Praying she wouldn't pull back, he took his time, stroking the line of her jaw.

His gaze dipped to the pale pink of her rosebud mouth. To taste those lips would be heaven. Up close, the fear in her gray eyes was visible. Holding still, he tried to silently reassure her. He had no intention of hurting her or hurrying her. Her eyelids fluttered down, the oat-colored lace of her lashes lying against her cheeks. Anticipation kicked his heartbeat into a fast tattoo.

He pressed his lips against hers. A desperate need to rush pounded in him. Now, while she was not turning away, he wanted more. When her lips parted ever so slightly, he tilted his head and deepened the kiss.

He was lost in her softness, the sweetness of her breath. She tasted subtly intoxicating, like an expensive wine, like a drink too fine for him. Desire fired in him with the explosive power of a need too long denied. Slipping his hand down her neck, he reveled in her satiny texture.

Her delicate fingers circled his wrist. Need tingled in his gut. In spite of everything, he yearned for her kisses. She was so beautiful. He'd been alone so long, and with each letter she'd sent he wanted her more. He'd dreamed of kissing her for months.

Letting her leave was the right thing to do, but first he needed to show her what marriage was all about. Life could be harsh, but there were rewards. If she had the heart to make it here, he wanted her to stay as his wife. He wanted her to have a fierce spirit.

If she could hold her own, he could be a good provider. Swamped by the sensations of her soft lips, his thoughts disappeared. Blood surged in his veins. He wanted to make her his.

Olivia didn't know how to react. Jack's tongue probed her mouth. She'd had no idea that this was what a kiss involved. Why hadn't Anna or Selina told her?

Jack withdrew but didn't lift his mouth off hers. His hand caressing her face felt caring, gentle. When she grabbed his wrist, she'd meant to push his hand away, but now it was as if she held his hand to her cheek. One minute he seemed to be refuting her as his wife, and now he claimed her.

He began the kiss anew, with a gentle brushing of his lips, then more pressure and prodding exploration. His urging made her feel hopelessly inadequate. Oh, God, please let her do this right and not foul it up.

She'd felt raw and rejected, and now she just wanted to fall into him, to pretend his disappointment wasn't real.

She'd dreamed of him kissing her, but now it was as if he was pulling forgiveness from her soul. If she allowed him to see how badly she wanted this marriage to work, she would have no defenses left.

Softness invaded her bones and a riot of sensations settled low in her belly.

He nipped at her lower lip, as if he was giving her time to assimilate this new experience. Except her yearning for him crashed against the knowledge that he'd told her their marriage only had a month to work. Her confusion swirled. Did he want her? In spite of her failings, did he want her?

His tongue invaded her mouth again and her eyes popped open. His unshaven skin was so close, the dark stubble blurred before her eyes. Not knowing how to deal with this new onslaught, she pushed back. He responded with a low groan.

She clutched at his buttery soft shirt, wadding it tightly. Had she blundered into a response he liked? Her insides coiled. Experimentally, she touched her tongue to his. The rough burr was not unpleasant and not like anything she'd ever tasted before. His kiss intensified, insisting on contact and swirling play. Her heart skittered in her chest and sparkles danced along her spine.

His hand on her ribs made her jump as if he'd touched her lower, below her skirts. How did he manage that?

She tentatively released her fistful of his shirt and smoothed the wrinkles. Uncertain, she laid her hand on his arm. His arm muscles were bunched and hard, bigger around than she could grip.

What little gentleness he had offered dissolved. His kiss grew insistent. He held her head steady. Unable to move away, she was coming apart. Only he was holding her together. Her heart fluttered and tension screamed through her muscles. Was it supposed to be this scary and thrilling?

Jack pressed against her. His wrist in her grip felt solid, strong. His thumb stroked her cheek. She clutched his wrist tighter, hanging on for fear of falling. His mouth left hers and he nibbled at her neck as he lowered her to the ground. Grass bent beneath her and the smell of earth, prairie and him filled her nostrils.

Strange little jolts coursed through her. His palm caught the outer curve of her breast. Short pants burst from her mouth.

She could think no further than the riot of sensation coming from his touch.

He returned to her mouth and Olivia was lost. His weight pressed against her and his whiskers scraped against her face, but a tingling in her lips spread down, with curling tendrils reaching her stomach then lower.

The solid length of him, hard where she was soft, bore down on her. He stroked her neck with the hand she wouldn't free and caressed her shoulder with the other. But when his fingers closed around her breast, Olivia jolted.

A sound like a cat's yowl left her mouth. An answering groan rumbled deep in his throat. Embarrassed by the animalistic sound, she wanted to turn away, but Jack didn't let her.

He rubbed his palm across her confined breast, eliciting wild sparks. She felt as if she was falling and falling. Her elbows came in as if she could thwart his trespassing touch, but all she succeeded in doing was pushing his hand to her buttons.

He touched his tongue to her lower lip, and then drew it into his mouth in a new kind of play that had her arching toward him. The button at the base of her throat opened.

Sanity shot through the sensations he evoked. What was he doing? It was the middle of the day. They were in the open, in a grassy field. It was too fast, too heady, too confusing for her to sort out. She tightened her fingers on his wrist. Her ringless fingers.

Her second button came free. The thought of his hands against the bare skin of her breast sent jolts of raw energy thrumming through her.

Panic at the power of the sensations rocked through her. She couldn't do this here, now. Undressing should be done in the dark, not in daytime when he would see the ugly scar on her thigh.

A lady shouldn't even *like* what he was doing to her. Olivia dug her nails into his wrist. She twisted her head away. "Stop!"

Jack went still.

Her breasts heaved against his solid chest and a hardness pressed into the juncture of her legs. An echoing heaviness in her lower half made her regret panicking, but so much was happening she couldn't take it all in.

As if coming out of a trance, Olivia noticed the

sounds. The chicks peeped, bugs hummed around them. Jack's labored breathing tickled her ear. Was he as affected as she was? His rough cheek pressed against hers. He gently stroked her hair back from her face.

One of the horses wandered close. His head dipped and he grazed not five feet from her. The loud munch of the horse's grinding teeth startled her. Thin ragged strips of clouds scudded across the brilliant blue sky. The world had not ground to a halt around them.

Where were the chicks? The horse was too near. She twisted, trying to count them. "Are the chicks all right?"

Jack lifted his head. "They're fine." His voice was gruff.

He touched her tender skin at the side of her mouth. He scowled down at her. His brown eyes went flat in a way that squeezed her heart. Closing her eyes, she shut out his expression. She released his wrist and covered her burning face. She wouldn't have felt more exposed if she were naked.

Why was he looking at her as if disappointed? A terror stole her breath and made a cold sweat slide down her spine. Had she been that inept? Had he forgotten he was kissing *her*?

"I'm sorry," she mumbled. "I… We… It's the middle of the day." What mesmerizing power did he have to persuade her to roll on the ground like an animal? Her heart beat wildly and she was edgy and hungry for something she couldn't name.

"Why didn't you say I was hurting you?" His finger dabbed at the skin beside her mouth.

"I-I-I'm hurt?" was all she managed. Her thoughts refused to sort in any kind of order. Her lips felt puffy and sensitized and not entirely hers. Only then she noticed the stinging burn around her mouth.

Jack rolled away and rubbed his chin. "I should've shaved."

He turned his wrist over and stared at the half-moon indentations her nails had made in his wrist.

"I need to water the horses." With that bland statement, Jack rocked up to his feet and stalked away.

Olivia raised her hand to her swollen lips. She'd never felt less ladylike in her life. What had he done to her?

Chapter Seven

In the spring there are many places where snow-melt cascades down the rock faces. The water catches the light like fine crystal and casts off small rainbows.

Night closed in. Jack searched for familiar landmarks. Another eight or nine miles lay before them. His eyes were scratchy. He'd been awake for more than a day and a half. Olivia had fallen asleep sitting up, and he'd wrapped his arm around her shoulders and pulled her against him.

She felt fragile against his side.

Something had shifted in him this afternoon. He didn't want to care about her, but he feared her eventual departure would hurt. He had nothing to offer a woman like her.

Life with him would chap her fine skin. Her lovely hands would grow calloused. The hardscrabble nature of his life would destroy her beauty. She would eventually resent him for not being a prince and, like his mother, leave to find a kindler, gentler world.

He tried to hurry the tired horses. While he'd been

kissing Olivia, the weather had shifted. Now clouds obliterated the night sky. He feared rain, or worse…a late-spring snow.

He never should have wasted time rolling on the ground with her. He'd meant just a kiss or three, not an hour of attempted seduction during which Olivia had never let go of his wrist. She hadn't exactly been throwing herself at him with unbridled passion, but she hadn't resisted…much.

He tried to understand what had happened between them. Had she participated because she felt she had to? If so, that bothered the hell out of him. She wouldn't even look at him afterward. She'd covered her face as if she couldn't bear the sight of him.

That he'd unknowingly hurt her made him feel like a great lugging beast. In the future, he would shave before he risked her tender skin. He pulled the blanket around her.

"Are we there?" she mumbled.

"No. Go back to sleep."

She straightened and shifted away from him. Missing her warmth, he sighed.

"Can you see anything?" She leaned forward.

"Not much. I know where we are, though."

"It smells different."

"Like rain."

Rubbing her arms, she tilted her head back and looked at the starless sky. "Should we stop?"

"No." Their best bet was to make it to the cabin.

"Will the chicks be okay?"

Jack shrugged. He'd warmed rocks for them when they stopped for supper. "We'll see."

She twisted as if she could see into the wagon bed and under the hides. "Was it my fault the chick died?"

"No, Olivia. Creatures die. There isn't always a reason." But his words mocked him. He figured he'd failed to keep the chicks warm enough. He hadn't made Wetonga happy enough. He wouldn't be able to keep Olivia cocooned enough.

She sighed.

"We're almost home." He rubbed his stubbled jaw. Her whisker burn might take a day or two to heal.

"Are you sure you can see?" she asked.

She probably thought they were lost.

"Yes. I've lived here a long time." Since he was seventeen and he'd married Wetonga and needed to provide her with a home. Wetonga would have been happier roaming with a tent. Olivia should have a mansion.

He stretched out a cramped leg. Olivia of the rigid posture had to be stiff and sore. "If you want, you could lie down in the back."

"I'm fine," she said.

"I'm beat."

She tensed.

He rubbed the bridge of his nose. A man admitting he was tired apparently violated the code of proper manners. That or she went rigid at the reminder of bed.

Her voice whispered through the darkness. "Should I drive?"

Jack doubted the horses could take more of her sawing their mouths, and he had to stay awake anyway. "No. You don't know the way."

"Oh." Her voice was small.

Her effort wasn't very helpful, but at least it was an effort. To show his appreciation, he patted her thigh.

She jerked away so violently she nearly tumbled from the wagon. He grabbed a fistful of skirt. As if he needed a reminder of how distasteful she found his touch. Her gut reaction was to flee or push him away. Or hold his wrist so tightly she restricted his movements.

A raindrop hit the back of his hand. Great. Just great.

Olivia didn't think the rain would ever stop, or that they'd ever reach his cabin.

Jack wrapped the blanket around her shoulders and hunched forward, peering into the darkness. Rain dripped off the battered brim of his hat. Her hat provided less protection. Moisture beaded through the woven straw and droplets ran down her face like tears.

She was shuddering and shaking with cold by the time they pulled up in front of a dark cabin. She couldn't see much beyond a porch with an overhang and a building that looked no bigger than the room she'd shared with Anna and Selina. Her new home, if Jack let her stay. She swallowed hard.

He set the brake and jumped down.

Pushing her stiff limbs, Olivia reached for the wagon side to climb down. Jack freed the horses from their traces. "Get up on the porch. Should be drier."

She could go to the porch and wait for further instruction or she could help and risk making things worse. She went to the back of the wagon and struggled to release the latches holding up the tailgate. Finally, one catch released and she reached to undo the other. Holding one latch open and straining to reach the other proved too difficult.

Jack's hand closed over hers. He released the stubborn latch and the tailgate fell. To avoid getting hit, she stepped back into his solid frame. Every inch of her was aware of him. She wanted just to lean against him and soak up his strength.

"Go inside," Jack shouted.

A black hole had appeared in the wall of the cabin. Jack must have opened the door. The inside looked darker than sin. Stubbornly she grabbed the chicks' box and made her way up the uneven stairs of rough-hewn logs.

Jack was right behind her. When she hesitated at the doorsill, his thigh pressed against her, forcing her into the dark hole. She felt a strange giddiness at the idea of his leg touching her so intimately.

Two steps inside she crashed into a sturdy obstacle. The crate jarred into her stomach, but at least she hadn't fallen on her face. The crate remained silent. The chicks usually peeped madly when shaken.

"If any of the chicks are alive, try to get them warm." Jack sidestepped around her. A deep thud indicated he'd set down a heavy object.

Rain pelted down, overly loud against the roof that didn't sound far above her head. She listened intently for the *cheep-cheep* of the chicks but heard only the thrumming rain. She ducked as if the dark was closing in on her.

The flare of a match lit the room and Jack leaned over to light a kerosene lamp on the bare plank table she'd run into.

He had matches?

Upward shadows on his face, along with the stubble on his jaw, made him look sinister. Olivia took a step back. Squint lines around his eyes stood out as he replaced the glass chimney. He never looked up at her. "Have to take care of the horses."

On his way out the door, he lifted his gun and placed it on pegs over the door. He stooped as he went back out into the rain. He pulled the door shut behind him.

"Welcome home," muttered Olivia.

Of course the horses needed to be cared for, and the wagon unloaded, but for all Jack's lifting her and carrying her around, he'd made no effort to carry her over the threshold. No, he'd pushed her across and her backside seemed imprinted by his unceremonious nudge.

Faintly breathless, she sat the crate on the table and draped the wet blanket over the back of a chair. Tools and contraptions hung from pegs on the log walls. The chinks in the logs were filled with a gray dried mud that in places had cracked. *Homey* was not a word that crept to her mind. Puddles in front of the door were streaked with mud. She swallowed hard against a lump in her throat.

Wooden crates were employed as all manner of furniture and crammed in the minuscule space. The table with three rough-hewn chairs occupied the center of the room. A small round black stove stood to her left, and a low bed covered with animal skins lay to her right. The bed she would share with Jack. Her heart tripped.

She forced her gaze away. The last thing she wanted was for Jack to return and find her staring at the bed.

Fearing what she might find, she peeled back the skin over the crate. A forlorn chirp greeted her. With a relieved huff, she stripped off her wet gloves. Her hands were nearly icicles.

She put her hands around the lamp chimney and then cradled a chick, repeating the process again and again until they all fluttered and pecked at her hands.

She was so relieved, she didn't mind…much.

The door swung open and her trunk thudded heavily on the wood floor. The cabin seemed incredibly small with him inside the space.

"They're alive," she said to his back.

Had he even heard her? She followed him to the

door and watched as he retrieved a heavy sack from the wagon and headed back up the stairs.

His steps were slow and his head bowed. She should help. The rain splattered off the roof at the edge of the porch, creating a curtain of freezing water. She ducked, then dashed to the wagon, lifted things out and stumbled inside as Jack returned outside. She placed the bags and boxes on the table and moved the chick's box to the floor.

Jack carried another sack over by the stove and set it down. They met at the door, not that they were terribly separated in the cabin. She squeezed her hoops through, but he pulled her back.

"Stay inside before you catch your death of cold," he told her. His hands were rough, not lover-like, as they had been earlier.

Nonetheless his touch made her quiver. "Let me help."

"You don't need to get any wetter." His grip gentled on her arms. His dark eyes searched her face while his lids drooped.

She shrugged free. He had to be exhausted, and she had been little help over the journey. "You're tired. I can bring in the rest."

The corner of his mouth lifted ever so slightly. "You're shivering and you're not dressed for the weather. I'll get the wagon unloaded and we'll sort everything out tomorrow."

"Fine, you unload everything onto the porch. I'll take it inside." Surely he could see the advantages of allowing her to assist him, although she didn't really want him thinking she was eager for their first night in bed together.

He rolled his eyes as he stepped back outside. Not

exactly an eager-bridegroom expression. Perhaps he wasn't in a hurry to get into bed with her. Olivia scurried as quickly as she could, but Jack piled up items faster than she could carry or drag them inside.

Supplies filled the cabin.

With the wagon empty and the skins draped over the porch rails, Jack threaded his way through the maze on the front porch with a sack of cracked corn on his shoulder.

Olivia tried to heft the heavy sack of oats. Although Jack had tossed it up on the porch as if it weighed nothing, she couldn't get the shifting weight to cooperate. When Jack didn't return to help, she dragged the heavy bag across the doorsill.

Jack knelt in front of the potbellied stove. The tiny yellow flames in its belly soothed her. After reaching into the box of wood beside the stove, he placed a log inside. He glanced over his shoulder and his gaze landed on the sack. "Get the lighter things. I'll get the heavy stuff." He turned his attention back to the fledgling fire in the stove.

Olivia ignored him, hauling the bag across the floor. She left a trail of oats. Had she split the bag? She struggled until she found the hole and, grabbing the punctured material with her hand and the end of the sack, she succeeding in getting the sack up against her thighs. Praying the fire starting would hold Jack's attention, she duckwalked over to the wall and set the bag down, careful to keep the hole to the top.

Jack turned and stared at the floor.

"I'm sorry. I didn't realize there was a hole in the bag. I'll clean it up as soon as I get everything inside."

He rolled his shoulders. "Chicken feed."

"What?"

He looked up, but his brown eyes looked tired. "The chickens and horses won't care if it's been on the floor."

Was he trying to ease her guilt about the spill? Olivia hesitated.

Jack stood, and she suddenly felt small. She swiveled and headed out to get another load.

He followed her outside. His hand landed on her shoulder. She jumped, her heart thumping.

"There's water in the pitcher on the washstand and in the kettle. I'll show you everything else in the morning. I'm going to bed. Put out the lamp when you're done."

He gathered an armful of the remaining items on the porch before returning inside. Shivering, Olivia gathered up more supplies and pushed through the door.

Drawing his shirt over his head, Jack stood near the bed. He untied his pants. When he started to shove them down, Olivia scurried outside. She slid items through the door. When she had everything off the porch, she slipped inside. Careful to not look in the direction of the bed, she shut the door. Then she tiptoed through the haphazard clutter.

His buckskin shirt lay on the floor and his pants were tossed across the foot of the bed. Unable to resist the sight, her gaze traveled up the mound in the bed.

His bare shoulder was above the fur and he lay on his side with his back to the center of the bed. One arm pillowed his head, the other lay draped across his broad chest. His eyes were closed and his mouth slightly open. His breathing was slow and heavy. If he faked sleep, he was very good.

She picked up his shirt and folded it. With most available surfaces covered, she put it on a chair. Slowly, being careful to not disturb Jack, she pulled his pants from the foot of the bed, folded them and added them to his shirt.

She half expected him to jump up and yell "Boo!" but Jack didn't move. She wasn't alone, but a cold ache in her bones suggested she might as well be. The blackness of the night glared in the uncovered windowpanes. The steady drone of the rain made the outside world seem hostile. She was trapped here in this cavelike cabin with a man who didn't seem particularly eager to have her here.

How had everything gone so wrong?

Jack woke with a start. His sleepy mind registered that he was home. Cool air wafting across his skin had woken him. Where had the draft come from?

The bed swayed.

For a minute his sleep-foggy mind thought of We-tonga, but the mattress stilled and his bed companion huddled away from him. Olivia. She shifted in tiny increments as if she didn't want to wake him while getting comfortable.

He rolled to his back, and she stiffened so quickly the bed jerked. Searching for the source of the cold, he looked at the door. The door was shut and the bar down. He'd lit a fire, hadn't he? Had it gone out? How long had he been asleep? He stared into the gray darkness. The rain had stopped. Olivia's breathing didn't drop into the steady rhythm of sleeping.

Holding a hand up in the air, he tested the temperature. Colder than he remembered. He felt as if he'd been asleep awhile. Was Olivia just now coming to bed? He could be disorientated because the rain had let up.

"Olivia?"

Her breathing stopped.

Not asleep, but not willing to admit she was awake, either.

He sighed. Pushing back the covers, he set his feet on the cold floor. He unsuccessfully groped the bottom of the bed for his leggings. Standing, he shook his sleep-muzzy head.

Carefully, he walked across the space, prepared to dodge supplies, but the walkways were clear. Squatting in front of the stove, he opened the feed chamber. An orange glow bathed his bare skin. A quick glance at the wood box revealed that Olivia had fed the fire. Why was it so cold in here?

Frost and white drifts piled in the corners of the windows. As he'd feared, the rain had turned to snow. Jack grabbed another quarter log and added it to the fire. It flared, catching almost instantly. He let the heat bathe him for a second, enjoying the comfort of being home, being warm, a woman in his bed. He glanced over his shoulder.

Olivia's eyes were shut so tightly he knew she'd been watching him.

He should get dressed and bring in more wood so it would be dry and ready to burn on what looked to be a cold morning. He'd rather slide back into bed with Olivia. However, by the stove was a hell of a lot warmer.

The light spilling from the open chamber illuminated the room. All the supplies were put away. Not everything was in the usual place, but the tabletop was bare, while the shelves were packed. Even the spilled oats were gone from the floor, the grain sacks neatly lining the wall next to the stove.

Stitching on the oat sack signified a recent mend. Jack ran his finger over the neat darning stitches. Obviously, Olivia had straightened up the place. Perhaps having her as a wife would have its advantages.

He shut the stove door and spun the draft dial near closed. It would keep the fire burning low. He straightened and banged his head on a pot. Leather thongs were looped through the handles of pots and were strung from the rafters.

Olivia's hands were curled in front of her scrunched face. White ruffles covered her wrists.

"I know you're awake." His blood stirred, as if she might welcome him back to bed. He knew better, but his body raised a flag of hope.

She drew up her knees and curled into a tight ball. "I'm trying to sleep." Her voice was strained, little.

She'd never sleep knotted up like that. She needed to realize he wouldn't attack her. Willing his blood to cool, he crossed the room, sat, then slid under the furs.

A near chirp left her lips.

He scooted to the center of the bed. Olivia hovered on the far edge. He wrapped an arm around her and pulled her back against his chest. He half expected her to grab on to the side of the bed, but she was too light to provide much resistance.

She trembled.

"The house looks nice." He hadn't been married for nearly a decade without learning a few things.

Searching for a good place to rest his arm over the top of her, he found her icy hands. Her bare, icy hands.

He shouldn't have asked her for the ring back. "We're in for a cold night. It's snowing."

"How do you know it's snowing? You didn't look outside."

She had been watching him enough to know he hadn't gone close to the window. Had she liked what she'd seen? His member pulsed. "Snow is drifting against the glass."

She didn't respond.

He wanted to turn her toward him and kiss her again. Between the snow and her stiffness, her partial welcome this afternoon felt eons away. The dark of the night was a good time to share intimacies. He moved his hand to her side, but the rigid stays of her corset barred him from getting close.

He sighed and tried again. "Is there anything you'd like to know?"

"Why don't you have sheets?"

Wetonga had considered sheets a white man's oddity, and he'd been sleeping on furs so long that he hadn't given a white woman's expectations a thought. "Furs are warmer."

"Oh."

"Sheets in the summer would be nice." Calculating when he could go to town and pick up material for sheets reminded him of his exhaustion.

Olivia relaxed just a tiny bit. "I have sheets."

He brought his legs up against the back of her thighs. His body stirred.

Tensing, she seemed poised to scoot away.

He moved his hand to her hip. Wanting her to stay cuddled with him but not wanting her to feel trapped, he whispered, "Relax, I'm not going to hurt you."

The rough red spots around her lips made that a lie. He grimaced. He'd already hurt her without intending to. Kissing her would wait until he shaved. The rest would wait until she was ready, willing. *Eager* might be hoping for too much.

"But you're naked," she whispered in a shuddery voice.

"You have on enough clothes for both of us." He willed his body to relax. His staff throbbed and he resisted the urge to nestle against the crevice of her body. "I can wait until you're ready to be a wife."

But could he? As tired as he was, ignoring the lure of having her in his bed was difficult. When he wasn't exhausted, having her so near and smelling of lavender and softness would be irresistible. His thoughts swirled around the kisses in the meadow. She'd kissed him back, damn it. And she'd watched him when he'd put a log in the stove. His breath hitched and his rigid length suggested he should make her his wife now.

"I know I'm supposed to submit to my duty," she said in a tiny voice. "But—"

"No." His breath left him before he could stop what must sound like impatience. But it had been more as if he'd been punched in the gut. All his eagerness drained right out of him. Coldness crept in. He didn't want a wife who felt she had to submit to a "duty." He wanted a woman who wanted his touch, wanted his kisses, wanted him in every way.

Obviously, Olivia would never be that wife.

"But—"

"Just go to sleep," he told her.

Chapter Eight

Colorado sounds like such a beautiful place. I long for a sight of the mountains and the bison so thick upon the ground they resemble a brown carpet. Such things sound exotic to me. You have enchanted me with your descriptions of your home.

Olivia woke to the clang of a pot against the stovetop and the aroma of coffee. Last night she'd wanted to ask Jack what her duty entailed. She knew it started with kisses and ended with a secret undertaking that no one ever spoke about. Or, at least, people only referred to the marriage act in the most veiled terms. Even Selina had resisted Anna's probing questions.

But Jack had rolled away with from her, taking his warmth and dashing her nerve. By the time she was ready to venture another question, his even breathing indicated he'd fallen back asleep. She'd stared into the cold darkness for a long time before finally succumbing to fatigue.

The morning light brought the questions back to her mind. She didn't know if he wanted her to submit or didn't want her to, or only if she intended to stay. Certainly if she ended up going to California, she did not want to arrive with a baby in her belly. A heart-stopping fear yanked her out of sleep.

Olivia peeked one eye open. The frosty bare windows let in the light. In full buckskins, Jack stood at the stove. Her insides fell as if she'd been let down.

Last night, the sight of his long bare legs and the solid muscles of his backside had made her feel quivery. Similar to how his kisses made her feel. She shifted. Was the marriage act supposed to make her feel so…unsettled? She didn't like feeling out of control. It reminded her too much of the sickening plummet through the air when the train had crashed.

Jack turned. His gaze raked over her. "You're awake."

"Good morning," she mumbled awkwardly. What was one supposed to say to a man you'd shared a bed with?

He grunted. Was that a response?

He'd shaved. The smooth line of his strong jaw and the elegant height of his cheekbones gave her pause. The contrast of his frontiersman buckskins and the face that would have made a politician jealous had her staring. Who was he? How could he be so beautiful but so manly? He'd written to her of flowers and waterfalls, but she hadn't seen the soul of a poet on their journey from Denver City. No, he'd been pragmatic and angry. He didn't seem like a man who appreciated beauty.

"I'm fixing flapjacks, although it's almost midday," he said.

Midday? Flapjacks? Was that a peace offering amidst the implied criticism that she'd overslept?

"I'm sorry I slept so late." Olivia pushed up to sit. The room smelled faintly of smoke and wet wood. The chicks chirped as if singing for a meal of pancakes. Sizzling and popping noises emanated from the stove. She was hungry, she was sore and she wore her nightgown.

Her gaze darted to all corners, hoping the darkness last night hid an undiscovered nook. Four square walls. The open room didn't provide any place to dress.

Jack's gaze dipped to her grip on the furs held to her chest. His lips flattened and he turned back toward the stovetop.

"It smells lovely." Making sure her nightgown covered her ankles, Olivia thrust back the furs. "You should have woken me."

"I was letting you sleep. You had to be tired." His shoulders shifted. "But I was hungry."

Her gaze darted around the small cabin. How long would they be stuck together in this one room? What would they do?

The table was set with thick plates and tin cups. Either he'd been very quiet or she'd been sleeping like the dead.

He flipped a flapjack in the skillet and the aroma of butter drifted toward her. Her stomach rumbled.

"There's warm water in the pitcher." He gestured to a white enamelware washbasin and a pitcher with a red rim.

Using the empty flour sack hanging on a nail, Olivia washed. Jack had put her store-bought soap beside the washbasin. Her lavender-scented bar had fused with his brown bar. If only they could come together as easily as their soaps.

Using the dry end of the makeshift towel, Olivia wiped the moisture off her face. While Jack had kept his back to her, she still felt too uncomfortable to complete her morning routines with him in the room. Perhaps he would step outside for a minute. "I need to get dressed."

"Why? There's no one around. Breakfast is almost done."

Why, indeed? "I cannot sit down at the table in my nightgown."

"Fine. I'll serve you breakfast in bed." Was there a bit of a lilt in his voice?

She hesitated, torn by the idea that no one was around to make sure she behaved in a civilized manner and that Jack didn't seem to care. Were all the dictates of polite behavior worthless here?

"Olivia," said Jack softly, startling her out of her reverie.

"The table, then, since you have already prepared it." She turned and dug her shawl out of her carpetbag. After moving items off her trunk to the bed, she dug out a green work gown and hastily pulled it over her nightgown.

He hadn't turned from the stove.

"I'd like to see where we are."

He nodded toward the door.

She pulled on her boots and slipped outside. Blinding white greeted her. She lifted her hand and shadowed her eyes.

Tracks in the snow led to a structure with a roof sloped in only one direction, like a lean-to. The nicker of a horse came from it.

Water dripped off the eaves of the house and the stillness felt warm. Stepping off the swept porch stairs, she entered into a sparkling white wonderland. In the near distance, snow blanketed the mountains. Dark stands of pines interrupted the cottony covering, but they thinned out and disappeared as the peaks rose higher.

She caught her breath. Even though the landscape was foreign, she recognized the vista as one that would have an artist drooling to capture it on canvas. She could almost reach out and touch the far mountains. They were vast and towering, forbidding in their steep slopes. Yet tiny puffs of clouds danced across the treeless tips. If she climbed to the top, she fancied she could touch the sky, or at least a cloud. No wonder Jack loved this place.

Turning in a slow circle, she took in the vast landscape. Jack's cabin nestled in the middle of gentler mountains. They were rounded and covered with trees and not nearly so threatening or challenging as the mountains in the distance. The cabin rested on raised ground, not at the bottom of the valley, with a mountain rising behind.

The ridiculous urge to lie down in the pristine snow and wave her arms and legs and make a snow angel gave her pause. Anna would do that the kind of thing. As would Selina at Anna's urging, but Olivia could not behave as a child. Yet the landscape was devoid of signs of man. No one would see her.

As she looked back at the cabin, she saw Jack leaning against the porch pillar. A skitter of alarm shuddered through her. God, what would he have thought if she had dropped to the ground and played in the snow? He was probably already irritated that she had taken too much time.

She ducked her head and scurried back. Life out here was not for the faint of heart or the weak. She could hardly prove that she was neither if she spent her time lollygagging. Yet part of her no longer cared if Jack wanted her here or not.

This was her place, too. As mean and squat as the cabin was, she could make it better. She could learn to cook and garden. And Jack could learn to treat her as a lady.

Anna and Selina would say that she was putting her head in the clouds. She looked up at the mountain faces and the wisps of clouds draping them. Perhaps one day she would really put her head in the clouds. Sometimes clouds and dreams were one and the same.

Jack shook his head and returned inside. One look at him and Olivia had lost her joy at the sight of the freshly fallen snow.

How ironic that she could marvel at the Rockies yet find him repulsive. But the mountains were majestic. Perhaps their beauty would tempt her to stay.

He slid into his chair and dished a stack of flapjacks on his plate and a similar stack on Olivia's. Ravenous, he stuffed a quarter of his flapjack stack in his mouth. No sense in waiting as Olivia danced her way back inside.

He poured coffee for Olivia and himself. Leaning his chair back, he put the pot back on the stove. The red tin caught his gaze. He could have offered her tea.

The door opened and Olivia glided through. Her nightgown's lace ruffles peeked out around her throat and wrists. She looked like a princess in a hovel.

His chair thumped down on two legs. Jack rubbed his forehead. Until this moment he'd thought his cabin rather nice, better than most, but he had so little to offer a woman who probably thought she deserved gems and luxuries instead of crumbling bark from log walls.

She stood next to her chair, her color high. "It would be appropriate for you to pull out my chair."

He stopped chewing. She had to be kidding. Her chin lifted as if she wasn't. With his foot, he shoved her chair away from the table.

"That isn't what I had in mind." Her voice shook and her gaze dropped. With the reddish-brown spots around her pursed mouth, she looked like a lowly brute had ravished her. Him.

How long would she wait before sitting? She needed

to eat. As slender as she was, she didn't have reserves for the tough work ahead. She turned as if she intended to go back to bed.

Either guilt or shame made him pop up. She gracefully lowered herself into her seat, and he pushed in her chair.

"Manners aren't a big thing on the frontier." As an apology it stank; as an explanation it probably was worse.

"Thank you. Do you suppose that is because there aren't many ladies here?" She looked to either side of her plate.

He grunted. That was possible.

Olivia's forehead furrowed. "I don't expect that your first wife stood much on ceremony."

"Not on white man's ceremonies." Wetonga had understood her role and wouldn't have let him cook if she was around. Or at least she hadn't let him prepare meals until she had grown too ill to manage. She'd never insisted he follow Indian ways.

"Did you say grace?" asked Olivia.

She had to know he hadn't. Jack closed his eyes. "Bless us, our Father, for thy bounty which we are about to receive. Amen."

Olivia echoed his amen.

She blinked. "Wouldn't you expect to raise your children with proper manners?"

"We would need to have relations before children become a concern." He folded his arms and glared at her. His heart beat funny. Wetonga had been barren, which was why men in her tribe hadn't wanted her. He hadn't thought he cared.

Pink stained Olivia's cheeks and then her entire face. What would Olivia bearing his children be like?

He leaned toward her. The memory of her in his arms swirled in his thoughts. If she wanted children, she would welcome his attentions. His blood rushed through his veins.

Her voice barely audible, she said, "Yes, well, if you will force me to leave in a month, then I don't think I should risk… We should not have—" her voice dropped even lower "—marital relations."

"I won't force you to leave. You'll want to leave." He pushed back from the table, his appetite disintegrating. She'd twisted his words into a reason to avoid intimacy. The flapjacks churned heavily in his gut.

Olivia very slowly picked up her fork and cut away a section of her breakfast. "But you said—"

"Forget what I said."

Olivia's mouth tightened, but that was all the response he got from her. To hold out the lure of children and then snatch it away was like twisting a knife in him.

"Do you detest me that much?" he asked.

"I don't detest you." She pushed the triangle of flapjacks across her plate. "I think you detest me." She carefully set down her fork and lowered her hands to her lap.

"No, you're just not suited for life out here."

"You're wrong. If working in a cotton mill for six years didn't kill me, I don't suppose the frontier will." Her words were mild, but her glare was fierce.

He stared at her. Was she made of stronger stuff than he thought?

Her pale eyes searched his face. "I know I have a lot to learn. I trust you will teach me, or if you have any books I can read…" Her gaze circled the cabin.

His secreted books had been a sore spot with Wetonga. She thought a white man's need to put stories on paper shortchanged the community of stories told around the fires at night.

"I don't expect *Le Comte de Monte-Cristo* will be of much help."

Olivia's gray eyes sparkled, charming him. He'd never realized gray eyes could sparkle. The novel written in French was frivolous—a long-ago gift from his mother. He shouldn't have mentioned it.

"No, I don't suppose it will."

"I have an old almanac up there." He pointed to the attic space over the bed. A few boards nailed across the rafters provided storage. He should have bought a new almanac.

"Well, if we have that settled, we should eat." Olivia picked up her fork.

What had they settled? He couldn't go a month sharing a bed without wanting her. But if she meant to leave…they couldn't risk babies. His head hurt. "No. We haven't settled anything. I want a real wife."

"But you have me instead," she said ruefully, her head tilted to the side. "I will do my best to learn how to cook and take care of the house and garden." She smiled slightly. "And the chicks. I will become a good wife."

Was she that innocent or was she willfully misunderstanding him? "I want…" He searched for a polite way of saying what he wanted. He gestured toward the bed. "I want congress. I want to…" He wanted to mount her, make her moan with pleasure, bring them both to mountain-moving ecstasy. "Make babies," he finished ineptly.

Her eyes widened, and then she dropped her gaze. She looked right and left as if she couldn't escape the idea. Her skin fired again. Apparently "make babies" was a strong enough allusion to make his wife squeamish.

"Last night you said you didn't want me to submit." Her voice squeaked. "My duties…". She swallowed hard enough he could see her throat work above the lace and ruffles. "It's not that I don't want to be a wife, but…"

He growled. The words *duty* and *submission* should be banished. But he suspected it wouldn't take long before duty was enough. He stared at her. She couldn't possibly know of the pleasures she was denying them.

She pushed her chair back and twisted away. "I thought we agreed on a month trial. Is that too long t-to wait?"

"No." He shot out of his chair. With her sleeping beside him in bed, being unable to touch her for a month was impossible. "I don't know." He stomped across the floor, but his moccasins didn't make satisfactory noise, not to mention there wasn't enough room to pace. "Yes."

"Why?" She pushed on her stomach and clapped a hand over her mouth.

He stopped pacing and stared at her. She looked ill. At the thought of intimacy? Her shoulders shook. "Are you going to be sick?"

Her spine went ramrod straight and her shoulders squared. "If I have to go away, I don't want to be like Selina."

Was that supposed to make sense to him?

"The mill fired her. Our landlady tried to evict her. She couldn't find respectable work…. She thought Charlie would marry her."

The understanding dawned. "Selina is pregnant?" Her friend was with child and headed to California to marry an unsuspecting man.

Olivia winced. "She was. We waited until she had the baby to leave Connecticut. It was so hard on her. I don't want to have to start over in a new place with that kind of burden."

His thoughts swirled and his heart pounded. She would consider his baby a burden. "I'm not sending you away."

"Yes, but even when I arrived, the men in town thought I would not last. So if you are not satisfied that I can survive the winter here, you will demand I go."

"For the last time, I will not send you away!" He could get Olivia pregnant; then she'd have to stay. The thought shamed him as soon as it occurred. He hadn't expected immediate consummation of the marriage, but then he'd expected to be able to have congress with his wife before long—a week, two at the most.

"But you took back my…the…your ring," she whispered.

"You lost it in the creek," he fired back.

Her color drained.

Drawing a deep breath, he shoved his hand into his pocket and pulled out the gold band. He slapped it down on the table. The plates jarred. Olivia flinched.

The chicks peeped madly as if a Greek chorus to their argument.

"You act as if you can't stand my touch." He shoved the ring across the table.

Staring at the wedding band as if it might bite her, she shook her head.

"Wear it when you're ready to be a wife." He grabbed his rifle from over the door. "I'm going to go kill something for dinner."

"You didn't even eat your breakfast."

He shook his head as he grabbed a buckskin jacket and reached for the door. "Feed it to the chicks."

She stood. "Are you coming back?"

Not "when are you coming back," but "are you coming back?" With his hand on the door handle, he paused. "This is my home. I always come back."

Her voice was tiny and shook. "My mother always k-kissed my father goodbye when he left for work or for a trip."

As his parents had kissed before each trapping trip his father left on, except the last one. The one where Jack's mother had fussed over him, telling him he was a man now. Her attention had puzzled him. He should have realized his father's wait in the street indicated trouble.

He thumped his forehead into the door.

"Is that what I should do?" Olivia's tone was tentative. "To be a good wife?"

"Only if you want to." Jack held his breath. Duty or desire? Did she want to kiss him, or was she afraid she'd pushed him too far? Had she put the ring back on her finger?

Her touch against his upper arm was so light it could have been a butterfly wing's brush, but he felt it right down to his core. He leaned his rifle against the jamb and turned to face her. "So kiss me."

Olivia blinked and her cheeks were pink. She bounced up on her toes and leaned across the space separating them with her lips pursed.

"Like a wife," he growled just before her childlike buss landed.

The instance her lips touched his, though, he didn't care that her effort was more innocent than worldly. Shocks ran down his spine and his blood thickened. He reached for the only exposed skin he could see. Her cheek was so soft, her neck like silk, her texture like nothing he'd ever experienced before. The scent of her lavender soap swirled in his nose, a refined counterpoint to his roughness.

Her eyes widened while her color deepened to a bright red. Her lashes fluttered down, shuttering any emotion in their pale depths.

He needed her to feel what she did to him. Yet the space between their bodies gaped like a chasm. Thankful the cage of her hoops wasn't barring him, he pulled her against him.

Her lips were heaven, the press of her body divine. God help him when the tip of her tongue ventured to touch his. Explosions of desire fired in his groin. In three heartbeats he was as hard as granite. He'd never make it a month. He wouldn't make it a week. He might not make it to the bed.

Surely if she was making the kiss intimate, she'd returned his ring to her finger. The hope of having her on her back, willing, sent flames coursing through his blood. His blood was on fire and his breathing grew ragged.

"Olivia," he whispered against her lips. He needed inside her to relieve this frantic urge. Only the barest warning echoed in his head that to push her too fast would only hurt her. A woman's body wasn't as quick as a man's to rise to the occasion. And she wore all those damnable layers of clothes. "Touch—" he heaved "—me."

He dived in for a deep, long kiss. Impatient with the distance between them, he stepped forward. She stepped back—toward the bed. His mouth locked with hers; he pressed forward, seeking full body contact. Dimly aware of her hands on his shoulders, he caught her hand in his and pushed it down between their bodies.

As he placed her slim palm against his hardness,

she gasped. Her fingers curled, gripping him, and she broke off the kiss. He didn't care. He needed to catch his breath. His breathing was like that of a hard-worked horse. He needed more than kisses. He needed more than touching. He needed her naked and willing on his bed.

Her fingers stretched out as if to torment him.

He groaned low. Pushing against the slender length of her hand, he wanted to stroke her delicate fingers almost as much as he wanted her to stroke him.

Only a detail jabbed through his arousal-clouded mind. Her fingers were bare.

"Wh-what's wrong with you?" She pushed against his shoulder and tugged her hand free.

The slide of her hand provoked a wild sensation. Words were beyond him. "Shh," he said.

Pulses of pleasure made him wonder if he'd spilled his seed, but it was just a new agony of desire. He wanted her in the worst way.

With a slow awareness, he turned toward the table. The gold ring lay beside her plate. Untouched, unwanted. Her meaning was clear. A sharp pain jabbed through his breastbone.

The sting offered slim respite from his urgent desire. Olivia was too fine for him, a woman he could never have. That, as much as the years of abstinence, must have fueled this insane desire.

He spun away from her and reached for his rifle, cartridge pouch and jacket. "I'll be back by dark."

"D-dark?" she echoed.

His chest heaving, he reconsidered. Dark was happening later and later. "By suppertime. Keep the fire lit."

He snorted. One touch and he'd burst into flames. They wouldn't need a fire. *Merde,* she'd meant a goodbye kiss and he'd lost his sanity.

Chapter Nine

Before you answer, you should know that I am often gone for weeks at a time. As my wife, you would have to hold down the homestead in my absence. Winters can be harsh. Although to return to my cabin and find you waiting for me would be heaven.

Jack bent to brush snow off his buckskin leggings. He'd hardly been gone two hours, and he hesitated to return inside, but he'd shot dinner and staying out longer was pointless. He looked around the area in front of his cabin, trying to imagine the way Olivia saw it this morning.

Instead, he noticed all the work needing attention. As soon as the snow cleared, the chicks should be in their coop and their pen constructed. The horses needed a corral as well as a better barn before next winter. He didn't have time to teach Olivia life skills.

When he opened the door, vapor rolled out. He ducked under a curtain of wet white material to enter. The cabin was like an Indian sweat lodge. Hanging from every rafter were pantalets, petticoats and chemises.

They dripped like stalactites, leaving puddles on the floor. He threaded his way through the dribbling mess. No doubt he had a wife, or at least a woman in his space.

He tossed the rabbit carcass on the table.

The stove door stood open, the fire blazing, but he didn't see her. "Olivia?"

He drew off his rifle and had to remove a ruffled petticoat from the pegs for his gun. He hooked the petticoat back on the ends of the mounting pins. Turning around, he ducked, looking under the forest of undergarments. She was on her knees behind the bed. The lid of her trunk was raised, although she wasn't looking inside. Instead, she was hurriedly fumbling with the buttons of her dress. Her hair hung down her back in a tangled, dripping mess with snow slush sliding down the long damp locks.

If he had been a few minutes earlier, would he have caught her bathing? His calm disappeared and desire surged. His plan to avoid sexual intimacy went up in a puff of smoke.

"Washing day, huh?" His voice was husky and the raging heat made him sweat. He threw off his jacket. It landed in a puddle.

"I'm doing laundry, yes." She dug in the half-empty trunk and came out with an embroidered hand towel. Her back still to him, she twisted her hair in the hand towel.

He bent and picked up his jacket, but found the peg he used for hanging it occupied by a lace-cuffed nightgown. He swallowed hard and hooked his jacket on the edge of a chair back covered in long skinny stockings.

She stood and folded her arms tightly across her front. Her color was high. Embarrassment or just the heat of the room?

Her chest heaved as if she had been breathing hard. "Is there a clothesline I could use to hang the wash?"

"I usually toss stuff across the porch rails."

Her lips pressed together. Her pale green dress clung to her and dragged through the puddles on the floor. Obviously the skirt was designed for hoops. Except her hoops leaned against the wall beside the bed, and the material clung to her skin. Was she wearing anything underneath her dress? Jack's mouth watered.

"I don't usually have so much to dry."

He would need to string her a clothesline.

"I'm sorry for the mess, but I haven't been able to do laundry since leaving Norwalk and…do you have anything you need washed?"

Olivia wasn't looking at him. Instead, her eyes traveled to the rabbit on the table. She blanched.

The hand towel slipped and fell to the floor. She bent over and her wet hair tumbled down.

He swallowed hard when she snatched the towel. He didn't notice the usual stiffness in her spine as the wet hair that reached the curve of her bottom swung over her shoulder. Straightening, she pushed it back and wrapped the towel around it; a wet spot over her right breast drew his gaze. The thin wet cotton molded a tight tip. The urge to dip down and suckle had him breathing hard.

But he'd allow her the month. Unless she put on his ring. Like a moth to a flame, his gaze went to her slender hand. Her ring finger was still bare. He groaned.

He forced his eyes away before his staring made her more uncomfortable. Her corset hung over the back of the other chair. It looked like an instrument of torture and, from what he could see of his wife's form, not terribly needed. She was slim, her breasts high. He swallowed hard.

Merde, he was going to need to take another trip to the woods. He forced himself to think of his clothing. "I washed most of my things before I left to fetch you."

White sheets peeked out from under an intricately sewn quilt on the bed. He moved his gaze away before his fantasies traveled too far on that path. A silver brush lay on the inside shelf of her trunk. He seized on the sight as a way to divert his mind from the urge to kiss her.

As she toweled her hair, her breasts jiggled beneath the dress. Heat flashed under his skin and centered in his growing hardness. He wanted her.

He was an idiot for explaining the preacher's words. He should have acted as if he believed she would stay and then she never would have made her eminently sensible request.

He wiped his hand across his brow. He had to get out of the cabin before he attacked her and his promises and good intentions fell by the wayside.

He grabbed the door handle and pulled it open, relishing the wash of cold air.

"Where are you going?"

Jack closed his eyes. "To clean my gun." He collected his thoughts enough to grab the cleaning supplies and a chair. "My gun needs cleaning," he added unnecessarily.

Olivia stared at the shut door. Jack seemed...odd. Her breath left her in a shuddery rush. She felt odd. Did he know she wasn't wearing any undergarments?

She drew her brush through her hair, making short

work of the tangles. Weaving it into a single braid, she quickly coiled it and pinned it.

She shouldn't have washed every single undergarment she owned, then bathed, but she'd thought he'd be gone longer.

Jack had been looking at her the way men often looked at Selina, but then his face had twisted as if he was in pain and he'd gone outside.

The door swung open.

"Olivia, come here," Jack said in a low voice.

She grabbed a shawl and wrapped it around her shoulders before heading out of door. The cold hit her damp skin and raised gooseflesh.

The sun slanted in the sky, but there were still hours of daylight left.

"Look, in the woods," he whispered.

A line of tracks in the snow led to the shadows in the trees. Still as statues stood a doe and a speckled fawn.

"See them?" Jack whispered. He pointed with his rifle.

"You're not going to shoot them?" squeaked Olivia.

The doe's tail rose like a white flag. In unison the deer bounded off, leaping through the snow in a graceful zigzag.

Jack scowled at her. "I don't kill does with fawns."

"Oh." He'd called her to see their beauty and she'd sent them fleeing.

He held out the gun. "You need to learn to shoot."

She shrank back. Ladies didn't shoot. "No, I couldn't."

"The rifle's not loaded. Just get the feel of it."

She shook her head and edged toward the door. "I have to finish washing."

"That could have been a fox after the chicks." He

caught her and pushed her in front of him. The rifle butt pressed into her shoulder. "I'll set up a target for you to practice later, but you really need to know."

Olivia shuddered as he positioned her left hand on the front part of the stock. He stood a hairbreadth behind her. His heat radiated through her thin dress almost as if they were skin to skin.

"Make sure the butt is seated tight against your shoulder. Line up the sights," he coaxed in a low voice that she felt right down to her toes. "Slow your breathing."

She didn't think she could. All she could think about was her lack of undergarments and his proximity. He pulled his hands away and the gun barrel dropped.

"Hold it steady. The trick is to take the shot in the pause between inhaling and exhaling." His hands closed around her shoulders.

What would it be like if he moved his hand to her breast the way he had in the meadow, only without the heavy material of her corset in the way? Her nipples tightened, tingling as if he'd touched her there.

He continued his instructions and she tried to listen without thinking of how open her private parts were under her skirt, and how liberated her body felt without lacing.

She squeezed the trigger, the gun clicked and she jumped.

"Good." He backed away. "Try again."

A violent shudder racked her body. She spun and shoved the gun back into his hands. "I can't."

"You need to learn to dress right for the out-of-doors," observed Jack with the gun held across his chest.

Strangely enough, it wasn't cold that had her shivering. "Yes, absolutely." She felt positively wicked. Her lower half felt funny—not a bad funny, but melting and open.

She rushed inside.

Jack followed her a few minutes later. He put the rifle back on the pegs. "It's loaded now, so be careful."

Olivia nodded. She shifted from one foot to the other. The cotton slid against her bare legs. The sensation unsettled her.

"The shotgun, too." He pulled it down and showed her the mechanics. His dark head bent over the gun while he kept the muzzle pointed out the door. "You should know how to shoot this, too, only it will kick hard. The shot scatters so you don't have to aim. It's not good for a long distance, but it'll put a big hole in anything close."

She nodded her head. He looked strong and handsome. His hands were sure as he handled the weapons.

He put the shotgun back above the door. She never wanted to touch them.

He turned slowly and leaned against the doorjamb. His eyes traveled down her body, leaving heat in his wake.

"Olivia, I will agree to not get you with child, but I expect to have marital relations." His brown eyes held hers.

A wave of shock and anticipation assaulted her. A melting heat settled in her core. Her jaw dropped.

"There are ways to find pleasure without risking a baby."

"But…" She didn't even know what objection she could make. "You don't even like me."

He shook his head. "I'd like you naked on the bed. I'd like you a lot. Besides, you can't go around without undergarments and not expect me to notice. All I can think about is kissing you and more." His brown eyes undressed her.

A hot flush burning her face and all down her body, Olivia tightened her shawl. "I didn't expect you back so soon."

His eyes dulled and he gave a brief nod. "I won't rush you, but it will happen."

She swallowed hard. She should tell him she'd changed her mind, she wanted to go to the place the kisses led, but she stood rooted in an agony of indecision.

"I'll go get more wood." He pushed away from the door and went outside.

Olivia should be tired enough to sleep, but her limbs seemed infused with a hazy energy. Her hands trembled as she unbuttoned her dress. She eased the material down. The material brushed her skin and shattering sparkles cascaded through her as if Roman candles were exploding inside her.

If Jack turned over on the bed, would he see that she had put the ring on a gold chain around her neck? She should just wear the ring, become his wife in all ways, but she was afraid. Afraid of being trapped in a loveless marriage. Afraid of having a baby when she didn't even know how to care for herself, but more afraid of the way she felt undone by Jack's kisses.

She should stand and let her dress fall to the ground and slide under the covers naked as Jack slept, but her courage deserted her and she snatched the nightgown off the bed.

She needn't have worried. Jack seemed to be sleeping soundly, not peeking at her naked torso. He was so close, yet so far away. Gathering up the hem, she pulled the nightgown over her head. She stood and stepped out of her dress.

Jack might say he would not force her to leave, but he was deliberately showing her how incompetent she was. How long could she stay where she wasn't wanted, or only wanted in one way? Selina must be right about men and lust. Even though Jack didn't like her, he still wanted relations.

Sighing, she lifted the quilt and the furs Jack had piled on top and slid into the cool sheets. Wincing at how the bed swayed in response to her movements, she carefully scooted down.

Lying still as a mouse, she stared into the darkness. Jack's even breathing was comforting.

Restless, she rolled to her side. Jack's back loomed before her. The muscles of his shoulders drew her. All through the day she'd been aware of him. He'd watched her, and her every movement had felt exaggerated and awkward. She'd hoped that he'd turn to her in the darkness.

Reaching out, she traced the indentation of his spine. His skin was warm. Pressing her palm against his firm flesh, she ran her hand down over the bumps and ridges of muscle.

"Olivia," he moaned.

She snatched her hand back. "I thought you were asleep." Her voice sounded loud in the silence of the cabin.

"No." He rolled to his back.

Her heart racing, Olivia clutched the ring under the bodice of her nightgown.

"So you only want to touch me when I'm asleep?" His voice was low, in keeping with the night.

A shiver ran down her spine. The bed swayed as a result. She couldn't tell if Jack noticed. Wetting her lips, she tried to formulate an answer. "I don't know."

His laughter rumbled. "By all means, don't let my being awake stop you." He rolled to face her and propped his head on his hand. His gaze landed on her clutched neckline. It lingered there for a minute, and then he searched her face. "Are you afraid of me?"

Unwilling to admit to her cowardice, Olivia shook her head. Her stiff neck almost refused to allow her the denial.

Jack sighed. His breath wafted across her face and she shuddered again. "Why are you scared? I promise I won't get you with child until you put on my ring."

She wore his ring. It just wasn't on her finger, but as long as he didn't know, he wouldn't force her to be his wife. Her hesitation befuddled her—she should just pull the chain out over her nightgown. But when her hand refused to move, she made a tiny sound of protest.

"Is it more than that? It is, isn't it?"

"I don't know," she whispered. She tensed, waiting for an expression of his disgust and disappointment.

He pressed his lips against her temple in a gentle kiss. "Are you frightened because I hurt you in the meadow?"

Opening her eyes, she searched his expression. Faint furrows in his forehead seemed more like concern than disappointment.

"No," she ventured.

The corner of his mouth lifted and her bones went soft. Her breathing chugged faster than it should. Brushing the back of his hand across his beard, he said, "You should let me know if I am hurting you. I'll stop or I'll shave."

Did he intend to kiss her? Her mouth watered. "But isn't it supposed to hurt?" Her voice shook.

Jack's silence gave her an answer. He finally said, "No."

It was only right that she had lied to him and he'd lied back.

"Kisses should never hurt," he added.

A huff escaped her lips before she could stop it. She hadn't been asking about kisses.

He leaned closer. His mouth hovered just above her lips and his breath brushed across them as he spoke in a low voice. "As for the rest, if the woman is in distress, then the man is doing something wrong."

Did that mean he only did things right? She stared up at him, waiting for his lips to touch hers. Waiting for the funny feeling in the pit of her stomach to settle.

"The first time might be a bit painful, but it shouldn't be bad."

Without lowering his lips all the way to hers, he rolled back to his side and watched her. He was depriving her of his kiss. Had he decided his beard was too rough? Disappointment curled under her skin while she pondered his explanation. She'd heard whispers of pain and blood. "How bad? Will I bleed?"

Jack frowned. "You really don't have any idea, do you?"

"I'm sorry. I don't know what to expect or how it works or…" Words tumbled out as if his knowledge and the darkness allowed her fears to froth out of her mouth.

Olivia whispered, "Mama died before she would have thought to explain anything to me. I have mostly only been around women for the last eight years…and… and…you're so different." Jack's body and how it functioned was completely unfamiliar. "And why was that part of you all swollen this morning?"

Jack's teeth gleamed in the darkness.

How could he find her ignorance amusing? Olivia winced. Humiliation rushed through her. She wanted to escape, but there was nowhere to go.

He shoved the furs, quilt and sheets down, then kicked them to the foot of the bed. Her ears burned and she stared up at the boards across the ceiling.

"*Ma chérie,* explore all you want. And I'll tell you all you want to know." He rolled to his back and folded his hands behind his head. "I promise to just lay here and keep my hands to myself."

He was insane. She couldn't stay beside a stark-naked man lying exposed on the bed. Sleeping naked under the covers was bad enough, but to willfully flaunt his body was beyond the pale. She rolled to the edge of the bed and swung her feet to the floor.

"Ah, if you want more light, you can hang the lantern on the hook above the bed."

The cold floor nipped her bare toes. She couldn't move for fear he would think she wanted more light to see him by. The moonlight reflecting off snow outside and streaming through the uncovered windows and the faint orange glow through the stove grate provided plenty of illumination.

"The first time will likely bring a little blood, but nothing like your monthly," he said conversationally.

He shouldn't speak of such an intimate detail of her body. Olivia covered her eyes with her hands. She wanted to cover her ears, too. Her entire face burned. She wanted to cool it on the icy floor. She wanted to look.

"Come, Olivia, you can look even if you don't want

to touch. My body should not be a complete mystery to you."

She shifted on the bed, turning toward the head of the bed so she could see his face, but she kept her hand up as a blinder. "You will catch cold like that."

He laughed. "I highly doubt it."

"I'm glad you find my…my…" She couldn't help but see the broad muscular expanse of his chest, the dark tufts of hair under his arms, the sparse spattering of hairs across his chest. Her sarcasm was lost in a welter of yearning.

"Innocence?" he supplied with a lifted brow.

"Amusing," she finished. She had perhaps meant *outrage* or *shock,* but *innocence* fit. *Ignorance* perhaps fit better.

"I'll close my eyes, and you can pretend I'm asleep." His dark lashes fluttered down. "I know that if I was offered an opportunity to look my fill at you, I would not hesitate."

But he closed his eyes. She didn't understand him.

His chest rose and fell with a rhythm too rapid to be that of sleep. "I could spend hours watching you comb out your hair. It is the color of moonbeams."

Was he picturing her in his mind? Learning he had watched her brush her hair sent a new burst of heat tumbling through her body.

"Your skin is pale and translucent like fine china." She couldn't pretend he was asleep if he kept talking, but his lashes hadn't moved.

Ever so slightly, her hand slipped down her cheek. His washboard stomach came into view. She swallowed and looked lower. A dark thatch of hair surrounded the part that drew her curiosity. His male member lay sideways, reaching to the top of his thigh. As she watched, it throbbed and stretched higher and higher until it pointed toward his navel.

"That part swells and grows hard in preparation for mating," he said.

Olivia snapped her head away and discovered Jack's dark eyes on her.

"Do you understand how it works?" he asked softly.

Olivia pressed her lips together and folded her arms, as if that would help her hold in her rushing emotions.

He waited patiently.

"I've seen dogs, is it anything like that?" Her voice was all breathy and shaky.

"Dogs don't have much finesse, but the basic act is not so different." His strong, even teeth appeared again.

"Quit laughing." Olivia's frustration and fear rocketed to a new level. Before she realized what she intended, she raised her hand. He twisted away as she smacked him on the back of his upper arm. The *thwack* was loud in the cabin. Everything in her went rigid. What had she done?

Chapter Ten

I accept your offer of marriage. My friends will be traveling to California in late April. I will travel with them to Kansas City, where our paths diverge. I will be counting the days.

Mortified, Olivia put her hand to her lips.

Jack breathed in several deep breaths and relaxed back into his ridiculous hands-behind-his-head, elbows-out pose. "That wasn't the kind of touching I had in mind, but it was a start." His lips twitched.

He couldn't possibly be amused.

"I'm sorry. I don't know what got into me. I've never hit anyone before." She bit her lip hard enough to draw blood. Tremors raced up and down her spine. She was both hot and cold, as if she couldn't make herself of one mind.

"Perhaps, *chérie,* you are full of energy you don't know what to do with," he suggested softly. "Your body readies itself, too. Your private parts grow soft and slick so that I might slide him…between your legs." The duck of his chin left no doubt as to what part of his anatomy he was talking about. "That is the only part of the act that can lead to pregnancy. I will not do that until you wish me to."

Oh, stars above. "What more is there?"

Jack's eyelids lowered slightly, and he didn't try to hide his smile. "Touch me and let's find out."

"You already know." Her heart thundered and her lower parts felt wet and yielding. She drew up her knees and tucked her nightgown under her toes. She should have put on a pair of freshly laundered and ironed drawers, but the lack of undergarments had started to feel strangely wicked.

"Not what it will be like with you. I can imagine that your touches will be light and sweet. Your hands will be cool and I will crave your caresses like a man in the desert needs water. Go ahead, I will endure your exploration."

"Endure?" She scowled. "You make it sound like torture."

He reached up and grabbed the top rail of the bed frame. "Torture to not touch you at the same time. Torture that you are too yellow bellied to do what you want to do. Torture that I am not—"

She planted her palms on his chest. His skin was hot and his muscles flexed. His grip tightened on the bed rail. An echoing tightness spiraled in her.

"—kissing you," he finished with a hitch in his breath. "Of course, you could kiss me."

She didn't know what to do next. "What if I do this wrong?"

His coffee-colored eyes held hers. "The only thing you could do wrong is to stop."

She slid her palms out, tracing his collarbone under her fingertips. In the silence of the cabin, his breathing was loud. She ran her fingers over a flat, dark nipple and he jerked on the bed. She snatched her hand back.

"Don't stop," he said in a husky voice.

"I am hurting you."

"No, Olivia, your body is sensitive there, too, perhaps more so."

"But I don't like it. I feel I am falling and my body is beyond my control, like when the train fell off the bridge."

His eyes narrowed and he sat up. "You need to trust that I will catch you and just let yourself fall." He cupped her head with his hand and pulled her head into his shoulder. "You are halfway there already. I promise it will be worth it." His low voice rumbled in his chest and reverberated in hers.

She felt hopelessly inadequate and on edge. "Where is there?"

She felt his smile against her forehead.

"La petite mort."

"Little…" She searched her limited French vocabulary. "Little death?" Death?

"Not death so much as a release. For me I would spill my seed and you would find the most intense pleasure, like dying and finding heaven."

Her face grew hot. Her private parts tightened and released. "Oh."

"Are we done with this game, then, *chérie?* Are you satisfied with your knowledge of a man's body? You do not wish to give me *la petite mort?*"

He was goading her to continue. That part of him that had risen and stood at attention was just below her line of vision. He'd wanted her to touch him there earlier. "I can do that by just touching?"

"With your hands, or with your mouth, *oui.*"

She clenched her eyes shut and drew in a stiff breath. Her mouth there? She was not quite repulsed and not quite ready to consider doing that. She swallowed hard. "People kiss each other there?" Her voice squeaked.

"Yes. I want to kiss everywhere on you. Most especially there."

She drew back, but the tightening of *there* suggested that while her mind might rebel, her body liked the idea. If all people did such things, no wonder no one ever spoke of it.

He let out a shaky laugh. "Another time, perhaps."

She lowered her index finger to touch the tip, where a beaded drop of moisture rested.

His male part stirred. His grip on her head tightened and his breath caught. She tried two fingers and marveled at the velvety texture of his skin over the steely hardness.

His low groan tickled her ear. She lowered her fingers to the springy thatch of dark hair. He released her head and put his hands behind him on the bed. She regretted that he wasn't holding her. He pulled his knee to the side, allowing her access to all parts of him. She moved her hand to his muscular thigh. The dark hairs were soft to touch. The rigid shaft bobbed slightly and she answered the call, touching with all of her fingers.

His stomach quivered. "That's good." His words were strained, as if he had a hard time getting them out.

Shifting to her knees, she stroked his length. Jack's gaze focused on her pale fingers on his darker skin. He slowly raised his eyes to meet hers. She slid her fingers around the head of his shaft and his eyelids lowered, but he still held her gaze. Something broke loose inside her. She leaned forward and found his mouth.

Her kiss was awkward, too rough in its inception,

but Jack didn't seem to mind. He caught her head and pulled her down on top of him. Everywhere his body was against hers, her skin felt alive. Her hips rocked and she pressed her legs together and released them. Her body hummed with a wild energy that centered in her core. His hand closed over hers and pulled it away.

She moaned a protest, but he stroked the inside of her wrist and then laced their fingers together. His mouth moved on hers as if he would draw her into him. He ended the kiss reluctantly.

"'Livia, let me see you. Let me touch you. Let me take you to heaven."

His hand on her back gathered the material of her nightgown. She hesitated. Certainly she wanted to find where these wild feelings took her, but she was still afraid. If she let him remove her nightgown, he would see she wore his ring. He would also see the scar on her leg.

He kissed her again and rolled them so she was on the bottom. His heartbeat thudded, strong enough she could feel it against her chest. She couldn't stop him if he intended to finish this, but he lifted his head up and stroked her cheek. His kisses gentled and he slowly nipped her lips as if drawing their game to an end.

"All right," she whispered.

"All right, meaning yes, *ma chérie?*" Jack stroked Olivia's hair. He was fairly sure "all right" meant yes. She'd said "all right" when she'd agreed to marry him, but now was not a time for mistakes. She was scared enough without him appearing overeager.

Her gray eyes glistened in the moonlight, and she gave a short, jerky nod.

His tension, which had built to an unbearable level, crested and eased into a low hum. Even if she was not eagerly reaching for him, her unsteady breathing and trembling suggested she was affected, too. Perhaps her reserve would melt away with her innocence.

There were so many things he wanted to do for her, so many things to show her. He knelt on the bed and reached for the bottom of her nightgown. Already it had crept up, exposing her slender feet and shapely white calves.

He slowly drew it up to her knees. He anticipated kissing the back of those knees, running his hands down her calves, finding out if her high arches were ticklish. "You are beautiful, *chérie*," he whispered.

She lurched up and put her hands on her thighs, preventing him from raising the nightgown higher.

He wanted to rip the damn thing off, but he let go and drew his hands back to rest on his thighs. "You wish to remove it yourself? I would like that."

Her chin dropped. Then she spoke in a herky-jerky manner. "I... No. I have a scar. From the train wreck. My leg was mangled." She bit her lip and turned her head away. "It's ugly. I am not so beautiful."

He snorted. Responses tumbled through his brain. He wanted to protest that he hadn't desired beauty, or that no scar on her leg could mar the perfection of her face, her form, but what response would soothe Olivia? "Allow me to judge for myself."

Her fingers curled around the wadded hem of her nightgown. He held his breath while he waited for her to remove the thin layer of cotton between them. His heart thundered and anticipation surged low and hard in him.

Her fingers straightened, but she determinedly raised her pointed chin and met his eyes. The gray was so soft, like the morning mist on the mountains. Pink washed across her cheekbones. Her champagne-colored hair caught the little light and reflected it on her ivory skin as if she were a fey creature, magical and ethereal. By God, she was beautiful. His breath left him in a hot rush.

How could he tempt this angelic being to fall to earth with him?

She touched her breastbone and slid her fingers up to the ruffle around her neck. Slowly she pulled the tie at the base of her throat free.

He swallowed hard.

With her slender fingers, she spread apart the material and links of a gold chain shimmered against her throat.

He wanted to put his hand there, his mouth there and everywhere on her. Patience be damned, he could stand the wait no longer.

A faint scuffling outside intruded on their lovemaking.

Her head jerked toward the door. He held still and prayed the animal would go away.

A thud emanated from the front porch.

"What is that?" whispered Olivia, her fingers clenching her neckline closed.

"Merde!" A most untimely interruption. Jack clenched his eyes shut and waited for more noise to identify the creature on his front porch. Scuffling and thumping. Jack sprang from the bed and reached for his rifle. The door would hold against most animals, but Jack wouldn't chance being unarmed. He reached for the doorknob.

"Jack," Olivia whispered. "You're not dressed."

"Jacques," called the animal on the porch.

Not a bear. Jack whipped open the door. Cold air rushed across his superheated skin.

His brother-in-law, Antonga, lay at his feet. Long dark hair threaded with gray covered his face, and his furs glistened with moisture. A red-stained hand reached out. Jack shoved the rifle back on the pegs and grabbed the man under his arms.

"I had nowhere else to go, *mon ami*," grunted Antonga.

"What happened?" Jack dragged his brother-in-law into the cabin, with little help from the man. Antonga's skin was deathly cold.

"Bear. Pansook is dead."

"Olivia, light the lantern." He didn't spare her a glance as he dropped Antonga in one of the chairs. "Where are you hurt?"

"We kill deer. Bear come. Antonga hatchet…in… bear head."

Jack rolled his eyes. "You are a brave bear killer."

Antonga's teeth flashed in the dim light, but the man slumped forward. His head thudded dully against the table.

Jack stripped away the furs and skins. His hand came away sticky.

A match flared and deep gashes across Antonga's back were illuminated. Long claws had ripped open Antonga's back.

"Oh, God," whispered Olivia. She stared at the horrible wounds.

Jack peeled away the clinging leather, exposing more of the devastation. Antonga sucked in a deep breath.

He wasn't dead yet, but with wounds like these… Jack didn't finish the thought. "Light the lantern."

Dimly aware of his wife's fluttering through the room, Jack exposed more of the Indian's bloodied back.

A steady flow of blood seeped from the wounds.

Antonga needed a doctor. The man's dark skin was dusky and pale. The wounds would need to be cleaned, stitched and bound long before Jack could fetch a doctor.

Olivia finally managed to light the lantern. She averted her head from Antonga.

"Towels. We'll need towels and bandages, water. He'll need your sewing skills."

Olivia swiveled, and stared at him. "I can't sew him." She swayed.

Jack caught her upper arm. "Don't you dare faint on me."

She shook off his grip and took a step back. Quivering like a drawn bow, she reached for the wall behind her. She had gone so pale her nightgown was hardly lighter than her skin. "B-but, he's an Indian."

Bristling, he said, "So he is not deserving of aid?"

She hardly seemed aware of his impatience, her wide gaze on Antonga. He was no threat to her.

"Who is he? How does he know your name?"

"He's Wetonga's brother." Working quickly, Jack jumped on the bed and retrieved the whiskey bottle he had stashed above the rafters. "Damn it, Olivia, I need help, not a lady afraid to get her hands dirty."

"There's so much blood. Is he going to die?"

Great, that was not what Antonga needed to hear. His cowering wife would not be any help at all. "Shut up or go outside," he growled.

Olivia's gray eyes peeled away from Antonga and she straightened. "I'll get my sewing kit."

The Indian man watched her with black eyes. His blood-smeared leathery face crinkled in deep pain. His mouth snarled. "Pale Eyes better choice than daughter?"

Jack answered in a singsong language.

He must not have wanted her to hear the answer.

The Indian's mouth moved into a semblance of a smile and his high cheeks nearly overtopped his eyes. "Pale Eyes give you white sons."

She pushed away from the wall keeping her upright. Why did every Indian insist on calling her Pale Eyes? "My name is Olivia."

She flushed, realizing she hadn't insisted on the accepted practice of using her title of Mrs. and his last name, but she didn't feel so married. Grabbing a handful of her nightgown at her neck, she gripped the ring she'd been about to show to Jack.

Jack unsheathed his knife and laid it on the stove top. Moving lithely like a cat unconcerned by his nudity, he crossed the room and grabbed up flour sacks. She'd done nothing.

God forgive her, all she wanted to do was watch Jack. She pushed away from the wall and went to her trunk. Yanking out embroidered towels, she found her sewing needles. Carrying a card of sturdy cotton thread and the towels to the table, she swallowed hard. Her hands were shaking so badly she didn't know if she could thread a needle, let alone stitch flesh.

The wounded man had slumped forward again. "Bury me with my sister."

"You aren't going to die," muttered Jack. He grabbed a towel from her stack and pushed it against a wound. The cotton quickly turned red.

Her stomach revolting, Olivia swiveled away from the sight. What if this had happened to Jack?

"Firewater," rasped the Indian.

"Olivia, get him a cup and help him drink."

She set down the needle, found a tin cup. By the time

she turned around, the Indian had wrapped his bloody hand around the whiskey bottle.

Jack spoke softly to the man in a low patter that was unintelligible to her.

She tried to help the man drink, but whiskey dribbled down his chin. He pushed the bottle away. "Jacques honorable man," muttered the Indian.

"We have to get him in bed before he passes out. Hold pressure here." Jack didn't wait for her compliance but shoved her free hand against the bloody towels at the man's back.

Her stomach churning, she pushed as if she could hold his life force in.

Turning, Jack stripped back her quilt and sheets. He piled the furs over the exposed mattress. Would the man be more comfortable on furs?

The Indian nudged the whiskey up to his lips, and Olivia shifted her attention. He gulped noisily.

The Indian sputtered and Olivia realized she was practically pouring the alcohol down his throat.

"Sorry," she muttered.

"More," he answered.

She helped him to drink the last of the spirits. Jack lifted Antonga out of the chair.

They got the older man to the bed. Jack was moving before Antonga was settled. "Get the lantern."

Olivia tried to move quickly, but Jack beat her back to the bed holding his knife with the handle wrapped in a flour sack. He straddled the man's lower half.

"Hold the light so I can see."

Her heart thumped erratically in her chest. How could Jack be so calm?

She thrust the lantern toward the wall, looking for the hook. The light swung wildly.

Jack wiped the back of his hand across his forehead. "What the hell are you doing?"

Olivia swallowed hard and fought the bile rising in her throat. She had to get out of here before she was sick. "Hook?"

"There isn't a hook. Just hold on for a couple more seconds. I have to cauterize."

She closed her eyes and attempted to control the wild pitch of her stomach. Unable to stand it any longer, she set the lantern on the trunk and ran out the door.

Leaning over the porch rail, she gulped cold air until her stomach quieted. She dashed away the moisture leaking from her eyes. The mountains and woods that had looked so peaceful this afternoon had transformed. The deep greens and purples of the mountains had changed to a forbidding black mass. The snow looked cold, white and cruel. Her bare toes curled against the frigid wood. If a bear could attack Indians familiar with the wilds, what chance did she have in this place?

The door opened behind her. Her quilt landed around her shoulders. "He's asleep now. Are you all right?" asked Jack.

He sounded weary.

"Why did you tell me there was a hook for hanging the lantern above the bed when there isn't?" She rolled her eyes. She didn't even care about the answer, but her thoughts were so muddled.

Jack wrapped his arm around her and pulled her back against his chest. "I didn't want you getting out of—"

"Will he die?"

Jack made a humming noise. "Possibly. He needs a doctor, and he still needs to be sewn up. I'd rather do it before he wakes."

Olivia turned in Jack's loose embrace. He tightened

his grip on her. "There aren't any doctors around, are there?"

"In Denver City. I'll leave at first light."

Panic choked her. She had no idea how to help him. "You can't leave me here with him."

"I'll be back in two days. Three at the most. I'll take both the horses." Jack stepped back. "I've got to get back inside."

"Jack."

He turned.

"What if that had been you?" she whispered.

Jack's eyes dropped. "I carry my rifle in the woods."

But as he spoke, she had the feeling he was saying there were dangers. Hadn't he been saying that all along? He needed a brave woman, a calm woman and a helpmate. What business did she have here?

"And that is why it is important you know how to shoot," Jack's voice rumbled low.

Even if she had a desire to learn, her hands shook too badly when she was nervous. A bear would make her nervous. Hell, a squirrel would make her nervous.

She didn't belong out here. With her ignorance and fears, she was likely to make things worse for Jack. She belonged in a city, where knowing what time to call on an acquaintance was an asset. Jack deserved a woman who could face the danger and assist him when a crisis arose.

"I need to finish with Antonga. Will you help?"

He sounded resigned, as if he knew she wouldn't. He'd not commanded, had not insisted she help. He'd given up hope that she would ever be the kind of wife he needed. God forgive her, she didn't know that she could be.

The Indian's words echoed in her head. Jack was an

honorable man. He would not refute her as his wife, even if he wanted to. Even knowing that she posed more risk to him than bears or renegades. Her own words mocked her.

She had misunderstood. He had meant the trial period for her to realize she should not stay. He would honor his promises. She bit her lip hard.

Her body still hummed with a raw, awakened energy that his kisses had provoked, although it was banked under a layer of dismay. The pleasures of the marriage bed were not enough. If she was honorable, she would leave so he could find a woman who could shoulder the burdens of living in the Rocky Mountains.

The idea of leaving made her sick, but she folded her arms across her stomach. It wasn't too late for her to correct the error she'd made in thinking she could be a good wife to a man who truly needed a calm, brave helpmate.

Chapter Eleven

The snowdrifts against the back of the cabin have reached the eaves. The days are short and it may be some time before I can mail this. During the day the sun is so bright. It glances off the snow in thousands of sparkles. When you arrive the first wildflowers should be in bloom.

Jack rubbed his face. He'd done the best he could for Antonga. Olivia had stitched, although her hands had shaken badly. Gagging, she'd finally run from the cabin.

He wound bandages around Antonga's chest. His breathing was steady, but he had passed out. The whiskey and exhaustion might be the cause, or he'd fallen into the deep sleep preceding death.

Bloody towels littered the cabin. Reddened water and whiskey puddled on the floor. Olivia would hate the disorder, but his mind was on the question she'd voiced. What if it had been him?

Bear attacks weren't common, but animals could be unpredictable and dangerous. A knife could slip. A tree could fall the wrong way. Avalanches roared down the mountains with little warning. He could be injured in any number of ways, especially while out trapping.

What if he had been wounded like Antonga? Would he be bleeding to death while Olivia wrung her hands?

He wanted to justify her behavior, to think everything overwhelmed her. He'd thought that, with her beauty and gentle domesticity, he could ignore her lack of suitability and they could make a go of their marriage. He was lying to himself.

If she was to make it here, she would have to rise to the occasion sooner rather than later.

Convincing her to stay by tempting her with the pleasures of the marriage bed was foolish. He should push her to leave.

The door opened and Olivia whispered through, a bucket of snow in cold-reddened hands.

Her gaze darted away. She set a pan on the stovetop and scooped snow into it. "I'm sorry," she said. "I couldn't take it any longer."

She hadn't been the one taking anything. Jack closed his eyes. Antonga had been the patient.

Jack rose and leaned over to pick up the towels Olivia had handed him earlier. Embroidered flowers and ivy flowed along the edges. His mother had owned towels like these. She'd put them out for special occasions. Once he'd wiped his muddy hands on one. His mother's shrill displeasure had never left him.

Her pretty things were ruined. "I'm sorry about your towels."

"It isn't as if I'll have a tea party anytime soon." She shrugged. "I can make new ones anyway."

Tension in his shoulders, which he hadn't even realized was there, eased. Had she appreciated his pitching her quilt and sheets to the side, avoiding their ruin?

"I wasn't much help." She stared at the floor.

He resisted the urge to disagree, to say he wouldn't have managed without her, because it wasn't true. What was worse, it was a lie that could keep her here when she should leave.

"I just… I just… I don't have any excuse."

Had his mother left because dealing with a fur-trapping husband was beyond her ability to cope? Had she been as out of her element as Olivia was? He felt a twinge of empathy for his mother.

"If you are leaving in the morning, you should get some rest. I will clean quietly." Twisting the bloody towel in her hands, Olivia's shoulders rose. "Would you be so good as to mail letters to my friends?"

"Of course." He waited for her to move.

"You were remarkable," she said softly. "I don't know how you stay so calm."

"One of us had to," he answered.

She drew a stiff breath. Her eyes darted up and back down before she took a quick step back. "I suppose so. I will have to do better when you're gone."

"Yes, you will." He folded his arms across his chest. He felt a bit like he'd kicked a wounded kitten.

Jack washed the blood from his hands. The urge to close the distance between them and wrap her in his arms was almost unbearable. Unbidden, her exploration of his body popped into his mind. He shook his head to clear it. Keeping his distance was a better plan.

He turned toward the bed and pulled a few of the pelts not being used to the floor. He made a mound and folded the quilt and sheets into a nest between the bed and the wall. If she lay down with him, they would have to nestle tightly together. His blood surged.

Now was not the time to resume her education in marital relations. She might be pretty, but pretty wouldn't save his life if one day he returned to the cabin severely wounded.

Her ineptitude shamed her. She hadn't known the first thing to do.

She dipped a sack in the bucket of hot soapy water and scrubbed the floor. Durable towels made of flour or meal sacks made more sense than her embroidered ones.

Across the room, Antonga snorted.

Her heart racing in her chest, Olivia stopped. The rhythm of his breathing settled into a heavy snore. Every time Antonga's breathing changed, Olivia started, and then waited until a normal pace resumed. She blew out a shaky breath. Jack's ability to sleep amazed her.

But then he did what he had to do.

A lump formed in her throat. Jack wanted her to leave. She ought to, but she still was trying to impose order on the rough and dirty cabin. She rested back on her heels. The floor needed to be sanded and waxed. The table needed staining. The walls needed plaster and paint.

Antonga needed cleaning, too. After carrying a chair to the side of the bed, she positioned the lamp on her trunk. Olivia found Antonga's hand under the furs. Moving slowly, she pulled it out. Gently, she rubbed the wet, soapy towel over his leathery skin.

"What are you doing?" Jack asked.

Olivia started, nearly knocking the bowl of water off her lap. Holding it steady, she didn't bother looking at Jack as she returned to washing the Indian's hand and wrist. "Trying to clean him up a bit. Does he feel hot to you?"

Jack bolted upright and felt Antonga's face. He flashed Olivia an irritated look and lay back down. "No."

"Perhaps my hands are cold from the water," she answered softly.

Jack rolled to his back. "He may turn feverish. His bandages need to be kept clean and dry."

"I'll do my best."

His dark eyes watching her, Jack rearranged the covers. "You need sleep, too, Olivia. You'll need to take care of everything while I'm gone."

Her heart thumped erratically. "About that." Could she manage? "What will I need to do with the animals?"

He studied her a minute. "I'll set out hay for the mules before I leave. Just make sure they have water, not ice, in their trough. The chicks need to be fed and given water several times a day, same as you've been doing."

Olivia concentrated on cleaning around Antonga's whitish nails. "I do not believe I am suited for life out here."

She held her breath, waiting for his response.

"Not many are."

Her breath stole away. She tried to smile, but it felt as if her face were cracking. "You did not have to so readily agree."

"You are suited for a gentler life." Jack's voice was kind, but it did not soften the blow.

"I was raised to be a society wife, but that is not my lot in life." Olivia suspected she wasn't particularly well suited for that life, either. Large gatherings overwhelmed her. Her mother had had a vivaciousness that Olivia lacked. Was there any place for her?

"You did not expect to find society here, did you?" asked Jack.

"No. I thought I would find beauty." She'd thought

she'd find peace, a simple, honest man to love her and a home. Those hopes were too dear to share. Jack was a simple, honest man, but if she couldn't be a true helpmate, he wouldn't love her.

"California is better settled, with men at least. Outside of the Sierras it is temperate, never cold. The valleys are lush. It might be a better place for you." He spoke in a coaxing tone that grated on her nerves.

Olivia turned her attention to Antonga's dark skin above the white bandage. She wiped brown blood spots from his shoulders. Her vision blurred, but her voice remained steady as she spoke. "If California is so wonderful, why don't you live there?"

Jack sighed. "This is my home. I am a fur trader, not a miner or a farmer."

"I see," said Olivia. She didn't entirely. She wished she felt so attached to a place that she didn't want to leave it, but she hadn't felt that way about Connecticut. She hadn't had a real home since her parents had died.

"I need to be where I can trade with the natives or trap wild animals. I must be on the edge of the wilderness or else trek for hundreds more miles."

Olivia eased down the furs. She positioned Antonga's cleaned hand by his side and dipped the towel in the water to wash his lower back.

She pressed her palm above his hip, testing his temperature. Her hands were very white against the Indian's sagging skin. He was not as perfect as Jack.

"Why are you touching him like that? Are you not satisfied with your knowledge of a man's body?" Jack squinted at her stopped hands.

She pulled back and rinsed the towel in the discolored water. "I was not touching him that way."

"Yes, you were."

She hadn't been exploring Antonga's body the way she had explored Jack's earlier. "I have never seen any Indians before coming here."

"So you must examine him like a blind woman?" Jack's voice contained no amusement.

Was her husband jealous of her attention to an injured, unconscious man? Was there a sliver of hope for their marriage? "I was remarking at how white my skin looks compared to his."

Jack threw his arm over Antonga's shoulder. "Not so much darker than mine."

Jack's brown eyes met and held hers. She went very still. "Your skin is not so dark, although I don't think anyone is as pale as I am."

"My father's mother was a full-blooded Chippewa."

Olivia sensed the moment was important; Jack was likely trying to give her more reason to leave. Only, his being part Indian made sense. He was equipped to live in the wilds, and she wasn't. She looked down at the bowl of water and wrung out the towel. "You want me to leave, don't you?"

She waited, hoping he would deny it, but only the soft snore of Antonga echoed in the night.

Jack pulled his arm away. He stared up at the far wall. "It would most likely be best."

"I see." Olivia's heart turned to lead in her chest. "You are honorable enough that you will not force me to leave." Her voice shook as she spoke. "Is that what Antonga meant? That you hadn't known how unsuited I was when you promised to marry me? Is that what you told him?"

"That I honor my promises," echoed Jack dully.

"I understand that now. You wanted me to realize

how unfit I am for life out here. You want *me* to put an end to this farce."

Jack's jaw pulsed. He was close enough to touch, but he seemed as far away as the mountain peaks that scraped the sky. "If you are done, put out the light and come to bed."

His meaning couldn't be clearer.

She rearranged the furs over Antonga's still form and slowly stood. Her heart felt heavy, but she put her shoulders back. She took the bowl to the door to dispose of the water outside. A part of her that had always held back and resisted the urge to make waves broke.

This was supposed to be her home, her marriage, her place to be who she was. She was not supposed to be hiding in the corners to avoid being thrown out or noticed in a bad way. She was not supposed to be just tolerated here. She was supposed to be a welcome partner, not a burden.

"You knew I was unsuited the moment you saw me. But you are wrong to think I have no value. I am a hard worker and…" Speaking of her worth was harder than she imagined. "You should have known I wouldn't have the wilderness skills a woman born and bred here would. And you are cowardly for thrusting the entire decision on my shoulders. You should have voiced your concerns before marrying me." Before looking to seduce her.

She yanked open the door and stepped out into the cold, hostile world in the shadows of the Rocky Mountains. She was trembling. She wanted to hate Jack, but instead she only felt empty inside.

Gripping the rail on the side of the porch, she stared into the bleak landscape. If she hadn't misunderstood him in the beginning, she wouldn't have insisted that they didn't risk pregnancy. They would be married in all ways, and she'd be well on her way to loving him. And he'd be stuck with her.

Her breath escaped her.

Another hour this night and he would have seen she wore his ring on a chain around her neck.

They wouldn't be fighting about whether she would stay or go. But would have, should have, could have—it wasn't what had happened. Mistiming and missed cues were the story of her life. Ever since the train engineer had missed the signal that the drawbridge was open, her life had been off track.

"You have a softness for women of no value, eh?" rasped Antonga.

Jack rubbed his face and tried not to react with disgust. After all this time, he would have thought that Antonga would have acknowledged his sister's worth. And the snap judgment about Olivia was unfair. "I thought you were asleep."

"Off and on."

Jack pushed back the covers to rise. He was too edgy to sleep anyway. "I'll put out the light."

Antonga rose up to his side. "Do not bother. The flesh wakes me. The bear's spirit wakes me. That I did not send Pansook on to the Great Hunting Land wakes me." He drew in a labored breath. "I do not wish my daughter to throw herself on Pansook's pyre."

Jack paused, half sitting. Ute tradition was to place a man's body in a cave and then burn his possessions with him, including his wives. Jack went still at the thought of Tabby ending her life in such a way. "Do you hate that I did not marry your daughter?"

Antonga had offered Tabby to Jack after Wetonga's

death. Jack couldn't imagine marrying a girl to whom he'd given horsey-back rides. Tabby was barely a teen… and now a widow.

"I want my grandchildren to have one foot in the white world. I want to know the flood of settlers shall not vanquish them. I make my people learn white tongues. Why have you let O…li…vi…a think she has no value?"

"Olivia," repeated Jack, understanding the name could seem foreign to Antonga while to him it sounded lyrical, poetic, beautiful. He didn't want to discuss his new wife with Wetonga's brother.

Reaching for his buckskin pants, Jack glanced toward the closed door. He should not let her stay outside long. She might be angry enough to not notice the cold. The last thing he needed was her developing a lung fever.

Antonga reached out and caught his arm. "O…li…vi…a has gentle hands."

The urge to punch Antonga surprised Jack. The man was weak and ill. He posed no threat. Jack jerked away and yanked on his buckskins.

"Why do you push O…li…vi…a to do what you fear most?"

Pacing the floor, Jack ignored Antonga's observation. "She is not meant for this place. She cannot cook or tend crops. You saw her. She panics at the slightest crisis."

"Bear just scratch Antonga's back," agreed Antonga with a low cough that belied his humor.

She'd nearly drowned in a shallow stream, too. "She's panicked before when she shouldn't have."

Antonga shifted. "O…li…vi…a can teach children letters. The white man come. Knowing how to survive

in white man's world is her strength. You have lit too
many fires in the red man's land."

Antonga wasn't even making sense.

"You drank too much whiskey." Jack circled the
table. Cold wetness greeted his feet. Moisture seeped up
from the floor where Olivia had scrubbed and scrubbed
the boards. She was trying so hard to make his squalid
cabin into a refined home. But the homey touches just
got in his way.

"I have many years to see. When the white man
come, they make the world to them. The old ways will
be of no use when the buffalo are fallen to white man's
guns and the grounds are broken to grow grain or covered in buildings. Already they foul the streams looking for metal that shines. *Mon ami,* we cannot live the
life of our fathers much longer. The iron horse comes
and our way of life goes away."

A chill ran down Jack's spine. In the past few years
he'd had to travel farther and farther to chase down
beaver and red-fox pelts. Hunting parties of white men
would come and shoot more buffalo than they could eat
in a month, only to leave the skinned carcasses rotting
on the ground. If the Indian's way of life disappeared,
so would his livelihood.

"You knew these things when you sent for a white
woman," slurred Antonga. "You wish her to stay."

"Of course I wish her to stay. She is the most beautiful woman I've ever seen." Jack wished he could pull
the words back into his mouth. Even if Antonga didn't
make note of it, Jack had just put Olivia above Wetonga.
The thought startled him.

Antonga rasped a laugh. "Is time for Jacques' wife
to teach my people the ways of the whites."

"I cannot promise..." Jack rubbed his forehead. He

couldn't argue with Antonga with the state he was in. "I cannot require Olivia to stay."

"You can let her know what you wish."

That would be simple if Jack knew what he wished. Earlier in bed he'd wanted her to stay, but when she fumbled around, more hindrance than help with Antonga, he wanted her to go. Jack looked to the door. "I don't wish for this life to defeat her."

"Mmm, you think she is like the men who arrive with sparks in their eyes and leave in a few moons with ashes in their blood."

"Not everyone can survive the mountains." Not everyone should even try. Many prospectors came only to be defeated by the weather, the hard work or the isolation. They left stooped and drained. Jack didn't want Olivia to become a shadowy version of herself.

Antonga's answer was a snore.

Jack wanted Olivia to be calm and brave and capable, yet look as she did, smell as she did and taste as she did. He wanted her to retain that air of refinement, yet wholeheartedly be his wife in bed. He needed a woman capable of hard work, chopping wood, carrying water and cooking. He probably wanted too much and more than any woman would ever be capable of managing.

Olivia would have to go inside soon. She'd at least grabbed her shawl and her scuffs, but she shivered in the cool night air. She tried to rehearse what she would write to Selina and Anna. But it always came back to the fact that she was out of her element and in over her head. Even a native had seen in minutes she was unsuited for life out here.

The mature thing would be to put an end to the dream life she'd imagined with Jack.

The door creaked open. A triangle of light slashed across the narrow porch. Jack's shadow interrupted the light. "Are you all right?"

"I'm fine," she answered. "I just wanted a minute to think."

"You cannot think inside?"

The truth was she couldn't think clearly around him. He moved and images of him naked goading her to touch him flooded her thoughts.

"You should not stay out long."

Even now his voice made a shudder ripple down her spine. "Why? Should I be worried about bears?"

"Only if you see one."

His flippant answer nagged at her raw feelings of incompetence.

She swiveled as he shut the door. He had her quilt again. Although instead of draping it over her shoulders, he wrapped it around his own.

Heat stole over her cheeks. The cold air couldn't penetrate her heated skin. But she didn't want to warm toward Jack, not when she'd finally understood she needed to find a different path in life. She turned back toward the cold mountain landscape.

"What should I do if I encounter a bear?"

"Chances are, you won't."

She snorted. It was unladylike, but how could she learn to survive if he wouldn't share his knowledge?

He sighed. "Never run or it might think you're prey."

"Great. Am I to stand there until it goes away?"

"Usually, back away slowly." Jack pulled her backward.

"Oh." She plopped in Jack's lap as he sat on a wooden crate.

Not that she'd had much choice in the matter. Before

she could spring off his lap, he pulled her legs around so she sat sideways on his corded thighs. Nothing about Jack's body was soft. Heat flooded her face as her new-found knowledge of his body swirled in her thoughts.

"This isn't a good idea," she said stiffly.

"Keep me warm." His low voice vibrated through her.

He tucked the quilt so tightly around them she would have had to struggle to get free. He was warm, his chest bare under the quilt that smelled faintly of him. She would never be able to use the quilt again without thinking about him.

She laid her icy fingers against his smooth skin. He gasped. After standing outside she certainly wouldn't be able to warm him.

She fisted her hand and rubbed it against her thigh. The strange tension she had suffered from earlier surged through her.

Jack's hand closed over hers and stopped her sawing motion, but not her racing heart.

His palm over her fist, Jack rubbed his fingertips in a circle on her leg.

Her thoughts scattered to the wind.

"Antonga will think he owes me for saving his life." Jack's voice dropped. "If he lives."

Her disordered mind jolted with a thud. She shouldn't be thinking of…Jack's body or of the strange way he made her feel while Antonga fought for life. She straightened her hand, interjecting her fingers between Jack's stroke and her thigh.

"He already brings me his furs to trade, even though he could get more taking them to Denver City. It is probably why he was nearby."

He traced the length of her fingers, but he paused

when he hit her bare ring finger. "We may end up with his family camped at our doorstep, or worse. He already believes he owes me for taking Wetonga off his hands."

A subtle shift in his tone indicated his deep emotions regarding Wetonga. A wash of dismay swept through Olivia. She wasn't sure she wanted to know more, but she asked, "Why?"

Jack shifted her. Olivia feared she had probed too deeply.

But his voice rumbled through her. "She couldn't have children, so none of the men would keep her as a wife."

"How…?" asked Olivia.

Jack's chuckle made her feel naive.

Selina hadn't needed marriage to produce a baby. "Never mind." Olivia floundered. "Did you not want children?"

"Not back then." His hand rubbed along her hip. "I wanted her."

Her spine stiffened as his offhand words sliced her to the bone. It was silly to be jealous of a dead woman. But her feelings were too raw. She didn't know if Jack could ever love her. He might always be impatient with her nervous timidity. What difference did it make?

If she stayed, Jack's tolerance was probably the best she could hope for. He'd loved his first wife, but how could he love a wife he saw as a failure?

Chapter Twelve

Selina, Anna and I are busy sewing our trous-
seaus. Although with only one trunk each, we con-
fine ourselves to bare necessities. I can hardly
stitch straight I am so eager to meet you in person.

Jack knew he'd said the wrong thing by the way Olivia
turned wooden against him. Instead of railing against
him as Wetonga would have, Olivia went very still.
Even sitting on his lap, she managed a dignity not many
women could have pulled off.

"Do you think you could find another wife you want
as much?" she asked.

What the hell did she mean by that? The wind sighed
through the trees, and Jack didn't answer. He didn't
move.

She pushed against him.

"Olivia." He refused to let her up. "I'm not looking
for another wife." A hollow space opened in his chest.
Even though her leaving was best, he didn't want that,
but what he wanted wasn't possible.

She chewed her lip. "Won't you marry again…when
I leave?"

"You have three weeks before you need to choose." He'd wanted her to realize she was ill equipped for life in the Rocky Mountains, but it seemed too sudden. After her speech about being a hard worker, he'd thought, he'd hoped, he'd believed she intended to stay.

"It is what you want, isn't it?" She slid off his lap.

He didn't stop her from rising this time. He wanted her to be the perfect wife. Bold, brave and soothing to his soul. Someone who could weather the hardships of life with him and not leave in the end.

Tightening her shawl around her back just under her shoulders, she moved to the porch rail. "I don't know why you advertised back East for a wife when there were probably better-suited women in Kansas or—".

"Another squaw," he finished. "Antonga wanted me to marry his daughter."

Bark flecked off where she held the support post. She pulled her hand away and brushed off her palms. He was aware of every movement she made. In the way she touched things, in the way she stood, in the way she moved, she carried an innate grace.

"Antonga thinks I wanted a civilized wife to be ready for when the settlers come," Jack offered.

Olivia's chin dipped. She was beautiful in the moonlight, her hair reflecting the scant light and glowing. "Is that true?"

"It will be a long while before civilization reaches the mountains. Farming will be too hard here. The land won't support dozens of trappers." The newspaper hadn't offered the option to advertise anywhere else but on the Eastern Seaboard. Women were always in short supply in the territories, but young men left the East in droves.

She stood very still.

"It is not always like this, Olivia. I don't think you should just decide…so soon." He stumbled over the right words to say to her. He was torn between wanting her to stay and fearing that he could persuade her to attempt a life that would only defeat her in the end. "You should just understand life is hard here."

Her chin lifted. "Believe me, I understand." She took a slow breath and shook her head. "I will ask Anna or Selina if it will be all right if I join them in California."

The speed at which his marriage had died took his breath away. "Don't decide tonight."

"D-don't act as if you want me to stay."

"Too much has happened. You aren't thinking clearly," he said. He wasn't thinking clearly. The idea of her leaving was like being kicked in the stomach.

"On the contrary. I realized if a bear attacked you, I would have been terribly ineffective."

"You would have been better than an empty cabin."

"But you won't be alone long. Antonga will send you his daughter."

"I didn't want her. I wanted…" He wanted a white woman's cooking. He wanted a literate woman. He wanted a different sort of woman than Wetonga. Yet every difference he'd pointed out as a weakness to Olivia. He frowned. He wanted a woman who shoe-horned into his life without changing it.

When he didn't finish, Olivia spoke. "Everyone I've encountered has taken one look at me and thought I will not make it here." She waved her arm. "The men from in town thought I would leave. The Indian called me lazy. The minister…" Her voice quivered. "I don't know what everyone thinks they see. But you see it. Everyone sees it."

Restless, he stood and paced along the porch. "What

everyone saw was a lady too finely dressed for this hard and dirty life. They look at you and think you'll never chop wood or carry it. You'll never adjust to the dirt. You won't want to clean game or plow for crops. You'll miss the fancy clothes and carriage rides."

"Is that what you see?"

"That's what I saw."

She watched him with narrowed eyes. "But you think it will just be a matter of time before I leave?"

"I thought that. I thought if your leaving was bound to happen, I'd rather it was sooner rather than later. If you'd had the means, you would be anywhere but here. If you had any other choice, you would not have married me." He rubbed his fist over his aching chest. "Am I wrong?"

She turned her back to him.

He waited in vain for a protest that she'd wanted to marry him. That she'd chosen his advertisement from the others because something about him appealed to her. Instead, she stood still.

"I hope…" He had to swallow against a roughness in his voice. "I hoped that you might prove strong enough to stay. I have seen you work hard. I was wrong in thinking you would be incapable."

She made a sound of protest. "You have pushed me to leave from the first minute we met."

"My parents were as ill suited as we are. My mother was from a well-to-do family and my father is a fur trader like me. He didn't have the means to give her fine things or an easy life. She was never happy with being left alone for long periods. She didn't want to live close to the wilderness. After a while they just hated each other and she couldn't take it any longer. She finally left and took my sister away."

He swallowed against the returning frog in his throat. "I haven't heard from her since."

Olivia had gone very still and she turned toward him. "She abandoned you?"

"I wasn't a baby." He headed down the steps. He hated that he sounded like a sniveling brat who wanted his mama. He just didn't want to face that pain again, the endless wondering what he had done wrong, what he could have done differently. As a grown man, he knew he hadn't caused his parents' divorce. It wasn't anyone's fault, but he didn't want history to repeat itself. He didn't want to love Olivia and then have his heart ripped out.

"I wouldn't do that to a child."

"I know." She had enough forethought to not risk having children while in a marriage that might fail.

"My parents may not have abandoned me by choice, but I understand what it is like to be left behind."

He paused on the bottom step. "It isn't about children. It is that we are so similar to them. We will have the same problems, the same fights."

"Did your mother expect your father to change his trade? Did they know each other before they married?"

It wasn't the question he expected. "They knew each other well enough that I was born six months after their wedding. Why?"

"I don't know. If you do not believe we can succeed, we will fail." Her voice flowed softly through the night air.

He wanted to protest that they were different enough, that he didn't have the intense wanderlust his father had and that Olivia was not a descendant of a French *comte* as his mother had claimed, but Olivia's next tentative words cut him off.

"I cannot hold out against everyone pointing out how wrong I am for this life."

By everyone, she meant him. He turned on the step. She stood, gripping the rail, unmindful of the bark now. His breath caught. She looked beautiful and so vulnerable. He'd made her think less of herself. "I didn't mean for you to doubt yourself," he began.

"It doesn't matter. You have shown me I have choices when I thought I didn't." She bit her lip.

A stinging pain, as if a bear had clawed through his chest, stole his breath. This mess was largely his fault. If he had not been so sure that she would never make it when he'd first seen her, perhaps she would not have given up so easily. "Olivia, I want you to be happy. It was never my design to hurt you."

She lifted her chin. "No, of course not. You just wanted someone different than me."

She swiveled and glided through the door. Even the gentle way she snicked the door shut had finality to it.

A hand on her shoulder woke Olivia. She jerked upright in the chair. She must have fallen asleep leaning on the table after she'd finished writing her letters.

"You should lie down. The quilt is still warm," Jack said.

"What time is it?" she asked.

"Near dawn. I'll be leaving soon."

"You'll want coffee." She scooted the chair back, then stood.

A low moan from the bed froze her. Antonga moved restlessly. Her gaze darted to Jack. His expression was grave.

"It's best if I leave as soon as possible. He needs a doctor, or at least some laudanum."

"Should I give him more whiskey?" asked Olivia. The crushing fear that Antonga could die if she didn't do the right things for him nearly made her knees buckle.

Jack shook his head. "There isn't any more."

She crossed the room to Antonga's side and put her hand on his heated brow. His thrashing stopped. "Should we take him to Denver City in the wagon? Wouldn't that get him to a doctor faster?"

"The jarring wouldn't be good for him and would take too long. I can make it in a day if I push the horses." Jack filled leather saddlebags as he spoke. "I'll be back tomorrow night or the day after. These letters are ready?" He lifted the two envelopes from the table.

Olivia reached out to stop him. She'd poured out her heart in the letters, but sending them to Anna and Selina felt too personal. Jack stuffed them in a bag without waiting for her answer.

The finality that he was leaving her alone with a man who might die sent rivulets of ice-cold fear running down her spine. She desperately wanted to beg Jack to stay. She bit her lip hard enough to draw blood.

"I'm taking the rifle. The shotgun is ready." He nodded toward a second gun above the door.

Her knees wobbled so badly Olivia grabbed the bed frame.

Jack glanced her direction. "You probably won't need it."

Olivia tried to buck up under his scrutiny. She didn't want him seeing how badly she was shaking.

The saddlebags thumped on the table and he crossed the room. He wrapped his arms around her and pulled her to his chest.

"You'll be all right. I'll be back before you know it," he murmured against her hair.

Olivia just wanted to cling to him, but he would see how very cowardly she was. She settled for momentarily brushing her nose against his shoulder and gripping his arms. "Please be careful," she said.

He tilted her away from him and looked at her. The corners of his mouth curled. Olivia's hand shot to her head to be sure her hair had not tumbled down.

His thumb brushed across her cheek. A shudder of need rippled through her. How could the burr of his thumb evoke such a strong response? She blinked.

His eyes turned concerned as he touched her sore lip. Time seemed to stand still as he lowered his mouth to hers. His kiss was soft, a gentle caress of the place she'd bitten. Her lips parted and she wanted his warmth, his strength and things she couldn't name.

He lifted her and set her away from him. "*Merde,* I have to go, Olivia."

She stumbled. He held her steady, his coffee-colored eyes searching her face.

She dropped her gaze. Every fiber of her protested his leaving. She ought to be used to abandonment by now.

"Yes, of course." She forced her clenched fingers on his arms to relax and slide away. Trembling racked her body.

Pressing a shaking hand to her mouth, she tried to still her nerves. How could Jack raise her hopes and then dash them in the space of a few seconds? Why kiss her when they'd agreed to end this farce of a marriage? Why did it make her feel so undone, as if her legs had turned as flimsy as a rag doll's?

She sank down onto the chair beside the bed.

Jack shoved his arms into his jacket and grabbed his rifle off the pegs. He lifted the saddlebags and opened the door.

Trying to ignore him, Olivia adjusted the furs around Antonga with a heavy heart. He wouldn't want to hear her sniveling and complaining that she couldn't cope. Jack needed a wife who could hold down his homestead.

She squared her shoulders. "Don't worry, we'll be fine." It might be a lie, but it was the kind of hopeful optimistic thing one said, even if it wasn't true. She wanted to say more, but there was nothing more to say.

Jack pulled into Denver City well after midnight. He was bone weary and saddle sore. He hadn't ever ridden for so many hours in one day. He'd rested the horses, letting them graze for fifteen minutes every hour while switching the saddle, but their heads had dipped lower and lower with each plodding step. They were dark with sweat in the warmer air of the valley.

The attendant at the livery stable woke as Jack unsaddled the horse he'd been riding. The young man rubbed sleep from his eyes and wearily grabbed a curry brush. "Rid 'em hard, eh?" said the teen.

"I'm in a hurry to fetch a doctor." Jack found a second curry brush and started in on the other horse. The boy might be young, but working in a livery stable probably exposed him to what went on in Denver City. "Do you know one who might be willing to go into the mountains?"

Jack would have to wait until morning to fetch him. No doctor would relish his pounding on his door in the middle of the night, and the horses were spent. A return journey tonight would kill them.

"Doc Jenson is willing to travel for the right fee," said the young man. "What happened?"

"Bear attack. Killed one brave and badly wounded another."

The boy stopped currying the horse and squinted over the horse's back. "You ain't gonna want Doc Jenson, then. Might try that doc over at Kincaid's saloon. He ain't so picky 'bout his clientele."

Jack sighed. Perhaps Antonga was right—the natives would be swallowed whole by the invasion of the white men.

"Is he any good?"

"Doc Jenson's better," said the stable boy. "Other one's a drunkard."

Great. His choices were a worthless drunk or a doctor that would balk at treating an Indian.

Chapter Thirteen

Mon père, *the wedding is done, but I expect my bride will not stay. She reminds me of Mother and she has no better liking of me. She has friends she can join in California. I will need you to watch my place if I have to take her there.*

Olivia knew she should change her stained clothes in case Jack made it home, but she was too tired.

She laid her head down on the table in what had become her regular sleeping position for the past three nights.

Noise drew her out of a deep sleep. The furs rose and fell steadily over Antonga's still form, assuring her he had not succumbed to his injuries. She was about to lay her head back down when the jingle of a harness had her bolting upright. Was Jack back?

A stranger spoke.

She couldn't see out. Once darkness had fallen, only the interior of the cabin was reflected back in the windows. The uncovered glass made her feel exposed. Whoever was out there could see her, but she couldn't see him.

Footfalls thumped on the porch. The idea of using the shotgun terrified her.

"Olivia?" Jack called.

Relief washed through her like a spring torrent. She flew to the door and lifted the bar. Realizing how slovenly she looked, she stepped behind the door.

"How is he?" Jack's saddlebags thumped onto the table.

"Not well," she answered. The full answer was more complicated than that, but she turned her attention to the stranger with Jack. She attempted a welcoming smile. "How do you do, sir?"

The man wore a shiny black suit and carried a leather doctor's satchel. He nodded. "Hello, ma'am."

Relieved that Antonga's care was being passed into more competent hands than hers, she gestured toward the bed.

He took two decisive steps into the room and came to an abrupt halt. He swiveled and glared. "This man is not your brother."

"N-no." Startled by the venom in the doctor's voice, Olivia looked to Jack.

Jack focused on the bed. "He's still breathing?"

"You brought me all this way to tend an Indian?" Doc Jenson's face twisted as if *Indian* was a foul word he had to spit.

Olivia took a step back. Tension filled the tiny cabin. She wanted to tell Jack about Antonga, but the doctor's attitude stilled her tongue.

Jack didn't have the same qualms. "You're here. You can at least look him over."

"I don't treat Indians," said the doctor.

"Won't you have a seat, please? I'm sure we can discuss this like civilized people," said Olivia. She returned to her chair. That left him with the chair facing away from Antonga.

"It is too late for you to return tonight," said Jack.

"You'll have to forgive the mess." She bit her lip, not knowing what else to say. She was a mess; the cabin was neat. She'd stained the table with a strong tea brew and used the stub of a candle to wax it. She had also stitched covers for the crates in the room.

The doctor's gaze raked over her. Olivia resisted the urge to push back the stray strands of hair.

One of the chicks scrabbled out of the crate in the corner and peeped. Olivia scooped him up, put him back inside and secured the hide covering the opening. The crate barely contained them, but she was afraid to leave them out at night.

The doctor's gaze followed her. His expression relaxed.

"Henry likes to escape." Olivia smiled, hoping to break the tension. He liked to jab her hand, too. Annoying creature.

"We'll be happy to feed you supper after you've examined Antonga, Doc Jenson," Jack said in a steely voice.

The doctor bristled.

The stew Jack had made from the rabbit meat was gone. Olivia's heart stopped. "Would you like coffee or tea?" She could fix those, at least.

Jack placed his rifle on the pegs above the door and removed his jacket. He stepped toward the bed. Jack would want coffee. She should have had the pot on the stove.

The doctor hadn't moved toward the chair.

The awkward silence in the cabin was deafening.

Olivia grabbed the grinder and filled it with coffee

beans. "I know Mr. Trudeau will want coffee, but please don't let that deter you from having tea if you prefer."

Jack's eyebrows flattened.

"Coffee will be fine, Mrs. Trudeau." Doc Jenson reached for the chair.

Olivia sagged with relief, then looked toward Jack. His expression was desolate. Her stomach knotted.

"You're not from around here, are you?"

"I came from Connecticut." She vigorously cranked the handle.

"You're a long way from home." Doc Jenson sat in the chair and crossed one ankle across his knee.

Home. Her smile fell like a stone. She took great care with filling the coffeepot's basket with grounds. As she added hot water, the rich aroma wafted upward. Setting the pot on the stove to percolate, she asked, "H-how was your journey? It is a bit of a distance."

"We had pleasant weather." The doctor leaned forward and solicitously asked, "Do you miss Connecticut?"

"I miss my friends." She reoccupied her seat.

Jack eased back the furs covering Antonga. "Olivia!"

She started.

"Why in God's name have you tied him down?"

The doctor stood. "Your wife at least has the sense to know what she is dealing with."

Jack eased the bonds from Antonga's wrist. The wounded man moaned. Afraid the thrashing would begin again, Olivia half rose from her chair. "I can explain."

"Your wife's foresight is commendable. You never know when a savage might attack." The doctor turned back toward her. "I do not know what a decent woman is doing with a dishonest man."

Jack's face darkened and he clenched his fists. He turned away from them.

"Sir, would you give us a moment alone?" Olivia moved to the door. She attempted a smile.

The doctor hesitated, then stood and walked out to the porch. Olivia shut the door on the doctor. She folded her arms across her middle as she stared at Jack. He had hardly looked at her since his return. She hadn't dared hope for a kiss or even a touch. She knew he was worried about Antonga, but his failure to look at her scraped a raw place in her heart.

"He's been feverish and nonsensical. He kept writhing and making his wounds bleed afresh. Binding him was the only thing I could think to do."

Jack rubbed his forehead.

"You look tired," Olivia said.

Jack dropped his hand and time seemed to stand still. She read pain in his eyes. He lowered his gaze as if he didn't want her to see his vulnerability. "I've hardly slept in days. Perhaps I was wrong. I should have brought the other doctor, but Jenson is supposed to be the best."

"You will not win him with anger," said Olivia.

"I know, I know. But he has come all this way and I will pay. Why would he refuse to treat him? I don't want him in my house if he won't treat Antonga."

Olivia steeled herself. "Let me talk to him." Persuading the doctor was the last thing she wanted to do, but Jack was unable to restrain his bluntness or hide his low opinion.

Jack's eyes dulled. "I couldn't find a doctor for Wetonga."

Somehow, that he was thinking of his first wife when Olivia stood in front of him made her eyes burn. Looking down, she brushed at a stain on her arm. "There isn't any more stew. I probably spilled more of it than I could get into Antonga…." She shrugged. Her face heated and she shifted. "I tried to make biscuits, but not even the chicks would eat them."

"I'll cook something," Jack said. "Go see what you can do to convince the doctor to at least look at Antonga. I have no patience left with the man. I promised him twenty dollars, but if another five would change his mind…"

Olivia took a deep breath to calm her nerves. Jack trusted her to negotiate. She didn't want to disappoint him. Antonga needed an expert in healing. Wrapping her shawl around her arms, she reached for the door.

The coffeepot grated against the stove. A tin cup clinked down on the table.

"Here, take him a cup of coffee. It might help."

Did Jack not want to risk the incidental contact handing her a cup of coffee might incur? Blinking back the unbidden moisture in her eyes, Olivia picked up the coffee cup. Jack stood with a second cup and the pot in his hand.

A scrabbling from the chick's crate alerted her to Henry's imminent escape.

"Perhaps Henry is ready to be made into stew." Jack set the pot back on the stove.

"No!" Hot coffee scalded her hand. Her exhaustion made her careless.

She transferred the cup to her other hand and rubbed her hand against her skirt. What more damage could another stain do? "Henry might be Henrietta."

"Olivia," said Jack gently.

She shook her head and stepped outside. If her value

was in bridging the gap to the civilized world, she had to convince the doctor to treat Antonga.

"Here is your coffee, sir." She held out the tin cup. The doctor stood at the porch rail and looked out at the moonlit mountains.

He took the cup and raised it to blow on the hot liquid.

Olivia moved beside him. "It is beautiful here."

"Certainly the view is spectacular."

She'd watched her mother, as well as Selina, charm men into doing their bidding. She'd seen the smiles, the light touches, the seemingly meandering conversation and subtle flattery. Everything in Olivia screamed against plying her feminine wiles with this man. She breathed deeply to calm her knocking knees. "Have you been in Colorado long?" she asked softly.

"About a year and a half." He took a drink.

"How do you like it here?" she asked. "You could live anywhere, couldn't you? Good doctors are in high demand. Mr. Trudeau tells me you are considered the best doctor in the territories."

"I like it well enough. Denver City is growing by leaps and bounds. We'll be a state soon."

"To come all the way out here was very kind." Olivia bit her lip. "You must have a great concern for your patients."

"I like to help settlers in need." His words were stiff.

"I know that it is not your regular course to treat Indians, but could you make an exception in this case? It would mean a great deal to us."

"Your husband lied to me."

His response was abrupt and she feared she was doing a horrible job in persuading the doctor to change his mind. Keeping her words light, she said, "Are you sure he did?" Olivia touched the bandages she'd washed out earlier and draped over the rail. She should be resting her fingertips on the doctor's arm, but she was having a hard time forcing herself to reach out. "For he is normally quite honest."

Too honest sometimes, but that had been what had attracted her to his advertisement.

"Why would he tell me that Indian is your brother?"

"Not *my* brother, but the brother of his first wife."

"He was married to an Indian?" The doctor sounded incredulous.

"My husband has been living here for over a decade." Olivia managed to overcome her repulsion and place her fingers on his coat sleeve. "I cannot fault him for taking an Indian wife when no women of his own kind were available. Life here can be very difficult."

The doctor turned toward her. With his sandy brown hair and mustache, his countenance was pleasant enough, but she wanted to back away.

Olivia forced herself to meet the doctor's eyes. "Mr. Trudeau blames himself that he could not fetch a doctor to save his wife's life when she took ill. If for no other reason, my husband should not bear guilt that he did not do everything he could to save another member of the family."

She searched the doctor's eyes for an indication that she was getting through, but saw only disgust.

"I also fear he might blame me if Antonga does not get well. I am nursing him as well as I know how." Olivia couldn't hold his gaze as she shared the lie. Her cheeks heated.

Watching her over the rim, the doctor raised the cup to his lips. "That would be most unfair to you."

Uncomfortable with the turn the conversation had

taken, Olivia rolled her shoulders. She didn't want to cast Jack in a bad light, but she wanted to convince the doctor to help. "He traveled all the way to Denver City and will pay a good amount to treat a man many would not allow in their house. My husband is a good man."

"But you have had your differences," said the doctor.

She attempted to redirect the conversation, telling him of the past few days with Antonga. "You are a well-educated man—I can see that in the way you hold yourself."

The doctor's mouth thinned. Had she overdone the flattery?

She closed her eyes and steeled herself. Putting every ounce of pleading in her expression, she asked, "What would it take to get you to examine Antonga? No one need ever know."

Certainly neither she nor Jack would ever tell anyone the good doctor had sullied his hands on an Indian.

The doctor leaned closer and Olivia feared he might kiss her. A sick dread tightened her neck. She turned toward the mountains. Gripping the railing, she prayed for fortitude.

He covered her hand with his. It wasn't Jack's hand. Doc Jenson's shoulder brushed against hers. To not jerk away took every ounce of her will. "He told me his brother-in-law had been injured by a bear, and then he spoke about you. He spoke a lot about you. I can see why he is concerned about your ability to live out here. You do not look as if you belong."

"Yes, everyone thinks that." Olivia tried to laugh, but it sounded more like a nervous trill. Jack had shared their problems with a stranger. She felt flattened.

"I have a two-story brick house in town and there

are enough ill people to keep me well funded." The doctor hesitated.

She went cold.

"You are trembling. Are you chilled?" Without waiting for an answer, the doctor put his arm around her shoulder and drew her against his side. He smelled not unpleasantly of camphor and bay rum, but she longed for Jack's earthy scent.

"I—I think you misunderstand me, sir."

"I wonder that you choose such a hard life, when an easier path might be available to you. Women are in short supply in Denver City, too."

"Do you not have a wife, sir?"

"I have not been so lucky as to find a lady like yourself. I must admit, the lack of companionship has been a sore trial." He squeezed her shoulder.

Olivia thought her heart might leap out of her chest, it was pounding so hard. She wanted to shove him away. She wanted Jack to defend her honor, but Antonga was still likely to die. She wasn't so innocent that she no longer understood what the doctor was implying.

"When I leave, why don't you come back with me and live as my wife? I could give you so much more than you could have here."

"Is this the only way you would consider treating Antonga?"

Chapter Fourteen

I've made a terrible mistake. He wants me to shoot guns, chop wood and stitch horrible wounds. I cannot do these things. There is such dependence on each other, my ignorance could be fatal, not just to me, but to him, too. God knows, if he had been the one attacked by a bear, he'd be dead.

Jack stared out the window at their blended silhouettes. How could Olivia, who shied away from him at every turn, be encouraging that man to…treat Antonga?

The older man's unnatural stillness didn't bode well. His breathing was shallow and strained. Other than a pitiful moan, he hadn't responded to Jack's queries. Antonga needed a doctor's care. While Jack didn't think much of Doc Jenson personally—he had come West to avoid being conscripted into Lincoln's army—his reputation was good.

The doctor stood too close to Olivia. Jack's heart thumped uncomfortably. His dislike of the doctor's attitude likely led him to make too much of their proximity.

Cupping his hands around his face, he leaned up to the window. They faced the mountains. Olivia's dulcet tone was soothing, although the words weren't clear. The man's arm was around her shoulders. *Merde!* For a second Jack couldn't breathe.

Space appeared between their bodies, but it was too late. A knife thrust under his ribs couldn't have hurt worse.

Seething with jealousy, he clenched his eyes shut and backed away from the window. He wanted to kill the doctor; he wanted to strangle him and make him bleed.

He wanted Antonga to get better.

He couldn't interfere if Olivia was convincing the doctor to treat Antonga. But if he didn't… God help the man.

Jack unwrapped the ham he'd bought in Denver City. Clenching the knife so tightly his knuckles turned white, he viciously hacked off three chunks. Olivia was leaving him; he didn't have a right to stop her from taking up with another man. He sank the knife deep in the meat.

He thwacked a skillet on the stove. A loud clang reverberated through the cabin.

Antonga moaned.

Jack pressed his fingers against his temples. By God, she was still his wife.

The door opened.

"I have agreed to treat the man." Doc Jenson returned inside alone.

Jack managed a strangled "Good." But blood rushed in his ears. He couldn't stay in the cabin with the man. "I'll fetch your things."

That he could think of no better excuse to go outside than to wait upon the doctor made his blood boil.

The doctor picked up his leather bag and moved beside the bed.

Jack sped out the door. If he walked around a bit, his head might clear and the raging ache in his chest and head might ease.

Olivia was doubled over and gripping the side of the doctor's buggy. His mind raced to picturing her climbing in for a tryst on the buggy's plush seat.

Red clouded his vision. He grabbed her and swirled her around. "What did you promise him?" he hissed.

"What?" Her eyes were wide and her nostrils flared. "Oh, God!"

"Did you promise him anything?" His control was more illusion than real. She was his wife. *His!*

Olivia's face twisted as if she was in pain. "Nothing." She clapped a hand over her mouth and shook her head.

Her chest heaved and her eyes were wild. The signs of her distress cut through his haze. His anger folded into a disappointment deeper than anything he'd ever felt. She could only be so distressed if she had promised to do something that terrified her.

She lowered her hand and gripped his arms. "I thought he would make…offer…improper—"

"Proposition you," supplied Jack, ending her struggle for words.

"You would have stopped him if I had cried out, wouldn't you? I couldn't have tried to charm him if I didn't think you would stop him…if…if… I'm sorry. I wanted to calm down before I returned inside. I wanted to act like nothing happened."

What had happened?

"Olivia," he breathed, and drew her against him. Her slender form felt so right. She molded perfectly to him, her hips to his, her breasts to his chest, like they were meant for each other.

He hadn't dared touch her earlier for fear he'd want

too much. As he did now. He'd wanted to hold her from the first minute he returned home, but she'd ducked behind the door. Then she'd smiled at the doctor. His jealousy had started before she even went outside to persuade the man to examine Antonga.

Her arms circled his neck and she was still talking. "How could he suggest I'd rather live with *him* in the city?"

So the doctor had propositioned her. Had she agreed to anything? Jack's emotions had been buffeted like a branch caught in the worst rapids. Damn it, she was his wife!

"He finally said he would—"

Jack kissed her. Not a gentle, leading kiss, but a full, openmouthed, hungry kiss, catching her midword. He caught her head before he knocked her into the buggy's side and swallowed her squeak of surprise.

She tasted divine, like heaven and angels spiraling down to earth. Her arms tightened and she kissed him back.

Her response was like manna to his soul. The fit of her body against his had heat flashing through his veins, making him hard and hungry for more. Shudder after shudder of need rippled through him.

Too soon, she twisted away and shoved at his chest. "What did you tell him about me? Why would he think…?"

Jack gulped in the night air, searching for the sanity that seemed to have escaped him. "I told him about your train ride. I told him about your parents."

Her eyes narrowed.

He'd said a lot of things, about how he'd been stunned such a beautiful woman showed up on the stage. He'd probably told Doc Jenson too much, all the while being careful not to tell him the patient was a native.

"I told him you were probably meant to be living back East serving tea to dignitaries. I didn't want to hear him say another word about how the Indians should be herded onto reservations or killed outright." Jack sighed.

She looked over his shoulder toward the cabin. "He won't hurt Antonga, will he?"

The moment of connection was gone. They both should go inside.

"I came to get the doctor's things. He has a camp bed." Jack shook his head at the foolish and pampered contraption.

"Thank goodness, because I did not know how we should sleep."

He smiled at their vastly different reactions.

"I didn't think he would share the bed with Antonga, and the chairs are not comfortable for sleeping," she explained.

He ran his fingers along the side of her face. A wave of tenderness made him want to protect her, promise she'd never have to deal with another man's insults, pledge he'd never leave her side.

He opened his mouth, but he couldn't guarantee any of those things. He hovered on the edge of making vows he could never honor. Rational considerations and honesty won out. He pushed aside everything but the business of life. "Biscuits are in the oven and ham is frying. You should turn the pieces."

A faint furrow appeared between her brows and she nodded. For a second they just stared at each other.

He wanted to claim her, to mark her as his, to whisper, *Je t'aime, je t'adore,* I love you. The thought shook him.

He turned and reached blindly for the doctor's carpetbag and camp bed. He didn't love her; he just wanted to be sure she hadn't offered herself to the doctor. He couldn't have fallen in love with a woman so wrong for him. He couldn't love a woman who would be happier in a brick house in the city.

Olivia pushed open the door of the cabin. Her heart raced. She didn't think she'd ever understand Jack. He'd been angry, then he'd kissed her. Why was he kissing her when they'd agreed the marriage was over?

Why did his embrace and his kiss make her feel all squishy inside, as if she would melt at his feet? His touch had a power the doctor's didn't. She touched her lips, remembering the hunger in Jack's kiss. Impressions of quick changes to his body and the way he'd pulled her hips against his imprinted in her mind. Heat pooled low in her.

"Would you bring me warmed water, please?" Doc Jenson unwrapped bandages from Antonga's back.

Doc Jenson's request brought her out of a near daze. She did as he asked.

The doctor's knobby fingers carefully prodded the skin around the stitched slashes.

"I have been bathing him with cool water. It seems to give him relief."

The door opened and Jack entered. He sniffed the air. "Did you turn the ham?"

Feeling vaguely embarrassed, she crossed to the stove. "Not yet."

Jack set down the canvas-and-wood contraption he carried, as well as a heavy tapestry satchel. More things to crowd the space, but the cabin always felt small when Jack was in the room.

The undersides of the ham slices were blackened. She winced.

Reaching for a sack, she bent to open the oven chamber door and check the biscuits before those burned, too.

Jack's hand closed over hers, keeping the oven door shut. "Don't keep checking them. Wait until they smell done."

Surprised at the rush of longing that quickened her blood and sent her heart fluttering, she looked over her shoulder at him. God, she'd missed him. In the past couple of days, she'd yearned more than once for a glimpse of the dark line of stubble along his square jaw, his steady brown eyes and his calming touch. She thought she'd missed his help, his guidance in this strange world, but what she really missed was the way he made her feel as if she wanted to be part of him.

Olivia wanted to forget the food and fall into his arms. The hunger she felt was not about eating.

"Sir, if you would help him sit, I can get this medicine in him," said the doctor, reminding her they weren't alone.

Jack rubbed her side before moving away.

Her knees shook. Hot and cold eddies swirled under her skin and made her want to adventure into Jack's arms. When she wasn't taking care of Antonga, she'd thought about Jack and his insistence she explore his body. Her skin would heat and her insides clenched. Another man would never have been as understanding or patient.

But with two other men in the cabin, kisses and further exploration wouldn't happen tonight. Disappointment curled under her skin.

Jack propped up a limp and unresponsive Antonga.

The doctor pulled a bottle from his bag. "This potion will reduce his fever."

Guilt that she wanted to be alone with Jack swamped her. How could she be so selfish when Antonga was so sick?

The fog cleared from her brain. What was she doing thinking of pleasures of the marriage bed? She'd decided to leave. Exploring her yearning for Jack's interest wouldn't serve any good purpose.

No good purpose at all.

As they ate, Jack listened politely to Doc Jenson's diagnosis. The man didn't say anything Jack didn't know. Olivia pleated her skirt to hide a stain. Every small movement she made drew his attention.

The doctor didn't seem to notice that every time he mentioned a grisly detail of the wound or treatment, Olivia pushed her food around with her fork. She finally set it down.

"Yes, he's lost a great deal of blood. It seems as though I have done nothing but clean off blood for the last three days." She put her hand over a stain on her wrist, which looked suspiciously dark.

"He may take weeks to recover from so grievous a wound," said the doctor.

"Eat, Olivia," Jack urged.

Her gray eyes darted to his, and she looked wan and troubled.

"Although I hope to see improvement by morning." The doctor's gaze landed on Olivia's bare left hand. He smiled as his gaze rose to her face.

She smiled in return. "I hope he sleeps well tonight. His sleep last night was restless."

Jack doubted she was aware of the path the doctor's interest had taken.

"He should. I gave him a bit of laudanum. You must be tired, too."

Olivia made a languid, dismissing movement. "I'm sure we all are. You both had a long journey."

"I presume you can translate for him. If he is sensible, I should like to ask him a few questions," the doctor said.

"Antonga speaks English, French and Spanish, as well as several native tongues," said Jack.

The doctor transferred his gaze from Olivia to Jack.

Olivia touched Jack's thigh under the table. She undoubtedly meant it as a wifely gesture, to quell his temper, but his thoughts turned to the kiss they'd shared outside. Desire thickened his blood and made his heart race.

If she only knew she could set him off like an avalanche.

"Would you like more coffee, Doc Jenson?" she asked with a smile.

"Thank you, no." The doctor pushed back from the table. "I'm stepping outside for a minute."

Olivia stood and carried the dishes over to the chick's crate, where she scraped the crumbs and half her meal into their dish. She twitched her skirt so one of the stains disappeared into the folds. Wearing a dirty dress must be driving her crazy, and her hoops were adjusted down as small as he'd ever seen them.

"We should be able to leave the chicks outside soon," Jack said.

Olivia's movements stopped.

He held his breath. She could very well have decided

to leave with the doctor and was just sparing him the agony of knowing.

He wanted to beg her to stay, but she might be better off living in an environment she understood. She was tired and overwrought and if she intended to go with the doctor, if her smiles at the man were an indication of her state of mind, he shouldn't stop her. Wanting to put space between them, he moved to her trunk. "I'll get you a clean nightgown."

She jerked as if to stop him, but he was closer. In the cabin, whoever was closer was bound to win any race. She had arranged her brush and things on the trunk's surface. Propped up in the corner was the photograph he'd sent her.

"I can't change," she said. Her voice was strained.

He picked up the photograph to set on the bed. The curling edges were chipped. Had she been holding his picture so much she was wearing it out? Hope knocked at his resistance. "You'll feel better wearing something clean."

"But there are no curtains. Anyone can see inside."

The only person who could see inside was the doctor. "I'll hold up the quilt so you may change behind it." Jack moved her silver brush and mirror to the bed and lifted the trunk lid. He should build her a shelf to hold her things so that she didn't have to move them every time she wanted to get into her trunk. But there was no point if she was leaving.

A tintype of her parents and a small photograph of her and her two friends were inside. Only his photograph had been on top.

He was too tired to sort out what it all meant. Water splashed as she washed the dishes, and he stared at the tightly packed contents. Most women on the frontier owned a couple of dresses, not a trunkful. He pulled out a tightly rolled white cotton nightgown. "Do you want anything else while I'm here?"

The dishes clinked together and Olivia sidled up behind him. He clutched her nightgown as he stepped back. He wanted to hold her. She pulled out a pink dress and pantalets, petticoats and stockings. "For tomorrow," she said huskily.

"Will you leave with him? I'd rather know now."

Her head bowed forward, exposing the back of her long neck. He wanted to nibble on that neck, get her to throw her head back in passion. She was so close the scent of her skin intoxicated him. The silence settled heavily between them, leaving him aching.

"Do you wish for me to?" Her voice quivered.

"God, no!" His voice was too loud.

The door opened behind them. "Any change?"

The smell of tobacco wafted in with the doctor. Frustration burned in Jack.

Olivia lifted her head. "No, everything is the same."

Was it? Jack was no longer sure. Everything felt different. All he could think about was Olivia and how badly he wanted to make her his wife.

She closed the trunk's lid.

"I'll put on new dressings." The doctor pulled a chair from the table and placed it on Antonga's side of the bed. "I'll need your assistance to lift him."

Jack put the nightgown on the bed while Olivia finished putting her things on the trunk. She surreptitiously lifted the lid and shoved his photograph inside.

After Antonga was settled in with thick cotton bandages and given medicine, the three of them prepared for bed. Jack held up the quilt while she hurriedly shed her stained dress and pulled the clean nightgown over her corset and shift.

Jack had so much to say to her. Her gray eyes searched his face, but the doctor's presence prevented conversation. If he signaled he wanted her to stay, would she?

Olivia leaned over Antonga, refreshing the damp cloths on his brow. The doctor watched her.

Jack pushed the camp bed against the far wall. "You'll be warmest here by the stove." *And as far away from Olivia as possible.*

"I think he's cooler," she said. Her eyes met his across the room.

"That is a good sign," said the doctor.

Olivia startled and jerked her gaze to the doctor. She winced and drew her shawl more tightly around her shoulders. Jack moved to her side, blocking Doc Jenson's view of Olivia in her nightgown. He wrapped an arm around her waist as Olivia brushed Antonga's damp hair away from his cheek and tucked the furs around him.

"His breathing seems easier, too." She blew out a slow, relieved breath. "I have been so worried I've hardly slept a wink since you've been gone."

"You can sleep tonight," Jack offered.

"I don't know. Every time he moves I wake and check him. He seems so helpless."

She would make a good mother.

The thought startled him. He wasn't in the habit of thinking of his mate as a potential mother. With We-tonga he'd known children were impossible, but he should have considered mothering skills when advertising for a wife.

"I'll listen, you just rest." He guided her around to

the other side of the bed where the quilt and sheets lay on the heap of skins on the floor. He straightened them, then lay down and pulled her to him. Because they were reduced to using only a couple feet of space, they had to spoon together, her back to his chest.

As she wriggled to get comfortable, his blood surged. He pressed his nose into her hair and bit back his response without much success. She needed her sleep. They weren't alone. He wanted her anyway.

He fought his desire long into the night. After her breathing fell into the steady rhythm of sleep and the doctor's deep breathing had turned to a light snore, Jack shook with need. The faint scent of lavender and woman intoxicated him. The softness of her body, the gentle curves under his arm, the heat of her earlier kiss all served to drive him to the brink of madness.

As attuned to Olivia as he was, he knew the instant she woke. He pressed his mouth behind her ear.

"Jack?" she whispered. "Are you all right?"

"No."

She twisted trying to see him, but the throb low in his body only intensified with each move she made. He reached to untie the string of his leggings and push them down.

She turned and her hip forced his hand away. He couldn't stop the low groan that left his throat.

"What's wrong?" she whispered.

"I need you." He slid his hand under her hip and cupped her bottom and pulled her tight against his erection.

Her mouth rounded in a surprised O. He could just make out her delicate features in the moonlight and the flush that crept up her neck. He wanted to kiss her mouth, her face, her neck and lower. She was so beautiful.

She rocked her hips, adding more pressure. He gasped. Did she even understand what she was doing? He struggled with how to explain to his innocent wife what he needed. Crass words bubbled in his head about how to convey, without repulsing her, what would happen, but he dismissed them only to find his mouth was ahead of him. "I don't want you to leave me."

Merde! That wasn't what he'd meant to say.

Chapter Fifteen

She is too refined for the harsh life I lead. The mountains will destroy her beauty. Her skin is lily-white and easily burns. Her lovely gray eyes are so light the natives call her Pale Eyes. Her soft hands will be roughened with the work. Besides, she has never cooked. Please, come as quick as you can.

Jack's expression showed a vulnerability she had never seen from him. Something inside Olivia went soft and she wanted to take care of him. He blinked as if confused by what he'd said.

His words echoed in her mind. *I don't want you to leave me.*

Her unsuitability for his life was undeniable, but in spite of that the bonds between them had tightened. In the morning they would still be as wrong for each other as a camel and a whale together, but right here, right now, a powerful pull existed between them. She could no longer fight the yearning. The solid length of him curled around her had been part of her dreams, and she'd awoken wanting him.

His mouth landed on hers. His kiss conveyed hunger and need that touched a hidden part of her. It was as if his kiss could strip her naked and lay bare her deepest dreams. If he wanted her, needed her, surely anything was possible.

The touch of his tongue, the fullness of his lips pressed against hers ended too soon as he slowly drew back. His moist breath against her sensitized lips was almost as tantalizing. He trailed kisses to her ear.

"I need...I need..." he panted.

His breath tickled and his inability to convey a complete thought made warmth curl in her stomach. Hot tendrils spiraled lower.

"*S'il te plait.* I need...you to...help me." His hand closed around her breast. His hot breath feathered against her neck.

Her heart pounded while a strange sensation shot through her, making her liquid and tense. But as her body came alive, the other sounds of the room intruded. Antonga's easy breathing and the doctor's snore. "Jack," she whispered, pushing against his chest.

He pulled her tighter to him, trapping her hand between their bodies.

"I need..." he whispered.

His desperation was palpable. She thought she understood what he was asking for. She wanted it to be more than just a physical thing. She wanted it to be about her. "Little death," she ventured.

"Yes, release." He gave a short chortle.

Olivia turned away, not wanting to admit disappointment.

He pressed his lips against her temple. "I'm sorry. I've been lying here breathing your fragrance, feeling your softness. I can't hold back any longer. I need you."

Alarm tightened her muscles. Was he reading her mind? Did he really need *her*?

He was breathing words in her ear again, and she tried to sort through the flow. "I need you like I've never needed any woman. I don't understand it." He lapsed into French as what he said sounded like more than the sweet nothings a lover would whisper.

Jack's hips rocked. His male part was like an iron bar as he rubbed against her. She wanted to move her clothes out of the way and feel him against her skin, feel him within her. Heat rushed over her face.

He rocked harder, his face buried against her shoulder. "I'll be quick."

"Stop! You'll wake them," she whispered.

"I can't stop, Olivia. I'll go mad."

He pressed kisses against her neck, deep, open kisses that felt ridiculously good. She tilted her head to allow him more access. Wanting to ignore the other men in the cabin, she slid her hand out and held his head to her. But the sound of their breathing intruded on her, making her tense.

His hips rocked again. His palm brushed across her beaded nipple and the riot of sensation made sparks fly to her core. She bit her lip to hold back a yelp of surprise. The layers of her corset, chemise and nightgown should have offered more insulation from his touch.

She wanted his hand on her skin, not impeded by the layers of fabric. Jack slid a finger under the edge of her corset and brushed her nipple. A jolt of pleasure electrified her body. She moaned.

The doctor snorted and rolled over.

She and Jack froze. Their breathing roared like train engines. Then Jack shifted and rolled them off the pallet. His arm around her waist, he yanked the quilt from the pile and ushered her toward the door. Not allowing her time to react, he opened the door and thrust her into the night.

Her heated skin barely registered the cool air, but her toes curled against the frigid planks. Pausing only long enough to thrust his feet into moccasins, he wrapped the quilt around her. She leaned toward him, anticipating his kiss.

Instead, he lifted her over his shoulder and hurtled off the porch. His arm steadied her as he crossed the yard.

Jack tossing her over his shoulder was so primitive. Yet his firm hold was, in an odd way, gentle. A thrill of pleasure shot through her and moist heat rushed to her lower regions.

"Where are we going?" she asked.

"The stable," he answered. "Do not complain we will disturb the animals."

She giggled. "I shouldn't think of it."

Hope surged and her heart felt full. Jack wanted her to be his wife, to stay, to make their marriage work.

"You want me?" she whispered, marveling at the idea.

The rush of mountain air cleared his head and the trill of Olivia's laughter touched a place deep inside him. He didn't think he'd ever heard her laugh before.

Her question stopped him cold. For a second he hesitated. But then Jack flung open the stable door and carried her inside. "Yes, I want you."

The smell of animal and earth was strong but tempered by the smell of hay and leather. He turned her so she could climb the ladder to the loft. She twisted and looked as if she would speak, but he cut her off. "Go!"

Please.

He didn't want discussions to ruin the moment. He didn't want to make her promises with no meaning. He didn't want to burst out the words of devotion crowding out thought.

He pushed her up the ladder, his hand on her bottom supporting her weight so the rough rungs wouldn't dig too deeply into her bare feet. *Merde!* The stable loft wasn't the place he should be seducing his wife. Her first time should be memorable for its sweetness, not its stench. But with his hand cupping the smooth roundness of her bottom, he couldn't restrain his desire. He wanted her soft touch, he wanted her long legs wrapped around him, he wanted Olivia's reserve to disappear into passion.

Jack pulled the door shut, closing out the moon and starlight and sending the interior into blackness. He'd probably regret his lack of control in the morning, but right now he wanted her worse than he'd ever wanted anything in his life.

He was much quicker on the rungs. The loft was black as pitch. The animals' body heat warmed the air. Only the faintest light marked the hatch.

Olivia crawled over scratchy hay. "I can't see anything."

He spread out the quilt over the remaining hay and scooted her into the center of it. He couldn't see a blasted thing, either. He missed the soft glow from the stove that would have allowed him to gauge her expression. Olivia laid her hand against his chest. He put his hand over hers. Could she feel his heart pounding?

"I was dreaming of you," she whispered.

A desperate urge to make her happy swept through him. More than wanting to give her physical gratification, he wanted to move the moon and the stars for her. He wanted to imprint her with his passion in a way that she would find all other men lacking. He wanted her to be his forever. The thoughts shook him and scared him.

He kicked off his moccasins. Sitting beside her, he shucked his leggings. His shoulder brushed hers, and even that scant contact sent explosions through his brain.

Sliding his hand from her shoulder, up her neck to her pointy little chin, he found her mouth with his. His urgency rushed back like a stampede, driving, thundering, shaking the earth. Pushing her back, he kept his lips locked with hers. Her arms curled around his neck. He kissed her again and again until her chest rose and fell against his. Running his hands over her sides, the steel bands of her corset hindered his touch. She was wearing too many layers of clothing.

He slid up her nightgown and rolled to his back, taking her with him. "Take this off."

"Jack!" she protested.

He couldn't tell if her protest was from modesty or against his sudden movement, but he couldn't stand the layers between them. "Hush. I want nothing between us. I want to feel your skin against mine, please, *chérie.*"

"I want nothing between us, either." Her voice sounded wistful, uncertain.

Her words only served to remind him how much was between them. His promise to not risk getting her pregnant until she put his ring back on was still between them. Such thoughts would drive him mad if he gave them credence in this moment. He pushed the thought away.

He found her lips and kissed her until her breathing changed. He wanted so badly to rip away her pantalets and thrust up into her. His need was like a raging beast that didn't care what stood in the way.

But she didn't straddle him or even seem comfortable on top.

"Jack, I…"

Leaning his forehead against hers, he breathed in heavily. "Don't think, Olivia, just feel."

He elbowed his way up to a sitting position and swung her sideways to sit across his thighs, and then returned to kissing her.

Her arms tightened around his neck. He reached again for the hem of her nightgown and eased it up until he had to pull his mouth away from hers. The yards of cotton separated them for but an instant, but it was too long.

Rather than flinging it to the farthest corner of the loft, he looped the nightgown around his arm, then placed it on the edge of the quilt. They would need to find it again. He ran his hands down her back, skimming over the chemise, corset and pantalets she still wore.

"I'm scared," she whispered.

A burst of protectiveness curbed his greedy rush to gratification. A deeper need to connect, to be sure she was with him every step of the way settled in him. It rocked him, altering his world. He had to slow down and get her to relax enough to let pleasure roll through her and build until the waves of ecstasy broke. "Trust me," he said, and stroked her face. "You will like this."

One by one he unfastened the steel clasps down the front of her corset.

"Will you?" Olivia's voice trembled.

He laughed. "You couldn't do anything to prevent me from enjoying this."

"Except stop?" she whispered. Leaning forward, she pressed a kiss into the crease where his neck met his shoulder.

Heat flashed out from the warm, moist touch of her mouth and spiraled into a raging hunger. "Yes... Don't stop."

Her fingers splayed and she slowly moved them across his shoulders. Colors flashed behind his eyes and he could scarcely control his urge to grab. He wanted to touch every part of her, explore every inch of hidden skin. But her tentative stroke reminded him she was new to this and unsure of herself. He fought to slow down.

"It is my time to teach you, *chérie.*" Her corset free, he twisted to add it to the pile of clothes. Cupping her face, he leaned forward to kiss her.

Before she could protest, he pulled her chemise over her head and reached for the ties of her drawers. He set her beside him to draw off the last of her underclothes. "I truly wish I could see you."

He ran his hand down her cheek, slowly along her delicate neck. "You are so soft," he murmured, bending down to follow his touch with light, feathering kisses. He encountered the chain she wore under her clothes. Did it bear a locket or a cross? He didn't stop to learn as he traced the line of her collarbone with his lips. He cupped her breast, and she shuddered.

The darkness meant he had to explore through touch and taste alone. Her stomach quivered under his touch. As he touched the silky soft hair below, she shied away.

He moved his hand to her hip and kissed her again, pushing her back on the quilt until he could lie against her with her satiny skin against his, breast to chest, thigh to thigh and mouth to mouth. The feeling was intoxicating. His head spun as he throbbed with need.

He continued tasting her instead of risking a demand for surrender or a declaration of love.

Ever so gingerly, she slid her hand down. Her fingers wiggled between their stomachs. He wanted to shout encouragement; instead, he was caught holding his breath as his control threatened to break. He repositioned her hand on his hip. A few strokes of her delicate fingers and he'd be done for.

"Jack?" she whispered.

"You're doing fine," he gritted.

She shifted under him. "Are you in pain?"

"Oui, un peu." He realized he'd answered her in French, but he didn't bother to translate.

"Yes? What should I do?" Her breathless words were like a balm to his spirit. "Why don't you want me to touch…?"

He just needed her to allow him access to her center. "Open for me, *chérie.*"

She hesitated. "Does that mean you will…? We will—"

"Trust me." He interrupted her struggle for words. His heart threatened to pound out of his chest. Would she demand a declaration of his intentions before she spread her legs? His fear of what she might say splashed a cold wash over him. His arousal was so far ahead of hers.

"Olivia," he moaned, "don't think, don't talk…" *Don't ruin this.* "Just relax. I promise, I won't do anything you don't want. I lo—will pleasure you."

His near slip made him tense. Sweat beaded on his brow.

"But you—"

He interrupted her with a deep kiss.

Olivia's heart pounded. His frustration and urgency

were thick in the air. She wanted to ease him. More than she wanted anything else, she wanted to relieve the desperation she sensed in him. But she didn't know how. She felt as if she was swimming beyond her depth, but the water felt shockingly good.

Her body buzzed with an energy that was unfamiliar and frightening. Tiny sparks floated over her skin and lingered in the wake of his kisses. If she could concentrate upon his needs, his body…but more than once he'd moved her hand away as she tried to reach the iron rod that nestled against her thighs. The dampness between her legs grew.

A wave of yearning broke over her. She wanted Jack there. Would that alleviate his suffering? Surely it would. She inched up her right knee.

His moan swirled under her skin and made her want to do more to please him. He ended their kiss and dipped his head to her neck.

She tensed. Would he discover the ring on the chain? She'd thought he might earlier, and he'd learn she wanted to be his wife, wanted to bear his children, wanted to open to him. She drew out her left knee.

He settled between her legs, nudging them all the way apart with his hips. His male member prodded at the entrance of her body and she held her breath, waiting for the thrust of his hips that would end all doubt.

Instead, he seemed to have other plans, and he lifted his chest from hers.

Gripping his shoulders, she tried to bring them back together. "Don't leave now."

"Shh." He touched his lips to her shoulder. "We're not done." He cupped her breast.

Hot heat surged between her legs.

Slowly, he drew lazy, ever-tightening circles with

his fingertips while he lowered his head and nipped the softer flesh of the upper slope of her opposite breast. Her fingernails dug into his shoulders. When he reached her nipples, the jolt of pleasure that shot through in a straight line from her breast to her nether regions surprised her so much she nearly sat up. As if Jack knew, he cupped that part of her.

She ground against his hand and then wished she could sink back through the floor. Nothing in her response was that of a lady. Heat flooded her cheeks. Her body seemed a thing disconnected with her, intent on a terrifying path. He laved her breast. An invisible ribbon connecting sensitive places on her body together tightened.

She wanted to snap it or sever the wanton urges prompting her hips to roll, her body to crave his, her heart to fear his reaction. She couldn't catch her breath.

He didn't let her, as he switched his attention to her other breast and then slid down until his mouth pressed against her navel. She shuddered as his kisses dipped lower. He spread her with his fingers and she gripped a handful of straw.

Sensations beyond what she had ever experienced rocked through her. His mouth touched her intimately and a jolt rocked through her and made her hips buck. She was lost in a welter of sensations. Never had her body felt so sensitized, so full and expectant.

His tongue probed her, and her body seemed a mass of fire and energy, as if it didn't belong to her and she was on the precipice of losing control. Her legs quivered. She'd never felt so wonderful, so glorious and so mortified all at the same time.

His mouth was an odd combination of heaven and hell as every touch of his tongue to her made her shudder and moan. She tensed, trying to fight the sensations, to stave off the pending mortal explosion.

She could take no more. Pushing his head away, she tried to escape the madness. She whimpered and Jack allowed her to pull him back. He started to speak, but she thrust her fingers in front of his mouth. Drawing her fingers into his mouth, he sucked on them. Even that she found incredibly erotic. She gulped in air.

His finger dipped inside her, and she scrambled away from his touch. "I can't breathe."

Could she make him feel as if he no longer had any control over his body?

"Olivia, don't fight it so much," Jack whispered.

"Can I do this to you?" she asked.

"S'il vous plaît," he said with a lilt of humor coloring his voice.

"Can I make you feel as if you are dying of something so intense you cannot stand it?" She felt as if he was drawing her very essence out of her. She shifted to her knees and backed away from him.

A moment of clear thinking was all she needed, but her thoughts swirled in a maddening whirlpool of confusion. Was this love or just a physical exchange of pleasure? She needed it to be love to feel this intense, but Jack had said nothing of love. And if she loved him, wasn't she lost? How would she ever leave if she allowed this intense passion to take her beyond reason?

Jack shifted on the quilt and reached for her. He patted the place where she'd been a minute earlier. "Is that how you feel?"

She nodded and realized he couldn't possibly see her in the dark. "Yes," she whispered.

"Do you not like it?" he asked. He must have realized she was on her knees, because his voice came closer as he spoke.

"No," she said so vehemently even she knew it was a lie. "Do you?"

"Very much so."

She closed the distance between them, flinging herself against his chest. He wrapped his arms around her and gently stroked her head. That he could be soothing when he must have been feeling as frenzied as she felt, but for a much longer time, touched her deep inside.

A new mix of the heady physical sensations and a desire to welcome him into her heart turned her body to a quivering mass of need. She needed what he had been doing to her a moment ago; she needed him to know that she had merely panicked.

She wrapped her arms around him but only hugged him a minute before she slid her hands down over the firm muscle below his waist. She pressed her lips to his chest, imitating the things he had done to her. As she tongued his nipple, he shuddered.

She kissed lower and slid her hands around to the front and rubbed his thighs. She dipped her thumbs into the springy dark hair. He ran his hands down her back.

"Olivia, I'm not going to last long." His words sounded strained.

Gripping his erect shaft, she lowered her mouth to the velvet tip. Slowly she ran her tongue around the ridge.

Jack gasped.

Pleased with the idea that she could evoke the same wild pleasure, she nipped at him. His hand closed around hers and he folded her fingers around his member and then gripped her wrist, moving her hand up and down.

His low groan reverberated inside her. She wanted to make him groan more. She traced the path her fingers took with her mouth.

He throbbed in her hand and she heard him scrabble against the low roof as if seeking a place to hold for steadiness.

Groans punctuated his hard panting. She wanted him as mindless as she had been. Kissing the tip, she strove to imitate the kind of madness he'd inflicted on her.

He thrust forward and growled low in his throat. Encouraged, she took the head into her mouth. Following the edge of her hand, she took more of him.

His hand fisted in her hair as if he would pull her away.

"Do you know what you're doing?" he demanded.

No, but she wasn't exactly in a position to answer. She pushed him deeper into her mouth. Recognizing she had ended his ministrations when it grew too intense, she ignored his counterpressure.

"Oh, yes," he moaned.

She took that as an affirmation that she was doing the right things.

Disjointed words tumbled from his mouth, as if he could no longer be coherent. But she caught the gist of his warning and ignored it.

He thrust forward and she flowed with him, not breaking her rhythm. Jack groaned and shuddered. His member throbbed hard. His loss of control was so complete, she knew a moment of triumph.

His ragged breathing filled the air.

"Don't…move," he shuddered out.

She didn't resist when he pulled her up. He wrapped his arms around her and cradled her against his chest. His skin was damp and under her ear she heard the rapid tattoo of his heartbeat. It gradually slowed to a steady rhythm.

"You are incredible," he mumbled when his breathing wasn't so strained. He pressed kisses on the top of her head, her temple, and he tilted her chin for a kiss.

The tenor of his hold changed as he stroked down her back.

She caught the ring that dangled around her neck and was grateful for the concealing darkness. What would he think if he knew she was still hoping for a real marriage, that she'd believed he intended to make her his wife in all ways? If he just said the right words, she'd never leave.

Where were the words of love and devotion?

"Jack, what did you really mean when you said that you don't want me to go?"

He tensed, and she knew the answer. He didn't want her to go when lust made him hard, but now that she had relieved that ache for him, it didn't matter. She was mortified at what she'd done. A woman intent on ending her marriage should never play sexual games. No lady would ever sink so low.

All along she'd wanted to believe their exchange was unique to them, a special bond that only two people in love could achieve, but what did she know of it? Jack had been married before, so it wasn't even a thing that was just between them. She was simply the woman sharing his bed. It meant nothing. And nothing had changed. If he had meant for her to stay, then he would have risked impregnating her.

In the morning he would remember she still was not equipped for life out here in the Rockies. Perhaps he'd never forgotten.

How could she have been such a fool? She'd made

the same mistake as Selina had with the father of her baby. She'd thought the act conferred affection and permanence. It didn't mean anything of the sort to a man.

"I need to check on Antonga," she said in as steady a voice as she could manage.

Chapter Sixteen

My husband—he may not be that for long—is just as expected from his advertisement. Unfortunately, Anna was right. I am not what he wanted. He took one look at me and was disappointed. I cannot tell you how hurt I am, but it is my own fault. He says my sewing would be valued in California and I could have my pick of husbands there. But I cannot imagine another man who would suit me, so I am doomed to living out my days alone.

"Wait a minute," Jack whispered. He had been on the verge of declaring his love for her. He must have hesitated too long.

Only love could have made him feel as if he had truly died and gone to heaven. Her mouth on him had been much more than he'd bargained for and much more than he ever would have expected from his prim and proper wife. Never before had he understood the French moniker for what had just happened. But he did now. He had died a thousand deaths and lived a thousand rebirths. She was bold and brave in the ways of the night.

If he had not loved her before, he did now. But none of it made sense.

And one thing stopped him cold. If he declared his love for her, would that be as much of a trap for her as getting her with child? Would she stay in a place that made her miserable? And why in hell's name couldn't she have waited for him to catch his breath and bring her to repletion?

"Olivia, you are not satisfied."

She scrabbled away and reached for her clothes.

Perhaps he'd taken the wrong tack. "Perhaps you would prefer to hit me?" He searched for her in the dark.

"No," she said.

He wanted so badly to see her face, to read her expression. Instead, he grasped her leg. She twisted away.

How could she be so cold when mere seconds ago she had been a creature of pure passion?

"I just want to hold you."

The rustling of clothes stopped for a second and then resumed.

"Well, it seems we have to share a narrow bedroll of skins, so you will get your wish." She sounded prudish and distant, as if she'd thrown up a wall to keep him far away from her.

"Why won't you let me in?" he asked.

"Will you leave me nothing? I must sacrifice my dignity, my, my, my…"

"Your what, Olivia?" He tensed, waiting, hoping she would say her heart, her affection, her love.

"I should like to have my pride when I leave," she answered, so quietly that a hole opened up inside him.

He swallowed hard. She still intended to leave.

What was the surprise? She was too good for him, too refined for his kind of life. Hell, her clothes were too beautiful to waste on the isolation of a squalid log cabin in the mountains. If she was like his mother, she might stay for too long if he begged or insisted. She might trade her happiness for his, and that was not what he wanted.

He wanted her to be happy. If that meant they couldn't live up here together, then so be it.

Jack reached for his leggings. "Olivia, whatever happens between us—if you stay or go—I want you to be happy." Even if it hurt. "I do want that."

"I don't understand what you want." Her voice quivered.

He paused. She kept talking of what he wanted, and he'd been selfish enough to allow the focus to be on his needs. "This isn't about what I want any longer. What do you want, Olivia? What did you hope for when you came here?"

She breathed in a deep breath.

Unable to bear the distance between them, he scooted closer, but he didn't touch her. Cotton brushed against his arm as she wiggled into her clothing.

"I wanted to be married to the man who wrote of the beauty of the mountains and the meadows and even how the snow can reflect the sun in thousands of little sparkles. I wanted to not fear being tossed on the streets or how I would pay for my next meal. I wanted a home of my own."

Could he make the changes that would keep her happy? "Would a brick house in Denver City be more to your liking?"

She blew a long breath out. "Like the doctor's house?"

How did she know the doctor had a brick house?

He opened his mouth to say no, but she was already speaking.

"That would make things easy for you, wouldn't it? I could just leave with him and you wouldn't even have to take me to California to get rid of me." She scrabbled for the ladder. "Maybe he is rich enough he could pay you back for my train and stage tickets, too. God knows you made such a poor bargain."

If she hadn't been barefoot, Olivia would have run to the porch. She wanted to get away from Jack. The uneven ground had her picking her way and trying to ignore the jabs of pine needles, but the pokes were nothing compared to the squeezing pain in her chest.

That Jack could so callously suggest she leave with the doctor so soon after they had been intimate shredded every softer feeling toward him.

The man who had written of the beauty of his home had disappeared under a harsh pragmatist who could only think of the problems she created. Had he ever been the man in the photograph? Or was that just a dream she'd conjured up, just as he'd thought she would be a woman who could cook and calmly cope with bear attacks?

He scooped her up before she reached the steps. His mouth was a flat line. Rather than meet his gaze and reveal her heartache, she stared at his granite jaw.

She shoved at his shoulder. "I can walk."

"You don't have shoes on," he countered.

Even that was a reminder that she was a tenderfoot. But then the way she'd been picking her way toward the porch would hardly have dispelled that notion. She almost wished he'd tossed her over his shoulder the way he had earlier. Then she wouldn't have to look at him.

He stared straight ahead as his long strides bit off the distance between the stable and the cabin. "Don't leave with the doctor. He may be well-off, but you could do better than him."

Her heart stopped. Had she misread Jack? Hope tried to chase out the coldness in her heart like the first thaw of springtime. Curling her fingers into the quilt, she hoped for a little bud of brightness. If Jack cared for her a little, perhaps what she had done was not so horrible. "You don't want me to go with him?" she ventured tentatively.

He sighed. "I want you to do what would make you happy, but for Pete's sake, for all his skill in treating the sick, that man is a son of bitch. He wouldn't make you happy. He wouldn't make any woman happy."

She jolted a little at Jack's raw language. "I don't think I could handle his dinner conversations on a nightly basis."

"I noticed." The hardness in Jack's face eased. Drawing to a stop, he looked down at her. In the pale starlight she imagined she saw tenderness in his expression. His gaze dipped to her lips and his nostrils flared.

Heat flooded her cheeks. She bit her lip and turned away. Not looking at him was easier.

He spun around and plunked down on the edge of the porch. He settled her into his lap and enveloped her in the quilt in one fluid motion.

She struggled to disentangle herself. "We should go inside."

"Give me one minute, Olivia."

Stilling, she waited for him to speak. The quiet of the night surrounded them and everything was still. She tried to extinguish the hope that threatened to rob her of her will. He tucked the quilt under her feet.

At times he could be considerate enough he broke her heart, and at other times he was cruel in his dismissals. Her heart pounded as she waited for what he would say.

She couldn't bear another candid talk. There was no solution. She'd made the right decision to leave. Earlier, she had just gotten lost in his kisses and had been unable to resist the pull of pleasures to be had, pleasures to be given, pleasures that made a mockery of her decision.

She deserved a man who loved her for who she was.

He stared at the shadows of the mountain peaks across the valley. With her gaze, she traced his strong profile. The memory of his kisses stirred her to new desires. And still he said nothing.

"Perhaps it will wait until morning," she suggested, wanting to end this before she succumbed to her physical yearnings. "I have not slept much of late and it is the middle of the night. I am sure you must be tired, too."

"I don't see the beauty of the mountains or the meadows anymore," he said in a low voice.

Impatient with the time he was taking, as if he had settled on a trick to confuse her, she shifted.

He tilted his chin down and looked her in the eyes. "I see you. You have eclipsed the beauty of my mountain home."

Her breath left her. Certain she'd heard wrong or misunderstood, she stared at him.

He ran a finger down the side of her face. "I knew from the first moment I saw you that you were too good for me, too fine, too genteel. I never stood a chance in hell in giving you a life that would make you happy."

She frowned, ready to protest, but Jack wasn't done.

"This night has been like magic to me. I don't think

I have ever felt this wonderful before. I am sorry I did not create the same magic for you."

She was stunned. A flood of warmth rippled through her.

He smiled ruefully. His eyes softened. "A stable loft was perhaps not the best place."

"It was not so bad."

Jack tilted his head as if he was assessing her truthfulness.

"I preferred it to an audience, even if they were sleeping." She flushed, thinking of what she'd done.

"Too dark," said Jack.

"Thank goodness." Her cheeks were on fire.

"No, I wanted to see you." Jack smiled indulgently. "I wanted to take down your hair, but I feared losing the pins."

"Must we talk of this?"

"Yes. Why did you stop me?" His hand was beneath the quilt where he'd been holding it under her feet. He slid his fingers along her calf.

"I don't know," she whispered. She'd been afraid of shattering into a thousand pieces. She'd been afraid of losing herself. Mostly she'd been afraid of loving Jack in a way that she couldn't ever take back.

Hot and cold flashes raced through her body. With lightning quickness the banked fires in her blood blazed to life. She wanted his hand against her private parts. She wanted his mouth there. Worse yet, she wanted his male member spreading her apart, sliding inside her and finding the rhythm that sent him over the edge.

He leaned down and kissed her. A slow, long kiss, so sweet heat surged between her legs. Oh, God, what was he doing to her?

"Let me show you what you missed. Open your legs for me, Olivia," he whispered against her lips.

He hypnotized her with his touch, with his low, coaxing voice. He moved his hand over her knee and slid up the leg of her drawers. His warm hand was against her skin. His fingers skimmed over the scar on her thigh. A burst of fear made a shudder ripple down her spine.

She twisted away. "Don't!"

Her abrupt movement pinned his palm against the scars.

"Is it really your pride you're afraid of losing?" he asked.

He ran his thumb across the raised ridge on her leg and she pushed at his hand and rolled away as soon as he pulled back. Cocooned in the quilt, she thumped onto the porch.

"Don't. This confuses me."

"You are aroused. I can see it in your face, in the way your eyes shine and in the way your breath catches."

"Oh, God, don't look at me." She covered her face with her hands. "What would it change? I will still be unequipped to live out here in the wilds of the Rockies. I still cannot cook. I'm still ill suited to be your wife."

He launched to his feet. She peeked through her fingers. Folding his arms across his chest, he said, "I have become too accustomed to my own ways. I have tried to mold you into what I wanted and did not consider that you might need me to make changes, too." Jack sucked in a deep breath. "Perhaps I could consider building a place for us nearer Denver City."

"But you hate the city."

He rolled his shoulders in a semishrug and his forehead knit.

Giddy with the idea that he would go so far to keep

her with him, she smiled. "Would it be a brick house with plaster walls?" she teased.

"If that is what you want." He recoiled and stepped back. "They always need men for building...railroads...."

He didn't want to move to the city. And he was talking about more than moving. Her stomach fell. She shook her head. "Did your father try to do that for your mother?"

Jack bent his head down and put his hand across his eyes. "He didn't try to change his profession."

Suddenly she was bone weary. Her emotions had been on a wild ride, but now the truth had to be faced. "Bricks and plaster walls aren't what make a home. I cannot change to be what you want, and you would be miserable trying to give me the life you think I want." She stood.

"What makes a home, Olivia?"

He didn't need her, and he certainly hadn't appreciated her efforts to make the cabin a home. Her mouth opened before she could call the words back. "Everything I have tried to do to make this my home, too, you have undone."

"I kept hitting my head on the pans."

Okay, she could understand that. "You covered the quilt with your furs."

"My mother's quilts were never warm enough." He rubbed his moccasin along the edge of the bottom step. "Yours is better made." His words were a grudging admission.

She wondered at his concern for warmth when he stood bare chested in the cool night. But a larger issue was at stake. She would never fit into his world. She would always be the square wheel on the wagon if she tried. "You don't want me changing anything."

"I didn't," he said softly.

For a second they stared at each other.

A heavy rustling in the underbrush jerked her attention toward the dark woods.

Jack reacted before she could think. "Get inside."

She stumbled trying to unwrap her limbs from the quilt.

Jack scooped her up, thrust open the door and dumped her on the floor.

He swiveled, pulled his rifle from over the door and headed back out. He aimed the rifle toward the noise.

She hung on to the door frame. A dark shaggy creature separated itself from the woods and rose up on its back legs. The beast stood high enough to waltz with her. It sniffed the air.

"Good God, what is that?"

Jack lowered the rifle. "It's a grizzly cub."

"They get *bigger*?" Her heart threatened to beat out of her chest.

He grimaced. "Lots bigger."

"I thought you said that they didn't come around here."

"Don't usually."

The cub dropped to all fours and let out a plaintive wail. He sounded like a lost child. An urge to comfort the wild creature had her stepping outside.

Jack scanned the tree line. He raised the rifle to his shoulder and sighted down the barrel.

"You're not going to kill it?" she yelped. "He's a baby."

Jack lifted his cheek away from the butt of his rifle. "If his mama is the bear Antonga killed, he won't survive."

"But do you have to kill it?" How could Jack go from

the man who made love to her to killing baby animals? She closed her eyes, knowing she was overreacting but unable to stand the rise of resentment.

Jack sighed and turned his attention back to the cub. "Go inside if you don't want to watch."

As if sensing the danger, the bear plunged back into the darkness of the trees.

Jack sighed and lowered the gun. "I'll have to kill him sooner or later or he'll become a nuisance. He's not old enough to make it without his mother's milk."

"What is going on?" asked the doctor.

"Just a grizzly visit." Jack returned inside and put his rifle on the pegs above the door.

The doctor sat up. "Is my horse okay?"

Olivia cast Jack a dark look. "Everything is fine. The *cub* ran away."

But everything wasn't fine, and the doctor stared at a piece of straw in Jack's hair. She reached up to make sure she wasn't sporting any similar hair adornment. Doc Jenson turned to look at her just as she realized her nightgown was inside out. She dropped her arm and hoped he couldn't see in the dim light of the cabin.

He glowered at her.

Her cheeks burned. She turned to Antonga and re-freshed the cloths on his forehead and neck. His fever hadn't returned and his face had relaxed as if he no longer felt the pain.

The doctor snorted and rolled to his side with his back to her.

Never could she imagine doing the things she'd done with Jack with another man, not the doctor, nor Mr. Kincaid, who'd offered seventy-five dollars for her. Repulsed, she shuddered.

After adding wood to the stove, Jack moved behind her. "He looks as if he is resting easier."

"He seems better." She tucked the furs around Antonga.

Jack put his hand on her shoulder. Her skin prickled with awareness. She just wanted to lean into him and pretend everything would be better in the morning.

Leaning close to her ear, he whispered, "You will be a wonderful mother. Someday."

Olivia stiffened. She'd never be a mother. She'd never risk her heart again as she had with Jack. She'd already lost one family and was about to lose the hope of another. And they hadn't done anything to create a baby.

He caught her hand in his and brought it up to his mouth and pressed his lips to the base of her ring finger.

Oh, God, he was reminding her that he'd promised not to get her with child until she put his ring back on her finger. She'd misjudged him, not just once but twice tonight. A house closer to Denver he meant as a compromise, not as a suggestion that she leave with the first available man who would take her. Heavens above, if he'd intended to foist her on another man, he could have taken the seventy-five dollars from Mr. Kincaid.

She ducked her chin, her thoughts swirling. Would Jack want her when the doctor and Antonga were long gone? Would Jack want her after she'd burned another meal? Or after he had to carry her because she was winded or barefoot? Could he love her? Or would he grow to hate her when she couldn't be the brave and calm-natured helpmate he wanted?

She was so lost in his world. But she'd been lost since her parents' deaths. She'd clung to her mother's fine dresses and her jewelry as if they were the means to reclaim the genteel life she'd expected to live. The townsfolk of Norwalk thought she was putting on airs. At the mill, other girls thought Olivia spoiled and arrogant even when she worked circles around them.

In truth, she had probably appeared a pathetic creature who clung to the past. Mill girls didn't wear carriage dresses, or even own them. No wonder the woman who'd showed up on the stage had startled Jack. He hadn't known what to make of her, either.

Jack was strong and solid as the mountains where he made his home, and he knew exactly who he was and where he belonged. That he would even consider moving closer to Denver City or working as a laborer for her broke her heart.

She could pull out the ring and show him that she wore it around her neck next to her heart, or she could do the right thing and leave his life so he could find a helpmate rather than a mate who was a burden.

Chapter Seventeen

*She doesn't complain, but the expression on her
face when she first saw the cabin said it all. Nor
have I ever seen a woman own so many dresses,
all of them too fancy. She scrubs and polishes as
if she can shine the cabin into a castle.*

Jack woke to the smell of coffee. Not entirely ready to
wake up, he pushed back the quilt and sat up. A wife
fixing breakfast was too great a lure to ignore.

Fully buttoned from head to toe, Olivia stood by the
table. Her forehead was knotted and her tongue curled
over her upper lip as she stirred a bowl. He liked that
little pink tongue and the wicked way she used it. A
shudder of pleasure ran down his spine.

She looked at him and turned bright red. She spun
so she faced the stove. In her haste, her skirt dragged
over the cot hogging the space in the room.

The doctor snorted and pushed up on his elbows.
"Good morning."

"Good morning," Olivia returned brightly with her
tongue safely tucked away. "The coffee is almost ready."

"I'll go get the ham," said Jack, disappointed he no

longer had Olivia to himself and that her pleasant greeting had been reserved for the doctor. Jack rocked up to his feet.

Antonga groaned from the other side of the bed.

Olivia's face twisted. "He feels hot again."

"He needs more medicine." The doctor rolled to the edge of the cot and slid on his pants. But instead of going to the bedside, the doctor put on his shoes and headed outside.

"You don't have to be nice to him," hissed Jack the minute the door closed. He almost hoped the bear had returned and attacked the doctor.

"I'm just trying to be polite, since you won't." She thrust out the bowl. "Am I doing this right?"

"Looks fine."

"I'm not leaving with him." Olivia stirred with a jerky, unpracticed movement. "But I don't see any reason to be rude while he's our...your guest."

Her correction froze him.

"Jacques?" croaked Antonga.

Jack turned toward his friend. He consoled the man in his own dialect. He glanced toward Olivia. He should have taken the brief moment to tell her he loved her.

After a breakfast of rock-hard biscuits, which he resorted to dunking in his coffee to soften, he grabbed his rifle and headed for the door.

"I'll have to track that grizzly and kill him." Jack reached for his rifle. "Or the livestock will be at risk."

Olivia turned her wan face in his direction.

"Don't stray too far from the cabin until I find him." He tried to convey more with his look. To tell her to trust him, that he would keep her safe, but she had already ducked away with a stain of pink across her cheeks.

Checking for signs of bear, Jack circled the cabin.

In the softer ground by the creek, he picked up the trail. He followed uphill until the ground was too hard for paw impressions. None of the signs led him to believe the cub had a mother. He bent down, examining a rolled-over log. Roly-poly bugs and grubs still clung to the rotted wood that had been against the ground. The bear had not collected all the food before moving on. Jack frowned. The cub's inexperience didn't bode well for its survival.

The broken twigs and disturbed underbrush led him farther and farther away. He didn't want to be all day tracking the bear cub, leaving Olivia alone with the doctor.

Jack bent and checked the ground. Instead of concentrating on tracking, he kept thinking of Olivia.

Walking softly, he slowly circled, looking for an identifiable sign. Chances were the mother bear had attacked Pansook and Antonga. The two men had most likely unwittingly separated the cub from its mother.

The woods grew denser and the landscape more rugged. The trail steepened. The bear's claws had dug out divots as he scampered up the mountainside. Using branches for towlines, Jack hauled himself up a nearly vertical face. The meandering path straightened.

After struggling upward for about a hundred feet through dense trees, Jack cleared a ridge. The ground flattened. His path was easier, but following the cub once again became difficult, as the bear had no reason to claw his way forward.

He took his heading from the direct angle of the cub's ascent. He'd been away longer than he wanted and the sun crested high in the sky. Would Olivia attempt to cook a midday meal?

Jack sniffed. The forest had taken on a different

scent. The smell of raw meat reached his nose. It was probably what had the cub bounding forward. With luck, he would find the cub at a meal.

Pulling his rifle off his back and holding it ready, Jack crept forward. If he could smell the flesh, it had to be close.

The trees thinned a bit and Jack could see silver-tipped brown fur in a small clearing. Jack crept forward until he saw a moccasin. The beaded pattern was Ute. It had probably been Pansook's. Jack pushed aside the heavy branches of a low-slung pine.

The cub shook a mostly eaten carcass of a deer. In the way of the wild, the cub had been feeding on the dead man's kill.

A buffalo hide lay over a lump that must be Pansook's body. Several other pelts were scattered about the clearing; undoubtedly, Pansook and Antonga had been bringing him the furs.

On the far side of the clearing lay a mound of motionless silver-tipped brown fur. The mother bear. From his vantage, Antonga's hatchet in the bear's head wasn't visible, but he would find it after he killed the orphaned cub. Antonga would be proud to have it back.

Keeping his vision focused, Jack crept close enough he could get a clear shot. Bear skulls were thick. Bullets could ricochet and leave a hunter with an angry wounded bear and an empty gun. If Jack could shoot cleanly through the eye, the pelt would be worth a few dollars.

Jack moved closer than he would have with an adult bear and sighted down the barrel. When the cub stilled, he squeezed the trigger.

The young bear wobbled and then fell on top of the deer's bones. As the blue smoke drifted upward, Jack hastily opened the breach of his rifle and dug in the pouch containing his paper cartridges. The cub didn't move. His shot had been true.

Standing up, he took a step closer as he tipped the pouch to remove a hand-wrapped bullet and powder.

A deep roar startled him. Cartridges pinged to the ground around his feet. *What the hell?*

The grizzly carcass moved. It drew up on all fours. The mother bear wasn't dead. Jack froze, not believing his eyes.

The grizzly lurched drunkenly toward the cub. Blood stained the fur on her neck. *Merde!* Antonga's hatchet hadn't killed the bear, just wounded her.

Fumbling to load, Jack took a slow step backward. He was far too close to the man-killer.

The bear rolled her head in Jack's direction. Her nostrils worked. *Merde!* He'd gone upwind to get a frontal shot on the cub.

The next roar had a sorrowful quality to it. The bear nudged her lifeless cub.

Jack's heart pounded. Blood rushed in his ears, blurring sound. This couldn't be happening. He got the cartridge loaded and closed the breach and took another step backward. The bear snarled and charged.

With the bear thundering toward him, Jack barely had time to get the rifle up and fire a shot.

The fur rippled and she collapsed to one shoulder. In one stride she was back on all fours.

The massive paws shook the earth. Jack dodged behind the nearest tree, a spindly thing that the bear could shatter into toothpicks with one swipe of her paw.

Merde, that bear had more lives that a cat.

Jack ran.

Darting back and forth, he kept as many trees be-

tween him and the bear as he could and headed toward
the steep slope. He needed to find a tree he could climb
a good forty or fifty feet up to escape her deadly claws
and bared teeth. The only trees around him were spindly aspens without low branches.

The bear behind him stumbled and Jack prayed for
the beast to drop before reaching him.

She thundered behind and he didn't dare look as he
headed for the extreme slope. He went over the side. He
slid, careening down. He was half on his feet and half on
his backside and gathering speed. Branches slapped at
him. Underbrush threatened to snag his boots and send
him tumbling. Rotted leaves and pine needles greased
his descent. Trying to control his plummet, he grabbed
branches with his free hand. The bear crashed above
him. At the bottom of the slope, he reached into his
shot pouch, but his fingers touched nothing but leather.

He should have brought the shotgun. But he hadn't
expected to encounter a full-grown bear, and he hadn't
been concentrating. He should have made sure the
mother bear was dead, and he should have realized the
nearly devoured buck indicated more than one small
cub had been feasting on it.

Wildly, Jack looked around. The crashing stopped.
The bear hung her head over the ridge, staring, sniff-
ing. The working of the animal's nostrils troubled Jack.
She could smell exactly where he was, but whether she
would risk sliding down the escarpment had him holding his breath.

Slowly Jack slid the rifle strap over his head and took
a step back. He would need both hands to climb a tree
if she chased after him.

The bear's fur stood on end as she snarled.

Jack took another step back, scanning nearby trees for a suitable escape.

The grizzly seemed unwilling to take the downward plunge, but Jack wanted to be ready. He only had a single knife to use against her four-inch-long claws and bone-crushing jaws.

After a few minutes, the bear withdrew from the edge of the ridge.

Jack drew in a deep breath, but not being able to see the bear was almost worse than seeing it. He'd have to go back to the cabin and get more ammunition.

Walking slowly to not confuse the bear into thinking he was fleeing prey, Jack headed home.

He was nearly out of the trees when the forest stilled. The birds weren't chirping and the incessant chatter of chipmunks was absent. His muscles tensed and his hackles raised.

Spinning around, he couldn't see any danger. The newly leafing aspens with their silvery shoots shimmered in the breeze. The darker ponderosa pines with their tall straight trunks loomed overhead.

His disquiet grew. Bears didn't stalk humans, at least not in his experience. But if she was stalking him, then she'd marked him as an easy kill.

The cabin was close enough to smell the woodsmoke. He quickened his step. If the bear had followed him, running would only provoke her, but he didn't know how to deal with a bear intent on eating him. Most bears only protected territory or offspring.

He heard her before he saw her. Twigs crunched. Branches swished. The forest's deathly quiet was shattered by the thundering of massive footfalls. Instinct shattered his shock. He was so close to home and Olivia, and that damn bear crashed toward him.

Running, he yelled as loud as he could. He had to get to the cabin and the shotgun before the bear brought him down.

His feet pounded the ground. He zigged and zagged, putting as many trees of substance between them as he could. The bear crashed into a tree. The wood cracked while the light filtering through the branches lurched wildly. Jack doubled his speed. Surely he couldn't get this close and not make it. "Olivia! Shotgun!"

The bear clumped behind him. Jack could practically feel its fetid breath on his neck. "Olivia!"

With a roar, the bear shook the ground. Oh, God, he wouldn't make it.

The cabin door opened.

Olivia poked out her face. She went ghostly white. Had she opened the door just in time to see him mauled to death?

"Shotgun!" Jack turn sharply. The bear closed in.

The clearing between the trees and the house was the most dangerous. In open space, a bear could outpace a horse. He didn't stand a chance.

Still, he focused on Olivia's wide gray eyes as he left the comparative safety of the trees. If he could just make it home to her, he'd give anything. He should have told her he loved her when he had the chance.

She raised the shotgun, pointing it directly at him. Her hands were shaking and she looked barely able to support the weight of the gun. A shot in the wrong place wouldn't stop the grizzly. An inexperienced shooter's aim was likely to be wild.

"No," he yelled. She needed to let him shoot. Scattering buckshot in his direction was more likely to kill him than the grizzly. He was only a few yards from the porch. "Let me."

The snarling, grunting bear snapped at his heels. The chicks squawked and scattered as he raced toward the cabin.

The bear roared. Dread scudded down his spine.

Almost in slow motion he saw Olivia aiming, drawing a breath and squeezing the trigger. Death by shotgun or by bear mauling. Either way, dead was dead. Covering his head, he dived forward and waited for the pellets to shred his flesh or the massive bear to maul him.

Chapter Eighteen

He looks as he did in the photograph, only better.
His smiles are rare, but make my knees weak. I
get his frowns more often, and I just want to die.
I asked once if he had ever climbed to the top of
any of the mountains. He thought the idea silly
and frivolous. He doesn't think any better of me.

The shotgun punched into her shoulder and knocked Olivia off her feet. Her hoops popped up and her skirts tipped back. Unable to see Jack or the bear, her heart skittered. Her ears rang. Had she brought down the bear? Or had she missed?

"What the hell?" the doctor said from behind the cracked door.

His voice was tinny and faraway sounding, and she had left the door wide-open. The doctor must have pulled it shut.

"Jack," shouted Olivia. Her chest squeezed.

Doc Jenson was taking an inventory of her petticoats and drawers. She couldn't care less. The only thing she cared about was Jack.

Feeling a bit like an upended turtle, she scrambled to right herself.

The doctor opened the door. That had to be a good sign. "Oh, for goodness' sake."

His voice sounded normal. He moved to the stairs. He wouldn't do that if the bear was still a threat, would he?

Olivia scrambled to her knees. The shotgun clattered to the porch. She clawed at the railing. Her hand was shaking so badly she could barely cling to the top board.

Jack was on one knee, breathing heavily. He filled her vision. Their eyes locked, and he gave a small shake of his head with a tiny curl of the edges of his mouth. He was all right.

Her breath whooshed out and she closed her eyes.

When she opened them, Jack had buried his knife in the bear's chest.

"I thought you said don't run from bears!"

Jack wiped his face with his upper arm but continued slicing open the bear. "You shouldn't."

"Well, then, what in heaven's name were you doing?" she screeched. The terror pouring through her had nowhere to go and her relief disappeared under a burst of anger.

The doctor took a step back, looking between the two of them. They probably appeared crazy. Jack butchering a bear practically on the front stoop and her on her knees yelling.

"This one was intent on making a meal out of me," said Jack in an impossibly calm manner. "Didn't matter if I ran or not. Would you get the washtub and empty sacks so I have somewhere to put this meat?"

"So why didn't you shoot it?" Her voice came out –

shrill in spite of her efforts to control her tone. His reasonable tone only made her feel hysterical.

"I did," said Jack. "Your shot was better."

Olivia swallowed hard, fighting the nausea that rose in her throat. Her shoulder screamed with pain. She clamped her hand against it. Gritting her teeth, she rose to her feet. Tears burned at the backs of her eyes as the enormity of what she'd done hit her. Never in her wildest dreams had she imagined shooting a bear. Heavens, killing a bug made her squeamish. Another detail penetrated. *Her?* "I thought you said the cub was orphaned."

"Antonga wounded the mother bear. She wasn't hunting normally."

"So she decided to eat you?"

"Pretty much." Jack stopped hacking at the carcass. He looked at the doctor, and then back at her. "You did good, *chérie*."

His voice was low and soothing, almost like when he'd encouraged her in bed. But her brain froze on the idea that the bear had intended to eat Jack. Horror tightened her spine.

"We are safe now," he continued in the lulling tone.

She wasn't ready to be soothed. Her shoulder hurt like the devil. Her emotions were knotted into hard lumps. She wanted to shout at him in a way that would have shamed her mother and offended her father.

"So what am I to do if I encounter a bear? Wait until it eats me?" What would she do if a wild animal attacked Jack? The terror she thought she'd banished returned full force, making her every muscle clench until she shuddered from head to toe. The very idea of his falling prey to an animal with flesh being torn from his bones made her ill. This was a god-awful place.

Jack's shoulders slumped. "Climb a tree, preferably a tall one."

"I've never climbed a tree." Certainly if she'd ever had the urge to climb a tree—which she doubted—she would have been discouraged. Not to mention, climbing a tree in skirts had to be next to impossible. So she might as well consider herself bear food. "And I'm not about to start now."

"Fine. I'll kill every bear within fifty miles," said Jack in a low voice.

"Like you did that one?" she snapped.

"Olivia, help out or be quiet. Or better yet, go get the mules. I'm going to need them…and the shovel."

"What for?"

"I found Pansook's body and I killed the cub."

That was more than she wanted to know. Olivia swiveled, went inside the cabin, and then slammed the door. Never once in all his letters had Jack mentioned that the bears in the Rocky Mountains liked to eat people. She couldn't understand this place. She couldn't stay here.

Doc Jenson took a step toward the stairs.

Jack sighed. "You might want to give her a minute."

Although he was wishing the doctor to hell, Olivia probably needed privacy to find her composure. Her struggle to hold back tears was obvious. He was grateful that her panic had held off until after the bear was dead. More than grateful. Whole and alive.

But the doctor probably hadn't noticed her struggle, as he'd been looking at the eight feet of dead bear with awe. And Jack sure as hell didn't want Doc Jenson to be the one to comfort her when Jack couldn't do it himself.

If the man hadn't been standing there, Jack probably would have said a dozen different things or wrapped

Olivia in his arms. Truth was, he wanted to do much more than hold her.

Nothing like having the chance of death in the form of a grizzly intent on eating him, and then staring down the barrels of a loaded shotgun to clarify things.

He probably hadn't needed to butcher the sow so quickly, as Olivia's shot had opened a huge gaping hole in the neck, but he wasn't waiting for the bear to use her claws to rip him or her jaws to close around him before making sure she was completely dead.

Now he was covered in gore, and holding his wife would have to wait.

"You have a wound on your temple." The doctor hesitated. "You might want me to bandage it."

"Later," said Jack. As the doctor brought his attention to it, he felt the warm trickle of blood down the side of his face.

The doctor glanced toward the cabin. "I never would have expected her—"

"Amazing, isn't she?" muttered Jack. And he was an idiot. He'd not been prepared. He hadn't been concentrating, and he'd dropped his ammunition. Then he'd led a grizzly bear to his cabin and Olivia.

She had been magnificent.

His father would flay him alive for being so stupid. Maybe he should go live in Denver City and work as a peon. He didn't deserve her.

Jack pulled the rifle strap over his head and set the empty weapon to the side. He needed to reload before he went back into the woods, and he'd take the shotgun, too, but that was probably a bit of closing the barn door after the horse bolted.

"Is that the liver?" asked Doc Jenson.

Jack rolled his eyes. Obviously the man had never

butchered an animal. Jack's head was starting to ache and he had two bears to skin and butcher, a man's remains to gather up and bury, then two guns to clean, not to mention instructing Olivia on how to cook dinner.

"You know, you really ought to let me bandage that. How did you do that?" The doctor squinted at Jack's head.

Jack raised his hand to his temple and felt the even furrow going into his scalp. At the end, deep in his hair, he felt the hard lump against his skull. "*Merde, she shot me.*"

Olivia made her way along the path toward the stream. She juggled the buckets and lifted her hoops to squeeze between two trees. An evergreen branch snagged her skirt anyway. Snapping off the branch, she sighed. Sticky sap coated her fingers.

She set down the pails to rub the tree tar from her fingers before it attracted dirt. The sap resisted. Finally, she gave up and continued.

How did one ever grow used to the dirt? Her mother had always said cleanliness was next to godliness. Olivia would never grow used to the animals attacking without provocation, and a husband who treated the whole incident with matter-of-fact indifference. She needed him to hold her, to reassure her, to give her time to absorb what had happened; instead, he'd set her working on a dozen small tasks—while he butchered the bear.

A chipmunk with spotted stripes darted in front of her and rose on its hind legs to scold her. Even the wild animals seemed to have an opinion about her unsuitableness for life here. She knew she was being needy and too squeamish. Jack had to bury Pansook and take care of the cub's carcass, as well as all his usual chores, including cooking supper.

That she wanted him to comfort her at the same time her resolve to leave was hardening didn't make sense. She felt too much like the half-drowned girl on the riverbank who wanted her parents but had no one. She'd needed to stand aside as others who were in much worse condition were seen to. She was tired of standing aside and pretending she was fine when she wasn't.

The cool mountain breeze shifted through the trees, rich with the scent of pine. She closed her eyes and breathed in. In spite of the dirt, the deep stillness of the woods and the blue-green mountains stretching to the sky seemed mystical and foreign. She didn't know who she was here. It was as if she had stepped away from her own identity and was too close to a primitive self that she didn't like.

The roar of the rushing stream greeted her long before the air grew cooler. In spite of her tumble into the other stream, the sound was reassuring, almost musical.

Getting the water from a fast-rushing stream with her wide skirts proved difficult. Gathering up the material and the hoops, she reached out to fill the first bucket. Her bruised shoulder screamed in protest.

Carrying the water back always took her longer and left her elbows aching where the heavy weight of the filled pails pulled until her arms felt as if they were unable to bend.

There had to be an easier way.

"Why do you—"

Olivia shrieked and dropped her skirts.

"—wear your hoops, when they make it so difficult for you?"

Jack crouched upstream on the opposite bank, his

rifle held across his chest. His dark hair was damp and slicked back from his forehead. Her breath caught. The thought of what they'd done last night flooded her mind with memories of his texture and taste. Her skin tingled and heated.

"The pail is full." Jack nodded toward the water.

Water gushed over the rim of the bucket. She lifted it and stepped back. The drenched bottom six inches of her pink skirt's front turned almost red. Probably matched her face.

He looked very much a part of the woods in his buckskin pants and shirt that blended into the old pine straw that littered the ground. As he stood, his form separated from the forest and appeared distinct against the dark boughs of evergreens. Had he been there all along?

He was so much a part of this land that she didn't know that she could ever be a part of him. In her pink dress, she fit in like a flamingo.

"What are you doing?" She hoped she didn't sound breathless.

"Took a bath in the sun over yonder." Jack moved to the water's edge.

The stream was clear and rapidly flowing over the rocky bed. A good fifteen feet of water rushed between them. Fifteen feet of water and a world of difference. She would never fit in here.

Jack slung his rifle across his back and walked farther upstream. Disappointment curled under her breastbone, but then he hopped on a rock in the stream. He leaped from rock to rock until he was on her bank. He moved with an innate grace that reminded her of wild deer. She could watch him for hours, except she needed to take the water back to the cabin.

Setting the buckets down, she wrung out the hem of

her skirt and that of the petticoats beneath it. With each step Jack took toward her, her heart thumped.

Irrationally nervous, she grabbed the buckets and said, "The doctor needs more hot water."

Jack leaned against a skinny white tree. "Wait."

Olivia turned toward the path back to the cabin. "This would be easier if I had a handcart." She bit her lip. She shouldn't complain. Wishing she could flee his presence, she focused on the path and took a couple of steps. She had to go slow or she would slop water. "I mean faster."

"Why won't you look at me?" asked Jack.

"I look at you all the time," blurted Olivia.

With lightning quickness, he blocked the path. She stared at his chest and the uneven lower edge of his shirt.

"Yes, I can see that," Jack said drily.

The full pails of water tugged at her arms and made darting away impossible. Turning her head to the side, she fought the wave of yearning that swept over her. Going all mushy on the inside just because he was near was mortifying. Staring at a spindly white aspen sapling, she tried to regain her composure.

"Last night—"

"Last night shouldn't have happened," she interrupted. She willed the ground to open up underneath her feet. Upending in the creek would have been less embarrassing. What she'd done was bad enough; she couldn't talk about it.

"But it did." Jack folded his arms across his chest.

Her thoughts homed in on his smooth skin and the muscles under the soft leather of his shirt. When he was close, all she wanted to do was lean into him and soak in his strength. Or, well, now there was more she wanted to do to him, for him, with him.

She noticed everything about him—the way he smelled, the agile way he moved and the cadence of his breathing. He occupied her every thought. She tried to dismiss her rampant yearnings, but they blossomed with increasing intensity. She couldn't glance at his face or she would be lost. If he looked on her with pity she would come apart. If he looked on her with disgust she would die a thousand deaths. Her will to be her own person disintegrated into ashes.

The water in the buckets rippled with her quivering.

"It changed everything," said Jack.

No, it hadn't changed that she didn't fit out here or in his life. It just made her long for things that couldn't be. She wanted him to love her, but how could he when she was so out of place and inept? She stared at the pine straw on the ground.

"Are you cold?" he asked in a gentle voice.

She shook her head.

"Afraid?" His voice dropped lower. "You're shaking. There aren't any more bears."

She pursed her lips and blew out. "I don't want to even think about the bears."

"You were very brave." He reached out and tapped her cheek. Her knees almost buckled as relief swept through her. Why couldn't he have offered this small comfort hours ago?

He hadn't. And he withdrew his hand, leaving her bereft. Since the bear killing, she'd been turning over everything in her mind. His focus had been on immediate tasks, not her, not on her need to be consoled. This place didn't allow for emotional delays. Like him, she had to be sensible. "I shouldn't have shot. I almost killed you."

"He wasn't supposed to tell you."

"I heard you talking about removing the buckshot." She'd about collapsed in despair. Her efforts to save Jack had nearly killed him. "I was so terrified, I didn't think." She had been foolish and clumsy, just as she always was in his environment. She was not at all what he needed in a wife. "I am not very brave after all."

"You are amazingly brave. I will not hear you say you weren't." He shifted, his weight rocking toward her. "We need to discuss what will happen between us, *chérie.*"

"I don't think anything has changed. Not really. I have only shown how ill equipped I am to live here. I cannot see how this marriage will work. I…" She didn't know how to finish or even what she meant to say.

His jaw tensed. "I need to tell you a few things." He ran a hand through his damp hair.

She waited. Even though they were too different, from two diametrically opposed worlds, she hoped he would persuade her to stay. She still hoped he would love her. In spite of everything, she just wanted to be wrapped in his arms and held as if he couldn't stand to let her go.

"I would rather write you a letter," he began.

Her heart dropped like a stone. Blood rushed in her ears and the sound of the water and the birds faded. Letters were distant and formal.

Except his hadn't been.

His love of his home had come through so clearly in every word he wrote.

"I don't know if I could ever give you what it would take to make you happy," he began.

The wild ricochet of her hopes to her fears and back again hurt her chest. It was as if her heart was cracking open.

"Last night you were so bold."

A squeak wrenched from her aching chest. She ducked and moved to circle around him.

He put out his arm to bar her. "Now you won't look at me."

She stopped before his arm touched her breasts. "I can't. I'm ashamed of what I did."

"Shit!" He raised his hand to his head.

He sounded so revolted she risked looking at his chin. A sigh left her. Her path was no longer blocked, but she stood rooted to the spot. The tension hung thick and heavy between them. With a nonchalance she didn't feel, she ventured, "That word sounds less disgusting in French."

"Pardonnez-moi," he said.

They stood silently for a moment. Her gaze moved from the strong line of his jaw to the lips that had imprinted on hers last night.

The corners of his mouth tilted up. "Most things sound better in French and come easier for me, but you do not always understand, *n'est-ce pas?*"

"No." She wanted to ask about what he'd said to her last night, but she couldn't bear the thought of calling attention to what she'd done. What did his choice of the word *bold* denote? She couldn't think it was anything good. "I really do need to get back with the water."

"Olivia—" Even the way he said her name made her heart beat a little faster. "I am torn."

She should have pushed past him. Only pain would come of this conversation. Already her eyes burned.

"I thought last night would be pleasant."

Pleasant? She wanted to run, but she was frozen. His mouth was moving and she wanted to stop him, to scoop up the words and shove them back inside where they were better left unsaid.

"A relief, even."

"Stop, please stop!" she whispered. How bad was it?

He touched her chin and she turned to quicksilver. "It was beyond anything I could have imagined. If it is even possible, I want you more now, I want you to stay and wear my ring. I want to love you, but I do not want to say things that will keep you here if you will be miserable."

He *wanted* to love her? Her ears buzzed. But he didn't. How could he? "I think it will only be a matter of time before you despise me." Or she did something else stupid that resulted in his death.

"No. I cannot imagine that," he said tenderly. He tilted her chin up.

He'd known from the beginning how dangerous her inexperience could be, not only to her, but to him.

Fearing he could look into her eyes and see into her soul, she lowered her eyelashes. The heavy pails pulled at her arms but kept her anchored. "I don't fit into your life."

"Yes, but you are a damn quick study." His eyes crinkled at the corners as if he was restraining a smile.

She didn't understand what he found so amusing, but that he would laugh at her hurt. "I have more failures than successes."

His expression changed to one of concern. "The biscuits were almost edible, and you didn't burn the ham."

"My clothes are in the way." Her vision blurred. "I wore my hoops all the years at the mill, even though the others didn't. My mother taught me to always be mindful of my appearance. It was important to her. It is important to me."

Her mother had cast many a pitying look toward the poor women who dressed in slovenly clothes without corsets or hoopskirts. The idea of her mother looking down from heaven and seeing her as a disappointment made her cringe. But all that seemed so long ago and so faraway.

"You would look elegant in sackcloth."

Heat flushed her skin. "But I don't know who I am."

The wail sounded childish to her ears. She winced. She just wanted to go back to the house, where she didn't have to face talking to Jack after what she'd done last night. But more than that, she wanted him to wrap his arms around her and tell her everything would be all right. Even if it was a lie. But he hadn't pulled her to him or kissed her.

"I know who you are." His brown eyes were warm and bored into hers with such intensity she could not look away.

Her knees threatened to buckle.

"You are a beautiful woman who manages to hide a lot of passion behind a great deal of reserve." He leaned close enough for his breath to brush across her lips. "Most of the time."

She shook her head. "I am not brave or calm or much of a helpmate."

"*Au contraire,* you are calm when I least expect it. I thought you would have been angry when I ruined your pretty towels. And there are times when you push forward when you are afraid. You have an air about you, as if you are lost in dreams...."

Thinking of all the times Selina and Anna had accused her of being unrealistic, Olivia scrunched her nose. She had to be practical like him. It was the only way to survive here.

"Yet I could not have asked for better care of Antonga. You killed the bear. You surprise me and scare me and excite me all at the same time."

"I am not calm. All I want to do is scream or cry. All day long, I've just wanted to die." She'd been terrified the bear would hurt Jack. If she'd had time to think, she probably would have fainted.

Jack frowned. "Not many bring down a bear the first time they fire a gun."

She wanted him to touch her, hold her—but if she was leaving, if she wanted to prove last night hadn't changed anything, why would she want him to do the very things that confused her? Why yearn for the things that would make her want to stay? She shook her head. "My inexperience not only makes it harder for you, it makes it dangerous. I shot you and almost killed you."

"Olivia—"

"I cannot stay here and share this life with you." Her voice wavered and her eyes burned. "Don't say you will move to the city and give up this place. You love it too much, and you could only hate me for it in the end."

She took a couple of steps on the path toward the cabin.

"Olivia—"

She jerked around, water sloshing from the buckets. "Do not say anything. You knew how unsuited I was for this life when you picked me up in Denver City. I just didn't realize how easily my—my ignorance and panic could kill. I can't…I can't cope with you being gone all the time. I can't sit and think you might come through the door mauled by a bear or—"

"Bears attacks are not so common."

She waved her hand. "If not a bear, a snake—or I will do something foolish when you are not around to save me. I thought you could protect me, but you can't protect me if you are gone."

Jack's expression turned flat. He looked off into the trees. "You know I have to guide the doctor back to town tomorrow. I will be gone a couple of days. Antonga…"

"I know. I will stay with him until you are back. But I cannot do this forever. I wish I could, but I can't. I never should have allowed you to think I could be a brave and calm helpmate, because I can't."

She walked back to the cabin, wishing Jack would follow and offer a magical solution, but there weren't any.

Chapter Nineteen

*Before I close, I should tell you that Antonga was
badly mauled by a bear. Pansook was killed. I am
in town to retrieve a doctor, and must get back to
Olivia as soon as I can.*

"He will come," said Antonga.

Olivia moved away from the window for the hundredth time this morning.

"He said he would be here last night," she said. Her
heart twisted in her chest. Was Jack all right? Had
he fallen ill or been attacked by a wild animal? She
wouldn't ever be able to handle the waiting with equanimity. Not now. Not when she knew what could happen.

"He will come," repeated Antonga. "Delays happen."

"Yes, well, the nature of the delay concerns me,"
she answered.

"Come read more." Antonga sat down heavily on
the bed and sighed.

For Antonga to ask her to read more in her broken
French meant her fretting was irritating. The waiting
was making her crazy, but the last time Jack had left,

he'd come back with a bear at his heels intent on eating him.

Shaking her head, Olivia picked up the copy of *Le Comte de Monte-Cristo* and pulled a chair near the bed.

Sitting up straight, she read in the clear way that Miss Carmichael had demanded. She did her best with words that were unfamiliar to her, which was most of them. She'd just begun learning French when the train accident had occurred. She hadn't been schooled since.

Her mind drifted to worries about Jack. She couldn't glean much from the words she didn't know. She had thought she might improve her French, but asking for translations interfered with Antonga's ability to enjoy the story.

Antonga sighed heavily.

"Did I mispronounce this word?" Olivia asked. She held out the book and pointed.

"I not know what black worms say."

Mortified, Olivia pulled the book back. He wasn't able to read. "I'm sorry."

A few minutes later, he sighed again. "What is the purpose of keeping a captive locked away? A captive should be made to work."

"Prisons are punishment for crimes."

Antonga snorted.

Olivia folded the book over her finger. "What happens among your people if a man steals?"

"Stealing is a white man's crime. If a man of my people has much, he shares."

Olivia twisted her lips. "You must have some wrongdoers."

Antonga sighed. "If a man creates too much trouble, we have council and a man can be banished."

"That's all?"

"To live without his people is punishment enough."

Olivia frowned. She had been living without her family for a long time. And Jack was separated from his mother and sister. There was a sense of punishment in that.

She looked toward the window. Perhaps they needed each other to create a new family to fill the holes that were left by their past. She, at least, knew that her parents hadn't chosen to leave her. Given Jack's mother's desertion, it was no wonder that when she'd reminded him of his mother he hadn't reacted kindly.

"There is a place on top of Jacques' mountain where you can see for longer than a man can travel in a day." Antonga sighed heavily. "I am not healed enough to get there."

Although much improved, he was still weak, but she wasn't.

Olivia popped out of the chair. "Would you show me where to go?"

Antonga smiled. "It is not an easy climb."

Her enthusiasm waning, she perched back on the chair's edge. "I should like to try."

Jack would think climbing to the top of the mountain was frivolous, but she wanted to do it. And if Antonga thought she could, then she wanted to try. It would be one last way of shaking her fist at this harsh place before she left it for an easier one.

Jack rested his head against the horse's flank. He'd been pressing the horses hard and now was paying the price. The mare had pulled up limping yesterday. She didn't have a rock in her shoe or a hoof injury. He checked her often. As long as her leg wasn't swollen or hot to the touch he could keep her walking home, albeit at a snail's pace.

He hoped Olivia would not be too worried at his delay. He wanted so badly to see her, to hold her, but the extra time was likely only to solidify her decision to leave.

She deserved better than he could give as a trapper. But she was right—he didn't want to give up the beauty of his mountain home. To move to the hustle and bustle of a town and be unable to breathe the clean pine-scented mountain air would be suffocating.

The clearing around the cabin was silent. He pulled his saddlebags from the stallion and left the two horses standing as he climbed the porch stairs. "Olivia?"

"In here," she called.

He crossed the threshold. She stood at the stove, her face flushed and a strand of hair caressing her cheek. She was so beautiful it hurt.

The sizzling crackle of meat filled the air.

"I'm trying not to burn this," she said with a swift glance his way. "Antonga left, since I saw you were nearly home yesterday evening. He was probably tired of eating burned food."

"The mare is limping. I had to go slowly." His gaze darted to her bare ring finger. Jack's heart fell, but then she didn't know of his plan to give them a chance. "I have an idea I'd like to discuss with you, after I take care of the horses."

"All right."

He wanted to share his plans with her before she gave up on this marriage working. She had been willing to change everything; it was time he changed, too.

"Oh, and you have a letter."

"I do?" She darted away from the stove and bounced a little on her toes. "Is it from Anna or—"

She was excited enough about a letter from a friend to leave the stove, but not to greet him. He shouldn't have expected differently after what she'd said the last time they were together. Tension crawled up the back of his neck. Her words had haunted him. She wasn't equipped to be the wife of a trapper. He'd known that from the first time he saw her, but she wasn't without value. She was brave, bold and calm, just not in the ways that would work with his profession.

"It's from Connecticut."

Her head tilted and she narrowed her eyes. "From Connecticut?"

He dug it out of his saddlebag and tossed it on the table.

She stepped forward, picked it up and opened it. She perused the contents. Her hand went to her chest.

When he could stand it no more, he said, "Is it bad news?"

Her eyes darted up and her wide eyes glistened. "No, it is very good news."

He waited, but she continued reading the letter. When he could again stand it no more, he asked, "What?"

Olivia tore her gaze away as if it took force. "They found my father's money."

The aroma of burned meat and vegetables filled the cabin. She dropped the letter on the table and then rushed to the stove. "Oh, my goodness. I'm sorry. I wanted to make a hot meal for you."

"Don't worry about it." He stared at the letter as if it were a snake. Her father had money? "I'm not hungry."

She plunked the pan down on the table and picked up the letter again.

Her gray eyes widened as she scanned the letter. "I knew my father had made investments. I had no idea it could amount to so much." The letter fluttered in her hand and tears filled her eyes. She relayed how she'd hired a lawyer to track down her father's assets after she'd turned twenty-one, but the man had found little until now. "He says I have railroad stock worth tens of thousands."

"Yeah," said Jack. He tried to smile, but it probably looked as if he was baring his teeth.

Olivia's inheritance should have been happy news. But Jack couldn't have felt worse. The door frame bit into his shoulder as he tried to look unaffected by leaning into the opening with his arms folded. His stomach churned. Every reservation she possessed about leaving was wiped away. She could live anywhere, any way she wanted. She could own a dress for every day of the week. His plan seemed stupid in light of her news.

He wished the horse hadn't pulled up lame. He wished he hadn't gone to the post office while in Denver. He wished the letter from Connecticut had gotten lost in the war that was all the talk.

Her gray gaze met his. "What was it you wanted to tell me?"

He shook his head. "Not important."

"Tell me anyway."

"The war. Armies live on their bellies. If I raised cattle, I could be home every night." The words came out in a jumble, and he wished he hadn't said them. "It doesn't matter."

She watched him intently. Then slowly she said, "Antonga says he will return with Tabby."

"No!" Jack jerked as if he'd been kicked in the gut. "I already told him I don't want her."

She smiled softly as if her worries had been eased and ducked her head. She was so wrong if she thought any woman would do for him now. He only wanted her.

"I have to take care of the horses. The mare needs liniment..." He stumbled off the porch, wondering how he could have returned home so hopeful and now felt as black as the charred mess in the pan on the table.

Olivia had been sure of her plan, but now she waited nervously for Jack. She'd left the cabin almost the minute he'd entered the stable, only taking time to dash off a note. She'd have half an hour or so as he curried the horses, fed them and raked out the stalls. Finally he emerged. His dark hair caught the afternoon sun and she longed to run her fingers through it.

Her muscles tensed as Jack entered the cabin. He might think she'd gone mad.

Her heart pounded against her ribs as she watched. Time stretched on forever.

Her mind spun. Would he notice the new lavender curtains this time? Would he understand she intended to stay?

She'd spent the morning ripping apart her mother's carriage dress and restyling the yards of ruffled skirts into curtains. They would remind her of her mother, but it would also remind her she had chosen a new path for her life. A path where fancy dresses were a hindrance more often than not.

More time passed. She eased back from the edge and turned to watch the place he would ascend. He would come. She had to believe he would come.

Unless Jack had decided to wait until she came down on her own. She swallowed against the tightening in the back of her throat. What if he didn't want her to stay?

Had she misread the anguish in his voice when he'd said he didn't want Antonga's daughter to come? But she'd had time to think while he was away. He hadn't said he loved her, but then he hadn't written he loved his mountains either, but it had been clear. He'd been trying to tell her that, if only she hadn't been in a tizzy over shooting the bear and him.

On the way up the mountain, Jack's commandeered knapsack had contained the quilt, her brush and a jug of water. Now it was empty.

All along the way she'd left a path for Jack.

She curled her toes in the sun-warmed grass. It was lush and felt odd to her toes. She had not gone bare-foot since… She couldn't ever remember going bare-foot outside before coming here. Now a lot more than her feet was bare.

What she was doing was scandalous and entirely freeing, yet terrifying, too. She tried to will her racing heartbeat to slow, but she couldn't. If she was truly brave, she'd lie back and let the quilt fall open around her.

Jack had said again and again he wanted to see her without her clothes. If he still wanted that, she would let the quilt fall. She practiced in her mind, but her grip on the quilt tightened. What on earth was taking him so long?

When Jack discovered the cabin empty, he assumed Olivia had gone for water. Then he realized all the buckets were against the wall. He spun around. The quilt was gone from the bed. Had she packed it?

Confused, he turned around. Lilac curtains hung beside the windows. The letter was on the table. A note was scrawled on it. Reading it, his heart skipped.

He raced behind the cabin. Her hat swung in the afternoon breeze. He moved to the tree and untied the ribbons.

"Olivia?" He peered into the trees. Twenty feet away her hoops dangled from a branch.

"What the hell?" He retrieved her hoops and saw her pink shawl tied around a small bush. Next her yellow dress draped a pine bough. He moved quickly along a deer trail.

Gathering her clothes, he sprinted upward. His heart tripped and energy coursed through his body. Hardly knowing what to make of the clothing trail she'd left, he tried to stifle his hope. A rush of heat flooded his body as he added her corset to his pile. He swallowed hard.

Above him a rocky face loomed, impeding all but the most intrepid of climbers. Where was she?

He moved forward as if this was a dream. Her chemise was draped in a crevice between a large boulder and the cliff. Just beyond was another glimpse of white. Her pantalets.

When he finally made it up the last bit, not an easy climb with his arms full of clothes, he saw her. She huddled under the quilt with her legs drawn up.

"Olivia," he managed to get out between heaving gasps.

She tilted up her chin. Color crept up from her neck. Her pale hair was down and she pressed her lips together. Her shoes and stockings were in the grass. He dropped the pile of her clothes on the top rock.

"I thought you weren't coming," she said in a small voice.

"I just ran up a mountain." His heartbeat and heaving gulps of air ought to prove that. He dropped to his knees before her.

"Ran?" A slow smile broke over her face, making her radiate with beauty. Her gray eyes lit with mischief.

He nodded. "What are you wearing?"

"Only one thing," she said softly.

She'd kept on her chemise. He tried to not be disappointed, but his emotions were raw. The littered clothes could only mean she wanted a repeat of the night in the stable loft. He needed more, but he'd take what he could get.

Her toes ventured forward, and the sight of her slim, pale foot and pink toes fascinated him. The quilt loosened. She wiggled and her bare arm appeared, as well as her shins. He searched her ring finger, but it was still ringless.

He swallowed back his disappointment.

The quilt dropped and puddled around her hips.

She gave a slight shake of her head and her fair hair shifted across her breasts. A strip of milky-white skin down to her naval peeked between the long silky threads.

Heat rammed past his despair. Jack couldn't breathe. Words flew out of his brain and he could only experience the moment. Like Lady Godiva, Olivia was using her rippling mane to cloak her charms. Reaching out slowly as if she was a mirage that might disappear, he touched her delicate chin. She'd only been wearing the quilt and nothing else.

Her breath hitched.

He leaned closer until he could brush her lips with his. The sweetness of her kiss had his heart racing.

Holding her gaze, he traced his thumb along her jaw. "You are beautiful," he whispered.

"You're not even looking." She crossed her arms in front of her chest. The purple-and-yellow shotgun bruise on her shoulder made him wince, but he kept his gaze on her soft gray eyes. He wanted her too badly to question this gift.

"May I?"

"I don't know. You might react badly." She flushed a bright red. "You are a strange man. When I arrived, you looked at me as if I was a disgrace to womankind. And most men would be overjoyed to learn their wife is worth—"

He ended her tirade with a soul-deep kiss. The last thing he wanted to do was talk. Before she came to her senses, he wanted her beneath him.

Her eyes widened and then closed as she matched him motion for motion with her mouth.

Oh, God, he wanted her. He wanted to learn every inch of her. He wanted to caress her legs, her hips, her breasts. He wanted to learn every scar, every perfection. He wanted to taste her, all of her.... He wanted to show her how much he loved her. He cradled her head in his hands.

"—a lot of money, but you act as if it is the worst thing in the world."

"Olivia," he protested. He needed her here in the moment with him. "I'm looking."

Biting her lip, she went silent.

Careful not to alarm her, he shifted his gaze to her toes. Her knees were still folded up as if she would draw them up against her chest. He touched the ridges that marked the delicate bones of her feet. Moving his hand slowly, he slid it up to the porcelain skin of her shin. A throbbing low in him marked what the sight of her toes did to him. Even her trim ankles made him pant. He wanted those ankles locked behind his thighs, but that wasn't to be. Without the ring on his finger, he'd promised to not risk a child.

Curling his fingers around, he tested the gentle curve of her calf. He bent and pressed a kiss on her smooth knee. Sliding his hand over the white ridges of long-ago scars, he moved his lips along the disfigurement she had been so worried about.

"Don't." She slid her fingers in between his mouth and her thigh.

He kissed her fingers. "Does it hurt?"

She took her time answering. "No."

He could not love that part of her less. "If not for that accident, you would never have come here to me." He laced her fingers with his. "I can only be grateful for these scars. They only make you more beautiful in my eyes."

She made a sound that was too like a sob. His gaze jerked toward her face but never made it. He was caught staring at her breastbone. His heart jolted heavily in his chest. The sight of her lovely tip-tilted breasts with pale pink beading nipples should have been what held his interest, but that wasn't what snared him. His ring dangled at the end of the chain. "Olivia?"

Chapter Twenty

I will be on the mountain behind the cabin. Please join me. If you do not come, I will return before supper.

How like Jack to see the ugliest part of her as precious and beautiful. As if baring her body allowed him to see through to her soul. Yet Olivia's nerves jangled. With her inheritance she could leave and Jack wouldn't need to spare a thought for her welfare. Perhaps he wanted her gone.

"Jack," she whispered, his name coming out squeaky and breathless. He had been staring at her chest so long she feared something was amiss. She was not as voluptuous as Selina, nor was she as comfortable in her own skin as he was. Holding her shoulders back and keeping her arms down taxed her willpower. She had been so sure that her claim to attractiveness rested in her stylish clothes. In the darkness of the loft, disrobing had been easier.

He raised his brown eyes to meet hers and excitement and appreciation radiated from their depths. Delight shimmered down her spine, and she knew it would be all right.

He understood. He would take care of her. He would be gentle and patient. The coffee-colored depths of his eyes conveyed wonder as his full attention was locked on her. Other things were in his look, emotions and vulnerabilities he'd hidden before. She wanted to erase that hint of uncertainty in him. If he wanted her, she wanted him.

She reached out to touch his mouth, rubbing her index finger along his lower lip. "Kiss me, please."

He touched his tongue to her fingertip and then leaned forward to capture her mouth.

The press of his lips against hers broke loose the tethers of her reservations. She wanted his kisses, his touch and his weight pressing her into the grass of his mountain. His mouth moved against hers and her heart raced. Her body came alive with thousands of rushing tingles over her skin, under her skin, deep in her belly. She reached up to wrap her arms around his shoulders. The heat of his skin came through the soft buckskin of his shirt.

His taste swirled on her tongue. Warm, masculine heat enveloped her as he slid his hands around her ribs. Her hair shifted across her back. Every touch of her exposed skin evoked shivers down her back. As if he knew, he explored the length of her spine. Tingles radiated out from his touch. Then he pulled her close. Her bare breasts pressed against the soft leather, inciting jolts of tightening need.

One kiss ended and the next began before she could catch her breath. And she, too, let her hands roam. The corded muscles of his shoulders marked his strength. His solid physique reminded her he had no problems tossing her over his shoulder or pulling her out of a rushing stream. He would be there to pull her from danger.

Impatient with the barrier, she slid her fingers under the edge of his shirt. His skin radiated heat. Sliding her hands against his back, she relished the feel of him. Did her fingers leave trails of sparks the way his did?

She was impatient, yet he seemed determined to go slowly, to savor the steps. Her breasts ached for his touch, yet he took his time. The slow sweep of his hand had her buzzing with anticipation as it arrived at each new destination. Her heart beat faster and her mind sang with the idea that Jack was touching her, Jack wanted her and she wanted him. Oh, Lord, did she want him.

The way he touched her, gentle and firm, almost reverent, was making her shake with a familiar growing need. Memories of the night in the stable made her breath hitch. Heat pooled between her legs and her woman's place tightened.

His hands left her and a yelp of protest left her mouth. The corners of his eyes crinkled as he pulled back.

"Trust me, *chérie,* I am not finished." He pulled the quilt away from where it had pooled around her hips and stretched it over the ground. Her body thrumming with desire, she pulled her knees tight against her chest as he smoothed out the material. The sure and agile way he moved drew her like no other man could.

Gently cradling her, he laid her down. She gave up the last vestige of modesty and stretched out her legs. He kissed her gently, but then drew away again. She whimpered but let him go, expecting him to remove his clothes.

He didn't. Instead, he settled down beside her, his gaze sweeping over her nakedness.

Heat burned up from her chest, over her face to the tips of her ears. "Jack," she protested.

The corner of his eyes crinkled again. "I have to look at you, my love. You are so amazingly exquisite." He pressed his lips to her temple. "And you have denied me this treat too long."

In spite of her misgivings, a wash of heat traveled down her body and settled in her core. "But you are dressed still," she whispered.

"I won't be for long." His fingers brushed across one pebbled nipple.

She jolted. Scrabbling at his shoulder, she tried to bring him close to settle the ache in her, but he resisted her efforts, sliding down to press his mouth against her collarbone, her chest, the upper slope of her breast. Anticipation made her arch, trying to guide him, but he bypassed her tightened nipple, leaving her frenzied with want.

His fingers drew lazy circles on her abdomen until she was quivering from his touch. His mouth followed with nips until her hips twisted. Memories of the intimate kiss he had given her in the loft made her yearn for more.

He slid against her, and with his knee nudged her legs apart. She closed her eyes and bit her lip as she opened herself to him. Finally he ended the torture as he licked her beaded nipple and dipped his fingers into the wet folds of her body. What should have seemed like an unbearable intrusion only felt right with him. Pleasure climbed in her, building to a peak that terrified her.

His insistence on keeping his clothes on frustrated her efforts to touch him. It was as if he had erected a barrier between them. Did he not want her the way she wanted him?

Her eyes popped open and she stared at the blue bowl of the sky. "Jack?"

He moved lower, his mouth open, warm and wet against her skin, inside her hip bone.

"Don't fight the fall, *chérie*." He spread her apart with his fingers. "I'll catch you."

She fisted her hand in his hair. She couldn't stop the rising force in her body, but she wanted more than just a physical pleasure. Did Jack not want her in the same way?

"Jack," she sobbed.

His tongue touched that pearl of pleasure and she shuddered all over. For a second she could only hold her breath, and then she was gasping in the cool mountain air and twisting away. She had to tell him what she wanted, tell him she needed his pleasure worse than she needed her own. She had to…be brave enough to voice the words. "I love you. Please, I want you to make me your wife. I want you…inside of me."

His mouth stopped moving. The sky above her glittered a watery blue. He pulled back and just his ragged breathing against the sensitive nub had her near shattering.

She hovered on a cliff between sanity and madness and she didn't know where she would fall. Her heart pounded in an agonizing beat and his hesitation cost her. How could she feel so alive and broken at the same time?

She closed her eyes, fighting the sobs that threatened to erupt.

His shirt landed beside her head and then he was lying on top of her, his hot skin against her, searing her, imprinting her. Just holding him breast to chest made her world right. His hardness probed at her slick folds and a rush of warmth moved through her. His lips were against hers, his breath ragged. She could taste herself on him. And taste his urgency, his need. She no longer felt alone in this.

"Olivia...are you sure?" He brushed his thumb against the corner of her eye. "Look at me." His voice was rough.

She opened her eyes. "I'm sure."

In the deep brown depth of his eyes something flickered. "You can't leave—"

She wrapped her legs around his backside and pulled him against her, trying to complete the act. The head of his manhood nestled in her entrance, but her body resisted. She whimpered and wiggled, trying to pull him in.

He groaned and thrust his hips. The barrier broke with a pang that was gone almost as soon as her gasp of surprise left her lips. Watching her face intently, he narrowed his eyes as if the little pain he'd caused her distressed him. But she could only feel how he was filling her, stretching her, completing her. He trembled with a need she could feel through his skin. A need that matched hers in intensity and hunger.

The moment was so perfect, with the sun sparkling down on them, the crisp smell of pine and grass and only the heavens above them.

He rained kisses on her face. "I'm sorry to hurt you," he muttered in a rough whisper.

She shook her head and smiled. "No hurt."

His hips eased back and he rocked forward.

She gasped, amazed at the warm heat flooding her to her center. Nothing had ever felt so good, made her feel so whole.

"Olivia," Jack moaned. "I can't...hold back."

"I love you," she repeated, and kissed him with her eyes wide-open.

Breaking away from the kiss, he panted, *"Je t'aime, je t'adore."*

He rocked forward again and within her she felt the throb of his manhood. Rush after rush of warm heat lifted her higher.

"I love you," he moaned, and shuddered to a stop. All his muscles were clenched tight as if he was fighting for control.

She dug her fingers into his hard backside, wanting him to continue. But then he rolled, taking her with him, and pushed his hand down between their bodies.

"Come apart for me, *ma chérie d'amour.*"

He urged her with his circling fingers and caresses while she gave in to the spiraling climb toward a height that was dizzying. She strained toward the peak, her muscles clenching around his rock hardness. She swayed up and down, imitating his smooth rocking, while he played her body as if she was a precious instrument. His eyes never left hers. The intensity of her emotions rolled through her, changing her, anchoring her to him while she spiraled higher and higher.

As if the mountain was falling from the heavens, her body quaked and shuddered with a force stronger than the earth and sky combined. It carried her along, but all the while Jack urged her toward the bliss. Almost when she could stand it no longer, she fell, collapsing into his arms. A blast of pure fulfillment roared through her. Her insides pulsed and a low keening moan left her mouth.

Jack thrust up into her, making the pleasure almost an unbearable thing, and his groan followed fast on hers. The throb of his manhood echoed her release and yet it was the hard cadence of his breathing, the twist of his face, his groan that held her enthralled as she floated on the last waves of her climax, and he found his.

Never had she felt so right. She was where she was supposed to be, right now, right here on the top of the mountain joined with him.

He pushed the curtain of her hair back and held her to his perspiration-slicked chest. Her heart beat against his in a matching gallop as their breathing slowed from heaving gulps to deep breaths.

He stroked her hair at the same time he cradled her to him. "Are you all right, love?"

She smiled and pressed a kiss to his chest. "Of course." She'd found her home. As she turned the words in her mind, she knew they were right. She had been searching for a place where she fit in, a place where she was wanted and needed, but she'd found home in his arms, in his kisses and caresses.

She was home.

Sprawled overtop of him, with their bodies still joined together, was the place where she felt wanted and needed, safe and secure.

Jack tightened his arms around her. The slight weight of her was the only thing that kept him moored to the ground. He was floating in an afterglow that astounded him. She was so perfect. Making love to her was beyond his wildest imaginings. It was more than physical, more than just bodily pleasure. Whatever was between them was right and made him feel whole. He was part of her and she was part of him.

Olivia was everything: bold and beautiful, brave and a soothing balm to his soul. There was a strength in her that she hid behind fancy dresses and elaborate coiffures. Her ability to remain calm in the face of a charging grizzly and fire the shotgun was beyond what he would have expected from any woman and most men. She had been frightened of baring her body to him, yet she had waited for him stripped naked on top of a mountain. That took a special kind of courage.

She belonged here. Even if she didn't know it yet, she was the woman he needed by his side. And he'd dismissed her as a frivolous piece of fluff when he'd first seen her. His mistake had nearly cost him the happiness only Olivia could provide.

"I'm home," she whispered against his chest.

"Good, because you're not leaving me now." His voice cracked. "Not now, not ever. You're mine."

She giggled.

The sound was as sweet as the crystal bell his mother had owned. He prayed that he could make Olivia happy. He'd done a much better job of making her miserable so far.

He was deadly serious. He'd tried to warn her. Running his hand over the gossamer strands of her pale gold hair, he said, "I won't let you go. You could be with child." But that wasn't the real reason he wouldn't let her go. "Damn it, if you left me, I would shatter."

Shatter like his mother's crystal bell that he'd knocked off the dining room sideboard while chasing his sister through the house.

Olivia lifted her head. Her rosebud lips were slightly swollen and the gray of her eyes had softened into a near blue. The sun had scorched pink swatches across her nose and cheeks. She was so achingly beautiful that his heart hurt. His flagging erection pulsed.

Her eyes darkened and her mouth opened with a soft

"Oh." As if experimenting with her power, she clenched her inner muscles.

The intense jolt of sensation jerked his head toward hers. "*Merde!* Don't move."

With an impish grin, she ignored him, of course. Worrying her lower lip with her pearly teeth, she rolled her hips.

In a quick move he flipped her onto her back. She squealed in alarm. He resisted the urge to rock his hips and let the lingering pleasure build to a new height. Instead, he pressed a kiss on the corner of her mouth. "You'll be sore if we do this again too soon."

"But it doesn't hurt now." Her expression was full of wide-eyed innocence. She didn't even have the wiles to fake a pout. Rather, she rubbed one foot up his calf and over the back of his knee.

He doubted if she knew what her play was doing to him. *Merde!* He was nearly ready again, although recuperation should have taken much longer. Resisting the temptation of her siren call was almost more than he could manage. He should withdraw, but he couldn't stand the idea of separating from her. He propped his weight on his elbows. "Stop tempting me."

"But…" Her pale eyebrows drew together. "Is it always like that? Because I don't think I've ever experienced anything so wondrous." She draped her arms over his shoulders. Her chin ducked a little, as if she was afraid she'd revealed too much.

"No." A thickness in the back of his throat surprised him. He pressed a kiss on her sun-kissed nose. "It was a thousand times better than I'd anticipated."

"But—"

He hushed her with a lingering kiss. If she wanted

comparisons, she won hands down, but saying so felt disloyal.

"Perhaps it was the mountain air." Bracing on his elbows, he lifted enough he could look down between them. Her pale skin contrasted with his bronzed skin, a bit like milk with honey. "Perhaps it is because you are so damn beautiful." He caught the chain with the wedding ring and dangled it in front of her face. "Or perhaps it is because you are wearing my ring. You do consider this wearing it?"

"I'm afraid it will fall off my finger again. I want to get it resized soon."

"I thought you were leaving me." His voice cracked. Lowering his body to meet hers, he swallowed against the emotion that threatened to overwhelm his intention to not risk making her sore. He wanted to recapture the magic between them. All it would take was the push and pull of his hips.

She sighed, as if the inch or two between their flesh had been a hardship. "I know. I won't apologize for making you wait for my assurances. You have put me through agony. And Antonga is sending Tabby to teach me to cook while I teach her letters. She can teach me how to live here and keep me from being afraid while you're gone."

"I won't be gone." God knew he never wanted to be apart from her again.

"Even better. For I really should prefer you home every night." She smiled a wicked smile. "But just think how many head of cattle my father's money will buy."

He shook his head and opened his mouth to protest. Providing for her was his duty. She put her fingers over his mouth.

"When you said that I could live anywhere I wanted

now, it occurred to me that I only wanted to live where you are. No place calls me. I only belong with you."

"And I with you, my love."

"Although I am partial to being on top of a mountain, so near heaven," she said mischievously. "I feared you might think it too silly to climb up here."

Not silly, but she captured a lightness and beauty he could forget to savor in the daily struggle to live. He wouldn't make that mistake again. He gave in to his building desire and pulled back and pushed deep inside her.

"Mmm, I thought you'd never get to that," she said, her eyelids lowering to a seductive half-mast. "I'm *not* sore."

He dropped the ring and moved his hand to cup her pert breast. "You will be."

"Promises, promises," she answered on a sigh as her hips rolled in answer to his slow slide in and out.

* * * * *

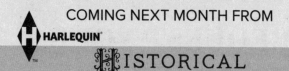

COMING NEXT MONTH FROM

HARLEQUIN

HISTORICAL

Available June 17, 2014

REBEL OUTLAW
by Carol Arens
(Western)

Colt Wesson Travers is headed for a life of tranquillity in Texas. But when he meets his delicious lodger, Holly Jane Munroe, he realizes that life is going to be anything but quiet!

A LADY OF NOTORIETY
The Masquerade Club
by Diane Gaston
(Regency)

Daphne, Lady Faville, is horrified to discover that the person who rescued her from a fire is Hugh Westleigh, a man with every reason to despise her! Will she find forgiveness in his arms?

THE SCARLET GOWN
by Sarah Mallory
(Regency)

When Lucy Halbrook arrives at Lord Adversane's estate, she knows her assignment is unusual—she must pretend to be his fiancée! But what Lucy doesn't know is that Ralph is hiding something....

CASTLE OF THE WOLF
by Margaret Moore
(Medieval)

Virtuous Thomasina is abducted after a high-stakes tournament. Trapped with her fearless captor, the legendary Wolf of Wales, she soon finds herself irresistibly drawn to the man beneath the armor.

**YOU CAN FIND MORE INFORMATION
ON UPCOMING HARLEQUIN® TITLES,
FREE EXCERPTS AND MORE AT
WWW.HARLEQUIN.COM.**

HHCNM0614

REQUEST YOUR FREE BOOKS!

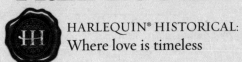

HARLEQUIN® HISTORICAL:
Where love is timeless

2 FREE NOVELS PLUS 2 **FREE GIFTS!**

YES! Please send me 2 FREE Harlequin® Historical novels and my 2 FREE gifts (gifts are worth about $10). After receiving them, if I don't wish to receive any more books, I can return the shipping statement marked "cancel." If I don't cancel, I will receive 6 brand-new novels every month and be billed just $5.44 per book in the U.S. or $5.74 per book in Canada. That's a savings of at least 16% off the cover price! It's quite a bargain! Shipping and handling is just 50¢ per book in the U.S. and 75¢ per book in Canada.* I understand that accepting the 2 free books and gifts places me under no obligation to buy anything. I can always return a shipment and cancel at any time. Even if I never buy another book, the two free books and gifts are mine to keep forever.

246/349 HDN F4ZY

Name _____ (PLEASE PRINT) _____

Address _____ Apt. # _____

City _____ State/Prov. _____ Zip/Postal Code _____

Signature (if under 18, a parent or guardian must sign)

Mail to the **Harlequin® Reader Service:**
IN U.S.A.: P.O. Box 1867, Buffalo, NY 14240-1867
IN CANADA: P.O. Box 609, Fort Erie, Ontario L2A 5X3

Want to try two free books from another line?
Call 1-800-873-8635 or visit www.ReaderService.com.

* Terms and prices subject to change without notice. Prices do not include applicable taxes. Sales tax applicable in N.Y. Canadian residents will be charged applicable taxes. Offer not valid in Quebec. This offer is limited to one order per household. Not valid for current subscribers to Harlequin Historical books. All orders subject to credit approval. Credit or debit balances in a customer's account(s) may be offset by any other outstanding balance owed by or to the customer. Please allow 4 to 6 weeks for delivery. Offer available while quantities last.

Your Privacy—The Harlequin® Reader Service is committed to protecting your privacy. Our Privacy Policy is available online at www.ReaderService.com or upon request from the Harlequin Reader Service.

We make a portion of our mailing list available to reputable third parties that offer products we believe may interest you. If you prefer that we not exchange your name with third parties, or if you wish to clarify or modify your communication preferences, please visit us at www.ReaderService.com/consumerschoice or write to us at Harlequin Reader Service Preference Service, P.O. Box 9062, Buffalo, NY 14269. Include your complete name and address.

HH13R

The warmth of her body against his, the scent of roses that always clung to her, her low, brandy-soaked voice all intoxicated him as much as the brandy had intoxicated her. At this moment he did not wish friendship from her, but something more. Something between lovers.

He resisted the impulse, but he did not release her. "I will bid you a friendly good-night, then."

He placed his cane against the wall and searched for her face. Touching her cheek and cupping it in the palm of his hand, he leaned down until he felt her breath on his face. He lowered his face and touched his lips to hers, slightly off-kilter. He quickly made the correction and kissed her, as a man kisses a woman when desire surges within him.

"Mmm." She twined her hands around his neck and gave herself totally to the kiss.

He was acutely aware of her every curve touching his body. His hand could not resist sliding up her side and cupping her breast, her full, high breast. He rubbed his fingers against this treasure and she pressed herself against him, her fingers caressing the back of his neck.

He wanted to take her there in the hallway, plunge himself into her against the door to her bedchamber. She would be willing. Never had a woman seemed more willing.

"Daphne," he whispered.

Some rational part of him heard footsteps on the stairs.

"Someone is coming." He eased her away from him. "We had better say good-night before we do something two friends might regret."

"I wouldn't regret it, Hugh!" She tried to renew the embrace.

"Not now." He pushed her away gently.

The footsteps were coming closer, nearly at the top of the stairs, he guessed. He opened her door and picked up his cane.

"Oh, madame!" an accented voice said. "I—I have come to assist you. If—if I do not disturb you."

"You must be Monette," Hugh said. "I have walked Mrs. Asher to her room. She is a bit unsteady."

He heard Monette rush over to her. "Madame! Are you ill?"

"Not ill," Daphne said. "Feel wonderful. Am dizzy, though."

"She drank some brandy," Hugh explained. "Without realizing the effects."

"*Je comprends,* sir," Monette said. "I will take care of her."

He felt the two women move past him and walk through the doorway. The door closed behind them and Hugh was left to find his own way back to his bedchamber to await Carter's assistance to ready himself for bed.

Sleeping would be difficult this night, he feared.

Don't miss
A LADY OF NOTORIETY,
available from Harlequin® Historical
July 2014.

4433

◆ HARLEQUIN®

ℌ ISTORICAL

Where love is timeless

COMING IN JULY 2014

Rebel Outlaw
by Carol Arens

Looking for peace, finding…trouble

Colt Wesson Travers is headed for a life of tranquillity in Texas.
Here, he'll finally escape the obligations demanded by his
notorious outlaw family.

But when he meets his stubborn lodger Holly Jane Munroe, his
illusions of peace are shattered. Colt is thrown right into the
middle of two feuding families intent on winning Holly Jane's
hand…and her grandfather's land! He quickly realizes that life
with delicious Holly Jane is going to be anything but quiet.…

Available wherever books and ebooks are sold.